HUNTED

BLOOD OF THE CHOSEN TRILOGY

D.L. BLADE

To my readers. Thank you for supporting this series and encouraging me to write the adult edition.

Here you go, besties!

SOCIAL MEDIA

Goodreads:
@D_L_Blade
TikTok:
@authordlblade
Facebook:
@dlblade
Instagram:
@booksbydlblade
Pinterest:
@DLBlade
YouTube:
@DLBlade
Newsletter:
www.linktr.ee/dlblade

AUTHOR'S NOTE

Hunted will complete the trilogy! It is a retelling, adult edition of my novel, *The Dark Deliverance*, published in 2019, and features mature themes and content.

Full content warnings can be found on my website, www.dlblade.com

PREFACE

The Gods rule the Upper World, the Underworld by the Devil and his demons, and the center—Earth—holds humanity whom the Chosen Ones swore to protect.

The secrets of a hidden realm will soon bring destruction.

In the darkest hour, on the darkest night, these four worlds will collide, and the gates of Hell will open.

CHAPTER 1

MERCY

The palms of my hands rested steadily at the center of Caleb's coffin. I glided my fingertips across the cool metal and moved over to where Leah had been laid to rest. I touched the silver metal trim of her coffin and stepped back. I stared at all four resting places, where a part of me would sleep ... for now, anyway.

I closed my eyes gently, feeling the heaviness against my lids from the lack of sleep over the past few nights. Each day since the coven had died flitted by quickly, but with each passing moment, I plotted my revenge against Maurice—the monster who took everything from me.

My coven's tragic demise happened unexpectedly because I was too blind to see what was right in front of me. Due to my ignorance, Maurice kidnapped and took me to California to be used for some twisted daylight spell. Meanwhile, Bradley, Lily's former fiancé, turned out to be a witch bent on revenge against my family, namely my father, Alexander, who had killed Bradley's wife years ago. He committed gruesome murders across town, stole our immortal dagger, and succeeded in killing me with it. Because of that, my coven had sacrificed their elements to bring me back to life, thus resulting in their deaths.

A single tear stung the corner of my eye as I tried to hold on to the hope that this wasn't it—that this couldn't possibly be it. The world seemed to slow down around me as the pain hit me, the pain of knowing that I may never see my coven again.

The pain in my chest felt like shattered bits of glass slicing my insides. The people who always helped put those broken pieces back together whenever I felt like giving up were no longer breathing in the air around me. It was my foolishness, my failure, my fault. I was unsure if I'd survive this without doing something to ease the grief.

The coven's elemental powers consumed me like a gale of wind swirling inside my body, unable to escape. The energies of the four tore at my soul, and I had to use the power of Spirit to constantly suppress the raging power with each unwavering breath.

I heard the quiet click of the door to the mausoleum opening behind me.

"Mercy, we're ready," Dorian's gentle voice called, pulling my thoughts toward his worried gaze. Another tear fell down my cheek, but I didn't sob or lose control; I couldn't cry like that anymore.

I had no tears left.

Could Dorian truly understand the level of pain I carried? I knew he had lost many friends in the past, but the universe had interconnected the coven and me. When they died, that link had broken, and my entire purpose crumbled at my feet.

I can't do this alone. My coven needs me to bring them back.

"I need another minute," I said, placing my palm back on Caleb's coffin and staring at the lid with unblinking, dry eyes.

"The coven did what they had to do," Dorian continued, this time walking to my side and placing his hand on mine to comfort me. His soft fingertips gently caressed my skin, and for a moment in time, I felt peace. "They would do it again if it meant keeping you alive."

And right then, that moment of peace that I had was gone.

"I would have stopped them somehow," I said. "It's my duty to protect them, not the other way around."

I turned to meet his brown eyes. I knew my unreadable expression wouldn't put him at ease. Dorian wanted me to be happy, but he couldn't rush my grieving process. He placed his hand against my cheek, and I allowed myself for a moment to let go again. I closed my eyes, leaned my head into his palm, and rested it there for a few seconds.

The death of my coven made me wallow in guilt, but I had a beautiful man in front of me who loved me, and I couldn't imagine a world where he was gone, too. While the touch of Dorian's hand offered comfort, I felt the wave of guilt drown me.

"Just one more minute, please," I said, lifting my cheek from his hand.

Dorian nodded slowly, and I turned back to Caleb's coffin. I heard the shuffling of his shoes across the concrete floor of the mausoleum, leaving me alone in my tormented guilt. Everything that had led to their demise was my fault. They wouldn't have died if I hadn't been so stubborn in doing things the way I wanted by myself. I would have seen it coming if I had just listened to my coven and stayed by their side. I would have been able to stop Bradley before he killed me.

All that mattered now was the mission ahead of us. I knew I'd eventually forgive myself for the actions that led to this fate and focus on taking down our enemies. But until then, I'd let the pain burn like a fire inside me.

The first order of business was that I was going to find Maurice and cut off his fucking head.

"I'll find a way to bring you back, I promise you," I said aloud, hoping that wherever the coven was, they heard me. I turned away from the four coffins and walked outside the mausoleum into the darkened cemetery where the others waited.

Dorian, Lily, and Joel stood outside the swirling black portal that would lead us to Los Angeles. Several weapons lay across the cemetery grounds. I bent down and picked up my new weapon of choice: a sword.

The star-like shine at the tip of the blade held my gaze, and my fingers trailed down the cool, flat metallic surface. I ran the pads of my fingers over the ornate inscription along the cross-guard, feeling the grooves of the engraving. The sword weighed heavily in my hand, but I gripped the worn leather hilt firmly. It was as if someone had made it specifically for me to fight my enemies with.

"I'd love to see the face of the person who originally owned this exquisite weaponry. It's enchanting," I said, turning to Joel.

"I'm not sure who it belonged to," Joel said, "but that symbol on the hilt is the sign of a knight. The inscription and artwork that wrap around the cross-guard are ancient. Most likely from the Renaissance era. Every weapon on that wall was chosen for a reason by the witches who took the safe house over."

"In other words," I said, my eyes sliding back to the sword, "I'd better take care of it." I clenched the hilt, swinging the blade down in a swift motion. I could hear the metal sing softly through the air. A smile pulled at my lips for the first time in days.

We had hundreds of weapons to choose from, but when I spotted this one yesterday as we searched the safe house for anything we could use, I would have sworn it called out to me. The witches that had occupied the lair before us had hung it on the training room's weapon wall, but no one ever seemed to use it.

Most people assumed that the only way to kill a vampire was with a wooden stake to the heart or to expose them to the lucent sunlight, both processes turning them into a pile of ash—a common misconception. That is what I had thought in the beginning, but as it turns out, decapitation by a silver-tipped sword would do the trick. The only thing I had fantasized about since I had awoken in Dorian's arms a few days ago was cleaving this silver sword through Maurice's neck. I'd cut his head clean off his shoulders and watch it drop at my feet. I'd finally be rid of that monster's smug grin.

I gave a swift nod to Joel, Lily, and Dorian, securing my sword in the scabbard at my hip, and stepped through the vortex.

—·⁕·—

Joel's portal landed us directly at the lobby doors of the building where Maurice had held me as a prisoner. The chances that he and the others were still operating there were slim, but we knew striking right away was a guaranteed way for us to get caught

8

D.L. BLADE

and killed. They'd be expecting us. I still held onto the hope that someone would still be there when we entered the building.

They had completely cleared the lobby out. The desk at the front, the couches in the corner, and the business logo right above the back wall, which read "Freedom Corporation," were now gone. There weren't even scraps of paper left behind.

"Shit," I cursed, feeling Dorian's muscular arms wrap around my waist from behind. He squeezed tightly, pulling me back into him for comfort. I turned my head around to meet his eyes. "I'm sorry, Dorian. We should have left sooner than we did."

It was now silent between us, and I wondered if the group questioned my judgment on waiting a few days before striking. Not that I didn't want to attack immediately. But I felt the vampires would have been waiting for us and taken us down if we had.

It was better to be cautious.

"Come on, Mercy," Joel said. "You know I would have made the same call to hold back, so we weren't expected. Your decision was the correct one. We'll use this opportunity to investigate unhindered."

Dorian released our embrace, turning me around until our eyes met again. He placed his hand gently on my cheek and rested it there. I hadn't realized how much my shoulders had been heaving with each breath I took until he brushed my arm slowly, creating a mountain of goosebumps and settling my nerves.

God, the way he could calm me with such a simple touch. Butterflies again bounced around in my stomach—a reminder of how foolish I was to deny moments like this after doing that damn spell last year.

"We're going to find that bastard," Dorian assured me. "I swear to you."

An empty promise, I thought. Maurice was always one step ahead of me.

Always.

We padded down the hallway, which lined the greenhouse. I remembered seeing several bunches of vibrant purple flowers in this area. They, too, had been cleared out, aside from a few lost petals crushed into pieces on the ground. It was as if someone had smashed them with their shoe.

Lily looked around and inhaled deeply. "This isn't lavender," she said. "What do you think it is?"

I bent down and picked up one of the crushed petals. "Joel, have you seen this before?"

As Joel opened his mouth to answer, Dorian said, "Wolfsbane."

I looked up. "Wolfsbane? What—"

"It paralyzes werewolves. Even the tiniest amount could cripple them for hours, preventing them from shifting," Dorian explained. "Their motor skills would be useless, and they'd be rendered vulnerable. It would be the perfect way for a vampire or witch to kill one without running the risk of being bitten."

An icy chill ran up the back of my neck, and a hard lump lodged in my throat. Whatever Maurice's plan was, it included the werewolves, too.

Great. No one's safe.

This wasn't a last-minute strike on their part; it had been planned in great detail and would soon be executed. Maurice would never be done with us until we put a stop to him.

I hadn't noticed until Dorian cupped my chin that I had been clenching my jaw, straining the muscles to the point of burning. He caressed his thumb over my cheek until I felt my body relax.

"Thank you," I whispered, not wanting him to release his touch, as it was the only thing keeping me grounded at the moment. We spent the past three days making up time for the centuries we had lost. I didn't want to leave that bed as we lay together under his sheets last night. The warmth of his new human body mingled with the sweat of lovemaking; it was all that held me together. It was those nights that brought me peace and eased my guilt and grief.

Despite Dorian's gentle touch, my thoughts turned to Maurice again, rage building back up inside me. I had never hated someone so much in my entire life. The constant obsession over killing him raced through my mind so often that I feared it would break me.

I turned to Joel. "The packs need to know what's happening. Not just Amber and Riley's pack but all of them," I said. "I'll reach out to Riley when we get back in town so they can send a warning to the others out there."

Riley mentioned that there were werewolf packs worldwide, but not everyone worked together with witches like theirs was willing to.

Amber, being the alpha, chose Riley as her beta. Together, they planned to increase their numbers and form their own colony in East Greenwich. There was already another pack in Providence covering that territory and another much larger one in Salem. That was as far as my knowledge went. Hopefully, they had enough information to find whoever else was out there. Who knew the depth of Maurice's insanity? And as far as the werewolves of East

Greenwich territory were concerned, he was just as much their enemy as ours.

"I'll update Noah so he can reach out to the remaining shapeshifters," Dorian said. "A few shifter families still get involved with the politics of the supernatural world, so we ought to be able to make some connections. Unfortunately, the rest stayed hidden after being nearly wiped out by vampires three decades ago."

"Vampires killed off shapeshifters?" I asked, surprised. "Yet Noah still worked for Maurice."

"Maurice raised him," Dorian explained.

I had not been expecting that.

"Wait, what?" I asked, shocked by this information. "Was Maurice a father figure to him?"

Dorian shook his head. "Not even close, but Noah eventually saw him like family. Maurice and his clan killed Noah's parents and older sister and brought him to their lair when he was only a kid. He remembers his family and life in Hawaii, and even though that was taken from him, the vampires always treated him kindly. They brought him up to believe they were the good guys, so he never felt the need to fight the clan."

I knew there was a lot from both their pasts that I still didn't know or fully understand, and this was one thing I never thought to ask Noah about. With Dorian, he worked for Maurice, who promised a roof over his head, blood supply, and protection. He joined that clan in the late nineties, and it was heartbreaking to think Noah was never given that choice.

"Noah—" Dorian looked past me as if lost in thought. "He battles between seeing Maurice as an ally and his enemy. His own vendetta against Maurice runs deep, but I also fear that a part of his love for the old clan that raised him might impede his judgment to act against them."

I understood that more than he knew. Or, at least, I thought I did. I often wept for my mom, who had stabbed me right through the chest. In her last days, she was evil beyond redemption, but my love for her never wavered. I even felt desperate to save her in those last moments before she took her final breath. Despite her cruelty toward me, I hoped a higher power meet her soul with grace and compassion.

Whoever or whatever that is.

Joel gestured ahead. "We need to keep moving."

We continued down the hallway, looking around for any clues that might indicate where Maurice had gone. All the rooms were vacant except one—the platform—still stained with blood and smelling of copper. However, the bodies of those sacrificed for the daylight spell were missing.

A yellow manila envelope sat on the corner of the platform. I picked it up, tore open the flap, and read the note inside. Dorian hovered over my shoulder to read with me.

Dear Mercy,

I know what you're thinking. I'm a sadistic monster and deserve to die. But hear me out. How would you feel if something trapped you in the dark for eternity, never to feel the light of day on your face?

Believe me, you would never survive as a vampire. Our greatest temptation runs in your veins, and we must fight now to abstain from giving in to our animalistic cravings.

The desire to drink your blood has tortured me these last few weeks while you were under my control. I wanted to taste you in more ways than just beneath my sheets. Honestly, the craving for you and your blood has haunted me since you left my lair a year ago. I've watched you closely. As you embraced your purpose on Earth, I've seen the woman you've become. Simply ... watching from afar until I finally took you.

I won't lie; the idea of you turning me human again has crossed my mind for a time or two. To have my soul back and let go of the monster. If I did, though, the guilt and shame I know I'd experience from the crimes I've committed would be my undoing. But then again, if you saw me for who I used to be, then perhaps I'd be worthy of your presence.

That being said, I won't apologize for what I've done. To you, to the people that I sacrificed, to anyone. I cannot take it back. If you're reading this, you either came for revenge, or you're here to collect the bodies of your fallen. You won't find them here. They've been cremated to save you time and energy and tossed in the ocean to feed the little fish.

Till we meet again, darling,

Maurice

P.S. I left you a peace offering, though, in the back room. The next time we catch up, you can thank me in person.

The bones in my fingers popped as I gripped the note, crumpling it into a tight ball and letting it fall to my feet.

"I'm going to kill him," I said through gritted teeth.

Lily bent down and picked up the paper, smoothing it out and reading to herself. Her expression was unreadable as she handed it to Joel.

After reading Maurice's words, he tossed the note back on the floor. "That asshole will never get to you again, Mercy," Joel promised.

"I told myself that after the first time that he held me as his prisoner. Look what happened," I reminded him.

I'd be a fool to ever believe again that Maurice would turn a blind eye after everything that had happened between us. His brother was dead because of me. I killed several of his vampire cronies, ordered an angel to take down his stronghold, and murdered his right hand, Kyoko, his only loyal friend.

No, he'll never be *done* with me, and he always found a way to track me down, no matter where I was. It was as if he had one hundred men always following me, yet I couldn't see them anywhere I went. There's no more terrifying feeling than someone watching you, tracking you, and knowing they could strike at any moment. I learned that lesson the hard way after Dorian and I were attacked, and I lost my memories.

"Never again," Dorian said, his eyes turning dark, as if thinking about Maurice was stoking a fire inside him, burning him up with rage. "I swear to you." Dorian gripped my waist and pulled me toward him in a possessive hold. It was as if he thought I'd vanish again if he let go. He pressed his forehead against mine and placed both hands on each side of my face. My heart beat wildly from the fierceness of his touch. "I'm so sorry I couldn't protect you before. I failed you, Mercy. I'll never forgive myself for that."

I shook my head quickly. "Dorian, stop. Nothing that has ever happened to me was your fault. They ambushed us that night. They followed me and knew exactly where I was the second that I arrived at your house. Maurice had it planned for months."

If anyone should have been apologizing, it was me. The moment Julian pulled me from the car, I should have used my powers instinctively before he placed his hands on my head and stripped me of my memories.

When Julian lay injured under the pier at the beach, and I had a foolish moment where I felt sorry for him, I shouldn't have. I should have killed that son of a bitch while I could. My shortcomings as a witch were the cause of what had happened. I took a step back from Dorian and glanced around the room. I spotted a familiar metal door, sending my stomach twisting in anxiety. "We need to check that back room," I said, pointing toward the door.

We entered the room containing the glass cells where they had caged me and the others like animals. A body lying on the floor in a tight ball inside cell number five immediately caught my eye. I felt numbness run through me as I recognized the blonde hair and petite frame.

Cami!

I hurried to the cell, yanked the door open, and kneeled by her side. It was clear Cami was alive as her chest heaved up and down rapidly, but I hesitated as I placed my hand on her shoulder.

Is this Cami, or should I expect Kylan to reach out at any second and grab me by the throat?

"Cami?" I said with a shaky breath. Her eyes fluttered open, and she slowly sat up.

Dorian kneeled beside me and helped me lift Cami to her feet. She staggered and looked dazed; the color of her cheeks had drained to a white pallor, like she hadn't slept or eaten in days.

"Oh, Cami," Lily whispered, "what have they done to you?"

"Lily, please grab me water from my backpack," I said.

Lily zipped open my bag, pulled out a water bottle, and handed it to me. I twisted off the cap and pressed the opening to Cami's lips. She gulped down a few swigs, but the last one, she coughed up, spitting water over my shirt. She slapped the bottle out of my hand, spilling the contents all over the floor.

"Cami?" Dorian called, his voice pitched with concern. "What did that taste like to you?" He leaned closer to her but quickly retracted, taking a step back. "Fuck." He grabbed my arm firmly, and I looked at him, confusion covering my face, until ...

"Oh, shit," I cursed as her eyes turned dark and blood vessels popped under her bottom lashes, protruding like cracks in a dry, sandy desert. She pounced on me, sinking her teeth deep into my neck.

I felt the blood rapidly drain from my veins. I gripped her shoulders firmly, feeling like I was going to fall flat on my back, but Cami's new, unnatural strength held me firmly in her grasp.

When Dorian and Joel tried to pry her off, I shouted, "Stop!"

I was growing weak and felt like I would collapse to the floor. But after another minute of Cami feeding on me, she released her bite. I felt my strength return instantly, and the wounds quickly healed. She coughed again and proceeded to vomit the blood she had drunk, which splattered all over the floor by our feet.

Cami wiped her mouth clean and looked down at her hands, which were now crimson. Horror filled her eyes. "What the fuck? Ew!"

I sighed with relief, as this was, without a doubt, the Cami we knew.

"Cami?" I asked. "Please tell me you can feel your heart beating?"

She nodded, pressing her stained hand to her chest. "Yeah, it is. Thank God. It felt like an out-of-body experience, where I was watching a monster version of myself before I woke up."

Cami looked up, and while her eyes were still bloodshot, the color of her cheeks was now a peach-colored hue. "I can't believe I'm actually alive."

"You and me both," I said. "Do you feel Kylan's possession at all?"

Lily ran to Cami and pulled her in for a hug before she could answer me.

"My God, you're alive! I can't believe you're standing here alive," Lily said. She pushed Cami back gently, sizing her up. "Mercy could have killed you."

"Well," Cami shrugged, placing her hand on her cheek, "Let's be thankful she held back." She turned to me. "I don't feel that monster inside my head anymore, but I don't think he's an entity that can be killed, Mercy."

I wiped a tear from my face—one I hadn't realized was there until I felt the coolness dripping down my cheek. Cami's words brought comfort to the fact that she was herself again, but that second part only made my skin crawl. Kylan's body was the only thing that died when I staked him at the cove, releasing his dark energy from the vessel that housed it and unleashing it out into the world. "I need you to tell us everything you remember happening to you in the last few days."

"Sure, but you'll need to sit down for this ... and I need some water," Cami said.

"Of course. I saw what looked like a breakroom near the main hallway," I said. "Come on."

We helped Cami to the breakroom and sat her at a table near the refrigerator. A few snack bars were in the cabinet near the back, so I gave Cami everything I could find. They hadn't cleared out everything, it seemed.

For that next hour, Cami explained to us what had happened since Julian took her. She didn't remember much after her breakout from the hospital, with Kylan still possessing her. She believed a few weeks had passed before the vampires tracked her down near her mother's house. Cami had been fighting Kylan with every excruciating step, but he was too strong, and her soul had almost wholly diminished from her own body.

Almost.

After they took her to face Maurice, she had the unpleasant opportunity to meet the "Evil Three," as she named them.

Julian had performed a spell that ripped Kylan's spirit out of her, and for a moment, she was alive, but barely. Cami's soul struggled to keep her body together. Magic warped her mind with so much darkness; all she wanted to do was die.

"It was terrifying watching Julian pull the spirit of a vampire from my flesh and into this other woman, whom they called Clara. I wanted to die, Mercy. I begged them to kill me." She bit her lower lip and looked down at the floor. "My life flashed before my eyes, but all I thought about was the bad things I did ... the thing I did in the hospital to my doctor, to you." It broke my heart that she felt the need to avoid my eyes.

Her knee bounced, and she fidgeted with her hands.

"That was Kylan, Cami. Not you," I assured.

"Am I ... am I going to jail?" she stammered.

I shook my head. "No, of course not. My friend's family owns that hospital. They know you were possessed. We covered everything up. I promise you're safe."

Cami breathed a heavy sigh of relief, but her hands still trembled.

I placed my fingers on hers and gave her hand a tight squeeze. "Continue. What happened next?"

She straightened her back as her knee slowed down its pace. "After Kylan left my body, Maurice did something to me," she said.

I closed my eyes and grimaced. "Fed you his blood?"

She nodded. "After they forced me to drink from Maurice, he placed his hands on my head, and my neck snapped." She closed her eyes tightly, and her legs started to bounce again, this time violently. "The next thing I knew, I was falling through this portal into another world." My jaw dropped as goosebumps trailed up my arms. "I know it sounds strange, but it was as real as speaking with you right here. I was dead, Mercy, and yet I saw things."

My stomach lurched, and I swallowed down my nerves. "What did you see?" I asked with an unblinking stare.

"Another world where the souls of the dead are lost," she finished.

I knew exactly where she was referring to, because I had been there: Purgatory.

Until now, the vampires I brought back to life with my blood couldn't recall that very moment when their souls left their bodies, let alone their time in Purgatory. This was the first time someone remembered what their transition from human to vampire was like. Though I had experienced it myself with my death, it had to have been much more frightening and confusing for Cami.

Cami bit her lower lip again and narrowed her eyes at me. She seemed to want to tell me something but was afraid to.

"Cami, what is it?" Lily asked.

"I saw your friend ... Caleb," she said, and my mind scrambled to grasp her words. "He ... he was there, begging me to find the link that tethered me to that world and return to you." Cami's voice shook with uncertainty. "It was so strange, but he grabbed my hand, and in an instant, I learned everything at that moment of your powers, your purpose, and who he was to you."

I blinked and caught my breath. Cami was always under Kylan's possession in any encounter with Caleb, even when he had visited her at Raven's. She had never learned what we were.

"That's a good thing, Mercy," Joel said. "Think about it. It means they haven't crossed over. So, the spell to preserve their bodies worked. They're still bound to Earth."

Despite what Joel had just explained, my nerves didn't settle. The room felt like it had been moving in a whirlpool, causing my head to spin.

"What about the rest of the coven?" I asked hopefully, finally finding my voice. "Did you see a brunette and two other guys around him and ... I mean, if Caleb were there, then they would be, right?"

Cami shrugged. "I was there for what felt like minutes before I was pulled back into my body when you brought me back today. Time moves ... differently there," she explained. "Just because I didn't *see* them doesn't mean they *weren't* there."

Cami yawned and rubbed her eyes. She was clearly exhausted from the recent series of events.

"We need to get you to a hospital," I told her. "I'm going to admit you into Raven's again, but you won't be stuck there. I promise."

Her head shook back and forth rapidly before saying, "Please, don't. I can't go back there."

"It's just temporary until we know for certain that Kylan is truly gone," I said. "No other facility will protect you as they can."

She looked at Dorian and Lily, as if needing their reassurance, too.

Lily nodded. "I think it's the best thing, too. Once they assure us you're fine, we will check you out and return you to your mom."

I squeezed her hand tightly and looked at everyone standing around, waiting for me to tell them what we had to do next.

"Once we admit Cami back into Raven's, then we'll come up with a plan of attack," I said. That tiny hope I had been holding onto resonated with my next words. "I swear to every single one of you that Maurice and his clan will die before he hurts anyone else that I care about."

As we headed toward the front of the building, my mind drifted to those who had died for that daylight spell. My father's and Abigail's bodies were treated like trash, and I couldn't give them the proper burial they deserved. I made a mental note to ask Desiree when we returned to see if she'd be open to at least holding a memorial service on their behalf with those who cared about them.

I dreaded telling Desiree that Abigail's body was now ash floating in the ocean. Desiree was already struggling enough with what had happened.

One moment, Desiree and Abigail were relaxing on Sunset Beach, and the next, Abigail went missing. When Desiree had gone to look for her, a hard object hit her over the head, and a few days later, she opened her eyes inside a hospital room. By then, it was too late. She had called to inform me what had happened, but they had already sacrificed Abigail. They hadn't left each other's sides for centuries, and now she had lost the one person she truly loved. Well, two people Desiree loved. She'd lost Caleb, too. After losing her mother and her brother within days, she needed space to grieve before I could approach her.

My thoughts returned to the present as Dorian wrapped his fingers around mine. He gave me a gentle squeeze, offering reassurance that we would be all right. I returned the gesture, and with the others following behind, we jumped into the portal, sending us back to East Greenwich.

CHAPTER 2

MERCY

Maurice was clever and calculating. He did nothing without a purpose.

For years, Maurice recruited witches to turn against their own kind, and convinced vampires to become just like the Hollywood archetype; ruthless, evil, and murderous. He had years of turning into a mastermind psychopath with no remorse for human suffering. He, and others like him, were beyond redemption. However, we had proof that vampires like Dorian, Abigail, and Desiree could be kind, decent people who would do anything to avoid taking a human life. Maurice took those desperate for survival and a place to fit in, promising them an endless supply of blood and a roof over their head. Now, he'd offered them something every vampire desired—to walk in the daylight while remaining immortal. That thought sent a bitter chill down my spine and coldness to my core.

Is that all the daylight spell would do for them? Would it give them strength? Make them invincible?

Those unanswered questions kept me up at all hours of the night. It created a constant battle between doing what I knew I had to do and knowing that if I failed again, everyone could die.

It was as if the elements themselves could sense my fear; my insides quivered, bringing my powers to the surface. It was overwhelming at times. The sensation differed from when I had lost control over my own powers. That had been due to a lack of control over my emotions and my temper. The powers felt like an overfilled dam, and one more drop would send it all cascading out in a violent rush. My hands constantly felt clammy, as if I were hot or nervous. It felt like those powers were reaching every surface of my body, threading carefully along my skin, trying to set themselves free into the world. I hadn't even attempted to use *their* magic yet now that I was the elements' new vessel. I was afraid to. Pulling energy from others was one thing, but having it and controlling it as if it were my own was an entirely different level of power.

A warm sensation drew me out of my spiraling thoughts. The tender touch of Dorian's hands once again found purchase on my skin, running his palm gingerly down to my belly. My thoughts were now back to the present, craving his touch. Always craving his touch. I let out a soft moan.

His hand stopped moving. "Why did you stop?" I whined, pouting my lips.

"You seem to have gone to another place just then," he said.

That happened often, thinking about what Maurice did to me, wanting Dorian's affection to remove the ghost touch from that monster's hands that seemed to not want to leave.

"Do you want to talk about it? About him?" he asked.

I shook my head. "I don't know."

Dorian had heard everything. I could never keep that from him, no matter how much I knew it would hurt both of us to say it aloud. I told him about what Maurice had done to me. He knew about the spell that altered my memories and feelings and that I had willingly given my body to him. It didn't matter how many times Dorian told me I wasn't myself in those moments, that the feelings I felt for Maurice weren't mine. That heavy guilt that I enjoyed and wanted it had weighed heavily on my conscience.

"Can we talk about something else?" I asked, looking up to meet his eyes. "I don't want to think about him right now."

Right then, a warm, comforting feeling came over me. It felt like a rush of warm water, settling gently over the surface of my skin like I had been floating. It happened often; the coven calling out to me, just barely out of reach but enough for me to know they were there, feeling my pain and attempting to heal it.

"Are you feeling them again?" My attention drew back to meet his eyes in confusion. "I guess I'm a little confused about how the coven's elements are inside you, and yet their souls are somewhere else." A playful smile touched his lips. "Can they feel me doing this?" His hand continued down my stomach until it reached between my legs. I rolled my hips slightly into his hand and softly moaned before he leaned forward, taking my lips into his mouth and sucking. His tongue slid over mine, and oh my God, I missed those lips.

This was what I needed.

I felt slightly disappointed when he pulled back again, but I didn't whimper that time. "God, I hope they didn't feel that." I laughed. "Leah may enjoy it, though." With a wink, he slid his finger under my underwear and pulled it back, gliding his fingers under the fabric and feeling my arousal. His touch was slow and teasing, as if he were savoring every second of it.

"I only wish to please *you*, my love. No one else." He leaned forward, grazing his tongue along my neck, his lips trailing up to my ear. He then hooked his fingers under the seam of my underwear and pulled them off. "Turn over," he commanded.

Dorian didn't have to ask twice.

I turned around, my knees pressing into the mattress. A pang of anticipation swirled within me, momentarily blurring the world around us. Dorian's left hand sunk into the crease of my hip, and the other found its way between my thighs, his fingers moving in a slow, circular motion around the bundle of nerves that ached for his attention. A tingling sensation spread through me like wildfire, parting my lips in a heady sigh.

He knew *exactly* how to touch me.

Even after all these years, it remained embedded in his mind—how he teased my body drove me insane, causing my knees to buckle.

I could feel him shift closer; his arousal was clear as a hardened bulge now pressed against my ass. I was wet and throbbing, aching for more of him.

"Dorian ..." My tone dripped with yearning. Dorian released his hold on my hip like he could read my unholy thoughts. He unzipped his pants, wiggling them down just enough to pull out his cock. The tip of his length pressed against my entrance, prodding at it teasingly. "Please ..." The word slipped out of my mouth, catching me off guard—I wasn't the type to beg, especially not in the bedroom, but with Dorian, I'd surrender every single time. Right now, my mind was slipping. It seemed like Dorian had just triggered something within me, something deep and primal that I had no control over.

"Please what, Mercy?" he responded, his tone deep and hoarse. His fingers applied more pressure to my swollen clit, the tip of his cock still pressing against my aching pussy. Dorian knew exactly what I wanted—my entire body was screaming it, and he just wanted to hear me say it.

"I need more ..." I murmured, my words mixing with my heavy breaths. Just like that, he obliged my pleas. His cock slipped inside of me effortlessly—I was ready. We both moaned simultaneously, sharing the moment of all-consuming pleasure as he penetrated me.

Dorian's hand found my hip again, gripping it as he began to move his hips. His movements aimed to enter me slowly and deeply, his other hand still tirelessly working against my nerves.

"Oh, God," I cried out, my hips now pushing back against his. He consumed every cell of my body at that moment. He owned me. The sensation swirled the world around me. My eyes closed over as I tipped my head back, riding that wave of pleasure from his cock and fingers.

"Mercy ..." he moaned my name—that sound alone raised goosebumps over my skin. "You're so tight. Fuck." He released his grip on my hip, using that hand to support himself as he hovered over me, his lips finding the back of my shoulder.

His mouth showered me with kisses, breaking some of my focus away from the way his cock filled me up. I tightened around him; it felt as if he was massaging my inner muscles from all the right angles, working his way deeper and deeper inside of me.

Dorian began moving his fingers against my heat, harder and faster, as his thrusts picked up their pace. We both ached for more, eager to devour each other, body and soul.

"Fuck, yes ..." I moaned; my breath hitched in the back of my throat as he found that spot buried in the depths between my legs—that singular spot that pushed me closer to that blissful high we were chasing. "Right there. Don't stop ... Oh, fuck."

Dorian listened to what my body demanded. He didn't quicken his pace, nor did he change his angle the slightest bit. The loud moans that broke from my lips uncontrollably encouraged him to continue fucking me ... just like that.

God, it felt good.

"Mercy ..." His teeth sunk into my shoulder, but he didn't pierce my skin. It seemed like he was trying to anchor himself and delay the inevitable while the pleasure threatened to consume us both.

My knees buckled at last, too weak to hold me up, my body dropping against the mattress. Dorian was tireless in the way he stimulated my clit, holding my hips in the air. My eyes rolled back into my skull. I was almost there—I could feel it.

"Dorian ..." His name rolled off my tongue one last time before my orgasm tore through me, soaking his hot length in the flood of my release. Loud grunts intertwined with my heavy breathing, momentarily leaving me lightheaded. The pleasure that flooded me seemed to tip him over the edge, too.

A moment later, his body tensed on top of mine, a loud groan echoing through the room as he came inside of me. I was so hyper-fixated on him, so oversensitive that I could practically feel him pulse. It was only then that he remembered to pull his fingers away from my tender clit, his cock slipping out of me as he settled on his pillow.

We were both breathless, still winding down, but a smile curved my lips as my gaze caught his.

"You never really answered me," Dorian said, turning to face me with a wide grin.

"About feeling them?" I asked, and he replied with a nod. "Yes, and no. I feel the coven's elemental power but not the people they were. It's not like I can sense them watching me, like they're ghosts listening to our conversations, or"—I chuckled at the thought—"feeling my arousal from what we just did."

Dorian interlinked our fingers, resting in the space between us, keeping his eyes on mine.

"A part of me, though," I continued, "feels like there's a protective shield around me. It brings comfort, you know?"

It was odd to have a conversation like this, but Dorian hadn't stopped asking me since I moved in. I noticed his frown as he stared into my eyes, and I wished, at that moment, I had the power to read his thoughts, like the ability that my father had.

The more Dorian hid from me and pulled away, the more it was clear that he battled an internal turmoil inside his head that I couldn't possibly understand. He knew the spell lifted when I died and that I loved him again, as I had all those centuries ago. I wondered if he was curious about how I felt about Caleb. Dorian had to know that I had gained all my memories about him and me, *not* with Caleb. The memories I had with Caleb were the same as I had with the rest of the coven; friendship with small moments of flirtation that would soon lead to the moments only Caleb remembered. Our bond spoke to me so strongly that I didn't have to have those memories to feel something.

Caleb had sacrificed himself for me. He loved me so much that he had laid down his own life, along with the coven, so that I could live and Spirit would remain on Earth. I experienced a pang of sorrow at the thought of how Caleb would feel watching me walk into Dorian's arms, especially after sacrificing his own life—his powers—so I could live.

I knew Dorian wanted to talk about it. I could see it in his eyes or his slightly opened mouth whenever I mentioned Caleb's name, but he wouldn't ask me the question that surely lingered in his mind.

He wanted to know if I still loved Caleb.

Every time Caleb's face popped into my head, my thoughts immediately drifted to Caleb's relationship before he passed—Melissa. I had stopped by her home a few days ago and told her what had happened to the coven. She was devastated and angry, and I watched her cry until she asked to be alone. She told me about their relationship and how serious it had become. I *was* happy he had moved on and found someone he cared for, but my heart shattered at the thought that they may never have that again. Even if I found a way to bring the coven back, it could be fifty years from now or one hundred, and Melissa would have moved on to the next life. Caleb could come back to face more pain and grief.

I hadn't contacted her since.

After I moved my palm over Dorian's hand, we rested a little longer on his mattress. I had been sleeping at his and Noah's place every night since we escaped, essentially moving in. Now that he was human, I feared for him being alone, and even though I couldn't die, Dorian still feared for me more than he needed to. He was obsessively checking the locks and looking out the windows. He'd circle the property each night, listening for anything out of the ordinary. It frustrated him that he didn't have vampire hearing anymore. But that was the least of what upset him. It seemed as if everything that had been taken away since becoming human frustrated him. He hated being a vampire, but after centuries of being undead, then losing the abilities that came with it, he felt powerless and inadequate.

Dorian kissed me gently on the forehead but wouldn't meet my eyes as he pushed himself to his feet, climbing off the bed.

An awkward silence loomed in the air.

Great.

"Where are you going?" I asked. My paranoid mind quickly analyzed why he was acting so strange and what it could mean, especially after Dorian had just fucked me on my knees.

Please, Dorian. Please tell me what you're thinking.

"Noah and I planned on going for a run." He paused by the mattress, and our eyes finally met. "What are you doing today?"

"Meeting Riley," I said. Of course, I was happy he took an interest in what I was doing, except he didn't press for any more answers about why I was meeting Riley. He smiled wanly and leaned down to kiss me. When I tried to bring him in closer, he pulled back. A gaping hole opened in my chest, but I didn't show him how much it was killing me. I flashed him a fake smile as he slipped away again.

Something is wrong.

CHAPTER 3

MERCY

Riley pulled up to Patricia's Witch Shop ten minutes after I arrived. I had been obsessing over Dorian and my relationship and why he pulled away this morning. I couldn't let go of how he was behaving, and it was driving me crazy.

Seriously, what the hell? Was it about Maurice? No. Dorian knows it wasn't my fault. Caleb? Maybe, but I've told him a thousand times he is all I want. All I need.

It wasn't just what he had done this morning that unnerved me. Dorian thrashed and kicked throughout the night like he was fighting something dark and haunting that he couldn't escape in his dreams.

Once Riley parked his car, I waved him over to mine.

Today, I couldn't think about what was going on in Dorian's complicated mind. As much as I was desperate for his touch again, he and I had just gotten back together after centuries apart. I couldn't expect our relationship to be like it had been all those years ago.

How could it be? I wasn't technically the same person. Though, I must say, his hands on me and his body inside of me are exactly how I remember from our life together before this.

Riley handed me my latte when I stepped out of the car, and we strolled across the shop's main entrance and toward the back. Riley rang the bell at the checkout counter. Patricia poked her head through the beaded curtain at the back of the shop seconds later.

"Mercy, what brings you in today?" she asked as she appeared through the curtain, the beads clacking together all too loudly. "And hello to you, young man."

Oh, just asking for a favor that puts you in danger.

I felt slightly bilious about what I was about to ask her.

"I'm good. This is my best friend, Riley," I said, gesturing to him as he held out his hand for Patricia to shake.

"Well, aren't you handsome," she said, gripping his hand.

I gave Patricia a nervous smile. "Do you have a minute? We were hoping you could help us with something."

"Of course. Let's head to the back. I don't have a reading for another hour."

As we entered the back room, I thought about the last time I had been here, when I discovered I was a vampire hunter. That was a pivotal moment in changing the course of my life.

She gestured toward the chair across from her. "Please, sit. How can I help you two?"

Fear caught my throat, and my mind scrambled. "Do—" I swallowed. "Do you know anything about astral protection?" I asked, my voice stammering and feeling a tad bit like a fool for asking her.

She studied my eyes carefully, shifting in her chair. "A little," she said. "Where do you want to go?"

I let out a labored breath. "Purgatory."

Just the sound of that name on my tongue felt wrong. It wasn't Hell or Heaven. We had no idea what that place was, but death had taken me there, and the idea of going back terrified me to my core. I had just asked her to put herself in an uncertain and dangerous position while I ventured into uncharted territory.

The energy inside the room shifted, and I snuck a glance at Riley. He looked as if he half expected Patricia to wave us off and close the shop, so we wouldn't come back for any more favors.

Her unblinking eyes stared at me for a long moment before she asked, "Why would you want to go to a place like that?"

I found it particularly strange that she didn't ask me what Purgatory was. I knew witches weren't completely aware of the existence of vampires, so how could they know about a realm that trapped their souls? Patricia didn't even know they still existed until she brought some of my memories back a year ago. But she was psychic, so some of her abilities allowed her to see and venture into other realms. If she had, did she even know what she was seeing on that other side and what that place meant?

I got right to the point. "Patricia, the future of witches and even werewolves is at risk."

Her eyes went wide. "I haven't seen anything that would indicate we're in danger. I usually receive visions of warning that I try my best to interpret, but we're safe as far as I can see."

"You wouldn't, though," I said, running my fingers over my cooling cup of coffee. "The vampire who is threatening us is working with a mind-controlling witch. Surely, he'd figure out how to shield our eyes from whatever master plan they're conjuring up."

Patricia nodded, her brow furrowing in concern. "That's true."
She placed her hand on mine. "But do you know what you're
getting yourself into?"

"You've seen it, haven't you?" I asked.

She frowned. "Only in my nightmares. Even if I could help you,
I won't."

My shoulders curved inward like I was shrinking into myself. I
didn't have another way to do this. I had never used the type of
magic that would allow me to visit another realm, nor did I have a
way to pull myself back before I became lost in it. Not even the dark
magic portions of Joel's spell books had any solutions for getting
me to Purgatory.

I felt Patricia's hand grip tighter on mine, squeezing for comfort.
"As much as I want to help, Mercy, I don't think it's wise. After last
time—"

"I know."

I understood her hesitation. When she performed that last reading on me, I learned that it drained her to where she couldn't get
out of bed for several days. Patricia wasn't even sure she'd be able to
reach my previous life since my spirit was only bound to this body,
but she did. She had opened my eyes to everything, but it had also
opened hers.

"Please," Riley said, finally finding his voice as if he had been
afraid to speak up until now. "She needs to visit her coven."

"Your coven?" she said, her eyes finding mine and holding an
intense gaze.

"My coven is dead," I said, watching her lips part. "Fortunately,
I was able to preserve their bodies through a spell in my uncle's

book. I need you to take me to Purgatory because that's where their souls went after they died."

She reached for me again. "Even if I could take you there, it's too dangerous. You're talking about astral projection into a world so close to Hell ... the Underworld ... that you can smell the fire and brimstone seeping through its walls."

The lump in my throat had now tripled in size, but I nodded. "I know," I said. "Which is why I need to contact them so we can take one step closer to freeing them from that world before it consumes them and severs the spell that we created to keep them bound to Earth. If they don't return to their bodies, my coven will have truly fallen."

Her brows furrowed. "You're basing all this on faith."

I shrugged. "Because faith is all I have left."

Riley reached out and put his hand on Patricia's arm. "Without this, we are walking into a war blind," he said.

She studied us for a hard moment then said, "Just this once, Mercy. I will see everything you see. I wish I could say I was powerful enough to handle a place like that, but I'm not."

I nodded. "I understand. Since your power is derived from Spirit, you can tap into my magic to amplify your abilities, and at any moment, if you need to pull me back, I won't resist."

She looked past me toward the curtain. "Let me lock the front door. Give me a minute."

Once she left to lock up the shop, I turned to Riley. "Yeah, I'm not going to lie, Riley. I'm fucking scared."

He reached out and grabbed my hand, giving it a gentle squeeze. "You're about to enter the world between worlds. I'd find it unusual if you weren't."

Patricia came back through the curtain and placed a pendulum on the table. She leveled a flat wooden stick behind it, parallel to ten metallic balls. Slowly, she pulled it upright and released it, allowing synchronized waves to move back and forth, creating a spiral motion like a snake slithering through the sand of a desert.

She reached out and grabbed my wrists, twisting my palms up and tracing her fingers along the lines. "Keep your hands up like this while I draw out your energy and connect with my own," she said. "Try to relax, if you can."

I slowly closed my eyes and felt a tingling burn on my palms with every motion from her finger pressing on the lines of my skin.

The tremble of my hand made tiny little rattles on the table. My body felt like it was being wrapped in a weighted blanket but not providing the comfort I needed to ease my fears. I felt Riley's hand on the ridge of my back, and his hand brushed up to my neck and back down until he reached my waist. His touch sent a warm sensation of comfort that helped my nerves steady.

Just a little.

Patricia uttered the spell, and I felt a strange vibrating sensation in my chest and the flow of warm, streaming water pulling through every limb of my body.

When I opened my eyes, I was no longer in the back room of the witch shop. I looked around a white hallway and recognized it as the entryway I had walked through when I was last there.

Holy shit, it worked. I was back in Purgatory. I looked down at my hands and body. The physical properties were no longer present, but I was still in human shape. I had become a shade made of glowing energy.

When I left the hallway and entered the open space, I eyed the same crowd of bodies walking shoulder to shoulder in front of me. It was like they were in this continuous loop, directing them into nothing but an endless tunnel. No one acknowledged my presence. I took a few steps before the world around me seemed to fade.

Everything around me disappeared, leaving me in another space, this one of unimaginable beauty. It was as if my body had traveled through space, leaving time behind me. This was a completely new area for me, even though I knew I was still in Purgatory. I quickly recognized this place as where I had seen Lily, Joel, and Dorian mourn my death.

I reached a vast, crystalline lake that I had not seen before. The water on the lake looked like flawless glass, without a breath of wind disturbing its surface. I then passed the bright cerulean blue body of water and glanced at a narrow opening near a tall, leafless tree. It had long, crooked branches stretching upward, like arms reaching for the stars. The tree was illuminated with a frosty white glow that connected with my own energy force, as if the two powers were pulling each other in until they could touch. I could only describe it as if my soul was being tethered by a shining, stretching rope, drawing me into the tree's energy. This tree was a part of me somehow, yet I had seen nothing like it.

The elements inside me that belonged to my coven suddenly hummed beneath my skin, almost knocking me to the ground, but I steadied myself, pulled my hands to my chest, and centered myself until I could continue walking. The elements were soon quieted.

I peeked up just as Caleb circled around the tree and leaned against its trunk. My body felt weightless as I stood there, still like a statue. I blinked and stepped closer, calling him by name softly, barely able to find my voice.

Caleb heard me, though, his head turning to face me, and his eyes grew wide with shock. I hurried toward him and leaped into his arms, and he pulled me firmly to his chest, burying his head into my neck. We didn't have physical bodies in this world, but our energy forces had become one, allowing us to feel a warm sensation of comfort and touch as if there were a solid mass covering our souls. I could feel Fire rise up, as if it knew its vessel was there, and it was eager to rejoin Caleb.

"What are you—" What looked like fear shone in his eyes.

I quickly held up my hand. "It's okay. I'm not dead. I'm not really *here*." I cast my eyes around. "Where's the rest of the coven?"

"We aren't sure where we are, so the coven went to explore this ... world. We thought if we found a window, a door, or perhaps—"

"No, I don't think you can leave, but I'm doing everything possible to find a way through magic." I looked around again, taking in the strange world around me. "I need your help, though," I said, meeting his eyes.

"I can't believe you're here," Caleb cried out, ignoring what I had just said. "You got the message?"

My forehead creased. "The message?"

"Cami," he said. "The moment she entered this world and her eyes locked with mine ... it was as if we were connected because of you, me having been the one to greet her at the gates, I guess. Of course, I didn't know if she'd recognize me, even from the times I visited her at Raven's. Kylan always had her mind in a magical force she couldn't break."

"She told me you had met," I said.

A wide smile reached his eyes. "We didn't have much time before that energy pulled her back out of this world. I had hoped she would remember me and could let you know we were okay." He reached out to my cheek, and I felt the power that bound us bounce off between us. "God, I wish so badly I could hold you right now." He placed his hand near my cheek. "Like, really *hold* you."

"I know." I looked down at my glowing, translucent hands. Caleb was nearly inches from my face when my eyes turned back up. I lifted my hand and placed it near his, but all that happened was that our palms glowed, bouncing light and energy off each other. Mine was significantly brighter.

"How are you here?" Caleb asked.

"Patricia is doing a spell as we speak to help my spirit project into this realm. I wasn't sure it would work, but it did the moment I thought about this place. I've been here before. Both times I died."

I didn't recall the first time I was in the spirit realm after dying on the gallows, but I vividly remembered it after Bradley killed me. I remembered seeing through to Earth like a window to Joel's backyard had dropped right in front of me. I wondered if the coven could see beyond this world and into ours as I had.

"How much time do we have?" he asked.

"We don't. As much as it pains me for this to end, I came here to get a name."

He opened his mouth to speak, but the ground beneath me shook violently, causing me to lose my balance. As I fell to my knees, he tried to catch me, but I dropped through his hands and landed on the grass. He was becoming more translucent, so much so that I could almost see through his stomach.

"What was that?" I asked, craning my neck to look up, peering past Caleb's body.

"You need to leave," he said. There was so much urgency in his tone, it was as if this was now a moment of life or death, yet I just sat there, shaking my head.

"No," I said. "Tell me why. What is that?"

His eyes went wide as he looked past me. I turned my head to follow his gaze. That was when I saw a black mist creep around a tree in the distance, heading toward us. The tree had become brittle, and the trunk turned as black as obsidian.

"Caleb?" I said, panic rising in my voice.

"We don't know what that is, but every day we're here, it moves closer." He kneeled with me, both of us still staring at the mist. "You need to get out of here."

My gaze turned back to him, and my eyes met his. "Tell me about the spell that helped reincarnate me."

"I can't," Caleb snapped as he reached out his hand to pull me to my feet. I could grab onto him that time and stood up.

"Stop being so goddamn stubborn, and tell me. You said a witch used the last remaining bark from the tree on Gallows Hill to bring me back. How? How is it that a tree can do that?"

Caleb looked past me again. "It's getting close. Have Patricia call you back," he said, ignoring my desperate plea for help. "Please, Mercy."

I stepped closer to him, feeling the beam of light bounce off my chest and hover over his. "What are you not telling me?"

Caleb shook his head. "I've hidden things from you. Unforgivable things. But this secret will change you. I'm sorry. We will find a way out of here without your help. Don't risk your life for us again."

"Enough! Tell me the witch's name who helped you." He shook his head. "Just give me the name!" When I shouted, the rolling sound of thunder echoed around me, knocking me off my feet. Caleb tried to grab me, but the dark mist had reached us. It stretched out and gripped me by the back of my neck, yanking my spirit toward the ground. The tingling feeling of fingers stroked my back, raising every hair on my skin. I heard Caleb shout for me in the distance as I watched the black mist circle my body, trapping me.

"Dante!" I heard Caleb shout, but my eyes wouldn't leave the dark entity that was so close now that I felt a spark of energy run through me. The spark felt malevolent, cruel, and all-consuming. Fear surged as I struggled off my stomach and onto my back.

Oh my God.

The mist hovered over me, paralyzing every energy force I projected. I could feel the heaviness of the black mist press down on me like it was about to consume my soul.

I couldn't move.

"Mercy," I heard a woman's voice call out. "Mercy, come back."

I felt a powerful jolt in my chest as my spirit was yanked from the black entity and flung back into my body with a flash of white light. My eyes shot open, and Riley had his arms wrapped around me in a tight grip. I was back in the witch shop.

"No! Why did you pull me back?" I asked, looking at Riley's chest. "Why are you cradling me like a baby?"

Riley released his hold. "Sorry, you were shaking so hard you were about to fall out of the chair, and Patricia felt a dark force surrounding you. Someone was trying to breach the spell."

"What?" I asked, turning to Patricia.

She panted, her shoulders heaving with every breath, the color completely drained from her face. "It was a demon, Mercy. They know you're trying to save the coven. It tried to cut off the link between this spell and your spirit to trap you there."

"What demon?" I asked.

Patricia arched her back and rubbed her palms, which were trembling slightly. "I don't know. Whatever *that* was, it was pure evil and powerful. I felt their dark energy. It felt heavy, and the walls of the shop were shaking. It was in-between worlds, and it somehow brought the two realms together." She looked down, averting her eyes from mine. "I'm sorry. It took all my power to pull you back. I can't do that spell again."

I nodded. "I understand." Yes, I understood, but I couldn't imagine not being able to reach my coven again. I had to save them. I had to protect them from that place and whatever evil had tried to catch me and was trying to break down the walls of Purgatory to enter our own world.

CHAPTER 4

MAURICE

I tapped my fingers impatiently against my right leg, waiting for Julian to join me at my new club, formally owned by Alexander Winchester, the now-deceased father of my greatest enemy.

Alexander had rented out this space for only a few weeks before he gave up everything to be with his precious little reborn daughter. A mistake he'd paid for at the jagged edge of my blade. He and the rest of those pathetic excuses for witches were now ash, floating in the Pacific.

Before I took over the club, I had been a member of Alexander's clan. In fact, he made me second-in-command. It drove me mad to have to answer to another, and once I learned who Alexander was and his connection to Mercy, I had to get the fuck out of there. It was only a matter of time before he realized who I actually was and what I had done to her, and one of us would take out the other. I thought if I could use my connections to find out everything I could about what was happening behind closed doors regarding Alexander's next move, I could use that to my advantage.

The only reason I found a safe passage here was because that angel bitch, Tatyana, had taken everything away from me and even burned down my lair.

Burned it to the fucking ground.

It didn't matter anymore. The fool was dead, and everything Alexander had was now mine. Marcus had introduced me to the Black Horse Clan, vouching my character to Alexander. The fool didn't even question the story, and I quickly became a member.

Marcus was also friends with Roland, Caleb's father. Roland trusted him, even though he was an idiot to do so. Roland had no idea that Marcus had been working for me all these years. Once Roland had tricked me into giving up Mercy's blood to make him mortal, I used Marcus to my benefit. Marcus fed Roland little bits of our plan so that Roland would share the information with the coven. It was how we were able to steer them where we wanted them to go.

I eyed the clock again. *Where the fuck was Julian?*

The door suddenly chimed, pulling my attention to the front of the room. After it had swung open, sunlight entered the club, washing over me and warming my ice-cold cheeks. The sweet victory made me grin.

I won.

The potion had worked, and now I would soon lead an army of vampires that would finally wipe out the existence of the last remaining witches and werewolves on Earth. These two despicable groups continued to suppress our race and stand in our way. Once the war began, we would have our ultimate victory, and I'd have my revenge.

Julian strolled past me and placed a small duffle bag on a table toward the back.

"You were *supposed* to have been here thirty minutes ago," I seethed through gritted teeth. "Where the fuck have you been?"

"Clara's body is having difficulty holding onto Kylan's spirit, so I had to try a suppression spell to help her out," he explained. "I don't recognize her anymore."

I huffed. "This is what that bitch wanted. She wanted him to take her body as his fucking puppet. Clara knew exactly what she was getting herself into."

His hand balled into a fist. Was Julian honestly going to challenge me right now? Would he be so reckless?

"We could have stopped Clara. Maybe talked her out of it," he said rather pointedly.

"Right," I grumbled. "Clara has always done what she wants. And she wanted to become a flesh sacrifice to the Original." Julian's glower intensified.

He's crossing a very thin line with me today.

Since we pulled Kylan into Clara's body, Julian wouldn't stop bitching about what Kylan was doing to her. I often wondered how hollow his mundane life really was that he couldn't just lighten up and look toward our future and what all this meant. Julian didn't see the big picture as I did. He was about to become a prince in my kingdom and have almost everything he wanted, yet this was what he was obsessing about: Clara's well-being.

"Where are they now?" I continued.

Julian leaned back against the bar, his arms folded tightly against his chest. "Clara is back at our lair, but we'll bring her in later today. It appears that Kylan is trying to figure out how to use her magic. She didn't exactly leave him a manual, and communication between the two is practically useless. Her soul is barely holding on to what's left of her body. She can't reach his mind, so she's stuck like a fucking prisoner."

"This conversation is boring me," I said dismissively. "Is the hangar ready for us or not?"

He nodded, but his nostrils flared. I had hit a nerve.

"That's all that matters now," I said. Julian huffed, but he didn't refute what I said. He knew I was right.

Bringing Kylan back at the time felt like a brilliant idea, but I feared he'd attempt to dismantle my operation or take it over. He had his own agenda, and I wasn't going to let him think I would step down in my role in all this. This was *my* army, and I wanted to be the one to take out our enemies. Not Kylan. I wanted to be the one to look Mercy in the eyes before I killed her ... for good this time.

Well, I might kill her.

Roland had relayed to Marcus what had happened after she escaped from me the second time. Her aunt's boyfriend had tried to kill Mercy with their dagger, but she'd ripped the fool's heart out. It excited me when I learned what she'd done to another witch without hesitation or remorse. The ruthless power she had; that was the Mercy I couldn't shake out of my thoughts.

Not to mention everything we had done when she was behind my walls and underneath me.

Fuck.

I had never felt so conflicted in my entire fucking existence. Mercy was alone now, her coven was dead, and all I had to do was retake her. *If* I did decide to kill her, now would be the perfect time to do it. I just had to find that damn dagger.

The front door chimed again, pulling me from my thoughts, and Marcus walked in, dragging a woman behind him whom I didn't recognize. She was tall, with thick thighs, hourglass curves, and long black hair that reached her hips. Her toned arms were bare, and she wore a tank top and tight black jeans. She looked like someone who could hold her own in a fight. Stunning, strong, and viciously delicious. Unfortunately for her, this wasn't a fight she'd ever be able to win.

Marcus tossed the girl onto the floor like a rag doll in front of us, and I cocked my head to the right. "Who is this beautiful creature?"

The girl glanced up but wouldn't meet my eyes. I could tell that Marcus had placed a restraint-type spell on her, which would explain her inability to fight. There was a look of loathing painted on her face, but instead of pissing me off with her obvious detestation of my presence, it only fueled me in this game of cat and mouse.

Marcus bent down, yanking the girl's long, dark hair back. "Look him in the eyes, dog," Marcus barked.

The girl's eyes turned bright yellow the instant she looked up, and she drew her mouth into a feral snarl, flashing her canines.

I wrinkled my nose. "And what pack are you from, little pup?"

When she didn't answer, I lifted her chin and dug my fingernail into her skin until she winced. She snarled right before she spat in my face.

I let out a low growl, rubbing my hand over my forehead before lifting my hand to strike her. The woman flinched, but she didn't attack. She simply kneeled there, quivering, waiting for me to hurt her.

A slight chuckle rumbled in my chest. The werewolf woman wanted me to draw blood so it would ignite her rabid beast's side, override the spell, and she'd transition to rip me to shreds.

Clever girl.

I placed my hand on her again, taking my chances of her striking back, but that time, I caressed her cheek with the back of my hand. "She's going to be our first test subject, isn't she, Marcus?" I asked, looking up at him.

A side smirk pulled on Marcus's lips. "She's all yours, boss."

It had been three hours of listening to her howl and pound against the steel walls of the walk-in freezer at the back of the club. We had her chained securely against a concrete support beam in the center of the freezer. By now, she had transitioned to her wolf form, so we needed to wait until she calmed the fuck down enough to turn back.

Clara sat in the corner booth of the front bar, panting heavily, as if her body struggled to take in the oxygen around her. Sweat poured from her forehead; instead of wiping it dry as a normal person would, the sweat dripped over her eyes and into her mouth.

I cringed.

Vile waste of space.

I watched Kylan struggle this last week to keep Clara's body from falling apart. I didn't quite understand how he was able to possess that weakling of a human, Cami, for so long, but inside of Clara, a powerful witch, her body looked as if she were dying. Her hair was matted, dark circles formed under her eyes, and the stench from her body caused me to gag whenever Clara walked over to me. She was becoming a rotted corpse. I kept my distance and sauntered toward where Julian was waiting.

I wondered how long Clara would last with Kylan possessing her body. I also wondered about the werewolf in that freezer. Their bodies were far warmer than humans, so the temperature shouldn't kill her. Would it be enough to keep her subdued and alive? It was the only place strong enough to keep her secure if the chains I had clamped around her ankles and wrists were to break.

"It's ready," Julian said as he handed me a vial of purple liquid.

"Is she supposed to drink this?" I asked.

Julian grinned. "You throw it at the ground next to her."

I looked at him with an eyebrow cocked. "And then what?"

"It basically works like a purple smoke bomb," he explained.

Julian had thought of everything, apparently. Would we really want to get that close to a wolf who had already transitioned and risk being torn apart? No. We had to think bigger than that.

"You can't miss, though. If you do, there won't be enough for them to breathe in and slow down their transition. When the vial breaks, the chemical compound with the wolfsbane will activate, creating a large smoke-like plume."

I bit the side of my lower lip. "And the glass is thin enough to break easily?"

"Yes, Maurice," Julian answered with a roll of his eyes.

"I don't want to wait any longer to test this. Bring the dog out," I said.

Julian pulled the wolf woman to the center of the main room, and she collapsed to the floor. She was naked, shivering, having ripped through her clothes in her transition to her wolf form. Maybe we had kept her in there too long. Didn't matter. She'd be dead soon enough. I took a few steps toward the shivering woman.

She recoiled but then froze, slowly lifting her head to meet my eyes. The look of loathing from this beast made it clear that, despite her warm-blooded anatomy, her blood was running cold with hatred.

"What ... do ... you want from me?" she stammered. Her teeth were chattering, barely able to form her words.

"Obedience," I said with a grin. "Aren't good dogs supposed to be obedient to their masters? I'd like for every wolf pack to join our side or suffer the consequences if they choose to remain loyal to those damn witches. If I gave you a choice right now, would you betray your own kind to survive? I'd treat you like family, as I have to all those who have worked for me. I won't degrade you to the point of calling me master with the title I'd give you. No, you'd be one of us. A part of our clan."

Her eyes turned yellow once more, and a low growl rumbled from her chest. She spat again at my feet, and I could see claws beginning to slide out from beneath her knuckles.

I smirked, letting out a low chuckle from amusement.

"Well, I guess I have my answer, don't I?" I tossed the vial into the air, backing away from the impact. It hit the ground before her, and purple smoke burst into the air, surrounding her. She dug her claws into the floorboards and howled as her spine contorted upward. The sound of pain reverberated off the walls, a delightful song to my ears. The smoke faded away, and I could see the bones of the woman's back straining and cracking, trying to shift.

With one last howl, her spine pulled back into her body, and she collapsed onto the ground, wrapping her arms tightly around her waist. Julian handed me a silver sword, and without hesitation, I swung it down toward her neck and sliced off her head.

CHAPTER 5

MERCY

D orian's wet towel hung loosely over the towel rack, and water droplets trickled down the mirror from the steam.

So, he showered after his run and took off again. Outstanding.

After I left the bedroom and entered the kitchen, I noticed a folded-up note on the kitchen counter.

We won't be home tonight. See you in the morning.

Love you, Dorian

I threw the note back onto the table and ran my hand through my hair.

Are you kidding me?

There was no explanation of where he was or why he'd left, and I felt a deep annoyance I didn't have a right to feel. I'd taken off plenty of times, and Dorian had always let me do what I wanted without checking in every two seconds. But this was the first time Dorian had left me alone in the house, especially without telling me where he was going. He didn't even send me any text messages during the day.

My mind immediately overreacted, but given how he had pulled away this morning after we'd had sex, I couldn't entirely rule out the possibility that he didn't want to be around me right now, and *that* stung.

He wonders about you and Caleb. He wonders if you still love him.
I cursed at that nagging voice in my head.

That was the voice that kept me up at night, wondering if I was making the right decision by starting a relationship with Dorian again before I brought my coven back. But I also thought about all the years we had lost and that Caleb, although stubborn and arrogant at times, would want me to be happy.

I didn't know what to do with myself tonight. This was also the first time I had been alone in this house since the coven had died. I couldn't rest at night anymore in my own place. The moment I entered my kitchen after they all died, it all felt wrong. All I thought about were the four people who were a part of me now lying lifeless in a mausoleum. The silence was choking me. I couldn't sleep. I couldn't eat. So, Dorian and Noah helped pack my bag and gave me another place to call home.

I had to distract myself, or my mind would enter dark places I didn't want it to go. Being alone meant thinking about my coven. Being alone meant wondering if Dorian still loved me and if I had done something to upset him. Why would he just leave like that?

I need to stop overthinking this or I will drive myself mad.

I entered the kitchen, placed a frozen dinner in the microwave, and looked around the empty dining area.

Netflix sounded good, but before I turned on the television, I pulled out my cell phone, dialed Raven's Mental Institution, and they connected me with Cami.

"Hey, girl. How are you feeling?" I asked once I heard her voice on the other end.

"Ready to go home," she said. "I know I'm not ready, but I miss you. I miss my mom."

I nodded, even though she couldn't see me. "I know. Your mind and body went through something none of us quite understand. It took a toll on you. All I want is for you to get well."

A soft sigh echoed through the receiver. "Thanks, Mercy. How are *you*, by the way? How's Dorian?"

I could only imagine her cute, dimpled grin as she asked that question.

As much as I wanted to tell her what had been going on and gossip with her like we used to, she wasn't ready for any more drama until she was fully healed. Still, hearing her voice tonight helped me relax a bit.

Just a little.

"We're good," I said. The phrase rolled off my tongue as if I had rehearsed it a thousand times in my head to make myself feel better. "We're," I said, leaning back in my chair, "getting things back to normal again."

She laughed. "Oh, come on. Will our lives ever be normal again?"

No.

"Yeah. Someday, I hope."

"Love you," she said.

"I love you, too. I'll stop by to check on your mom this week."

There was silence on the other end, and I heard a quiet sniffle. "Thank you. That would mean a lot to me ... and to her."

We hung up, and I gripped the phone tightly and closed my eyes. I wasn't going to cry. Not right now.

I sent a quick text to Shannon, whom I haven't spoken to in weeks.

> **Me:** *Miss you, bestie.*

A minute passed before the chime of a message came through.

> **Shannon**: *God, I miss you too. You'd love New Orleans. Visit once you save the world. Okay?*

I didn't know why it was so difficult to respond to that. If I could trade for a moment in Shannon's shoes to be an ordinary woman, pretending none of who I am or what I know is real, I would. Sure, it wouldn't last forever. Now that I know what's out there, I was happy to be the one to fix it. But shit, I needed a break.

I put my phone down, picked up the remote, and turned on a new comedy that had just been released last month. I was okay with a comedy tonight. Romance, not so much.

———

I eyed the clock once the credits rolled, which read almost midnight.

Can I even sleep?

I texted Dorian, asking if everything was okay, and waited.

And waited.

And waited.

My phone beeped after twenty minutes.

Dorian: *I need a few days. I love you. Please forgive me.*

My heart sank.

"A few days for what?" I said aloud to myself.

And what am I forgiving him for?

I turned off the television, put my plate in the sink, and padded to the bathroom to get ready for bed. Once I had changed and brushed my teeth, I went back to the living room and sat on the couch.

What is happening?

My hands felt clammy.

What are you up to, Dorian?

I grabbed my cell and dialed Riley.

"Hey," I said when the call connected.

He yawned, but it sounded muffled like he was trying to hide it. "What's up, Mercy? It's midnight."

"Sorry. I know you never talk to Dorian, but have you spoken with him tonight by chance?"

"I haven't," he said. There was a slight pause. "He's not there?"

"He's not, and he didn't mention where he'd taken off to. I do know he's with Noah, though. Dorian's been acting strangely lately, too. He's had these nightmares almost every night since I turned him human, kicking and flailing his arms. I've had to hold him steady and sometimes wake him. He always tells me he can't remember his dreams, but I don't buy it."

I didn't give Riley a chance to interrupt before I continued. "I was going a little insane tonight, so I texted him, and he did text back, but all it said was that he needed a few days and to forgive him. What the hell does that mean?" Riley stayed silent on the other end of the line, and it made my head dizzy. "You know something, don't you?"

"I don't know, Mercy," he finally said. "He asked me something the other day that I thought was a little strange, but I didn't really think anything of it until now."

My heart beat wildly in my chest. "What did Dorian ask you?"

"What it was like being a werewolf and where the other packs live. I just assumed he was curious about the manpower we had while we formed a plan to bring the packs together," Riley explained, and the clamminess of my palms returned when Riley continued. "He wouldn't, would he? Without telling you?"

Yes, he would. If it meant I couldn't stop him.

I sighed heavily. "How could I have missed this? He has been torturing himself, because he has lost all the power he had as a vampire. I knew he hated the feeling of being so vulnerable and weakened. But to go from one supernatural creature to another?"

"You know why he wouldn't tell you. Not saying that this is what's going on, but he's never asked me anything about what it's like being a werewolf. It's not like we talk about anything unless it's about you. I'm sorry I didn't bring it up earlier, but it didn't seem suspicious at the time."

I tucked a pillow under my neck, shifting my body around until I was comfortable on the couch, and looked up at the ceiling. "Don't apologize. This isn't your fault, and it's not up to me to tell Dorian that he can't become a werewolf. But if he's being turned and doesn't want me there while he goes through it ..." The pain of it all pulled at my chest. "... that stings."

"What do you want me to do?" Riley asked.

"Where's the nearest pack?"

There was a moment of silence on the other end until he answered. "The closest pack I know of is the one in Providence. They live close to The Black Horse, and yes, it's a pack I mentioned to him. We had been negotiating that territory for the last few months with their alpha," he explained. I heard a few clicks come through the line. "I'll wake Amber to get the exact address and send it over to you."

"Thanks."

After I hung up, I grabbed my car keys and waited patiently for Riley's text to come through with the address. I hoped it wasn't too late for me to hold Dorian's hand as he transitioned for the first time.

CHAPTER 6

MERCY

I glanced down at the address and then up at the numbers on the house. This was the place.

It was a two-story townhouse with a white picket fence surrounding the property. Riley had said that if Dorian had indeed sought out a pack, this was where he would have gone. Or, at least, the alpha who lived here would know where he might be.

I hesitated before I knocked three times and waited. A beautiful woman answered after a minute. Okay, she wasn't just beautiful; she was drop-dead gorgeous. Her long, wavy, chestnut brown hair fell to the center of her back. Her eyes were shimmery gray, and her skin was flawlessly tanned, almost close to Noah's complexion. She was also tall, maybe a few inches taller than me.

"I'm looking for Dorian and Noah," I said, irritation clear in my voice.

"You must be Mercy," she said. Her smile that followed looked forced as she pressed her lips together tightly.

The sound of her saying my name bugged the hell out of me, but I was relieved that she at least knew who I was. Dorian or Noah must have mentioned me at some point.

"Is Dorian safe?" That was all I wanted to know. She had to confirm that he was safe before I left. I didn't want to be here unless he wanted me to be. I hadn't even walked through the door and was already feeling unwelcome.

She nodded. "Yeah, he's safe." She gestured toward the stairs opposite the doorway leading to the second floor. "Come on in."

The woman escorted me to the bedroom at the end of the hall. I spotted Dorian on a bed, curled into a fetal position and holding his stomach. He looked to be unconscious but breathing evenly. Noah sat in the corner in a rocking chair. Once Noah's eyes met mine, he placed his phone on an end table and smiled at me.

"I told him you'd use a locator spell," Noah said, and he looked pleased to see me.

I shook my head. "I didn't, actually. I just put it together after I talked to Riley."

"Ah, well," Noah said, his smile slipping, "we didn't think about that part. Dorian's okay, though. Just running a fever that his body isn't used to."

The woman stepped past me and walked over to the bed, placing her hand on Dorian's brow. She pulled a wet rag from a bowl, squeezed out the excess water, and draped it over his forehead.

"This will cool him down a bit. It won't be as bad tomorrow," she said, as if she had done this a thousand times before. It clicked right then that this must be the Providence alpha.

"Was it you who turned him?" I asked.

It was a dim-witted question to ask. This entire situation was numbing my brain. As far as I could tell, we were the only ones inside the house.

I was well aware of the bond between a newly turned werewolf and their maker. Riley had explained to me in detail the continuous need to know if Amber was okay and the never-ending presence of the alpha. It also created a desire to be at each other's beck and call at any given moment. Amber felt responsible for how he had behaved as a wolf, and Riley felt obligated to submit to her if she called for it. Amber and Riley were also bonded as "mates," as Riley described it. Meaning that their ties ran deeper than the typical werewolf pack bond.

Was that how this was going to be from here on out? Dorian and her bonding and sharing moments I couldn't possibly understand? Would he reject me and take her as his partner?

She smiled thinly, but she didn't look up at me. Her eyes wouldn't leave Dorian's curled form. "Yes," she said. "My name is Davina. And I promise to take care of him, okay? He's part of *our* pack now."

Those words cut through me like a jagged knife, threatening to poison me with its rusty edge. Was she trying to agitate me on purpose? I clenched my jaw and stepped near the bed, giving her a hard stare. Noah tensed and stood from the rocking chair, taking a few steps toward me.

"Like hell he is," I said, choking back a sob as tears stung my eyes.

She frowned. "You don't get it, do you? I'm his maker, and when an alpha wolf turns someone, that new wolf joins that pack. That's how it's always been, and it will always be."

"Noah," I said, my anger still simmering. He slinked across the room, and for the first time, my massive friend cowered at me. He lowered his head, barely making eye contact.

"We knew Amber wouldn't agree to this," Noah said, his eyes shameful as his head stayed low.

"So, you asked a stranger?" I said, sticking my finger out and waving it in her direction. "What the fuck, Noah?"

Davina fixed me with an icy stare. "He's not a prisoner here. If he wants, he can walk out the door right now. But he *needs* to heal. So, I suggest not."

"But he's part of *your* pack now, right?" I turned back to Noah. "Riley and Amber can train him and—"

"*They* didn't turn him," Davina remarked. Her presence fueled a wave of anger inside me that made me want to ignite my powers in this room and show her she wasn't going to win this argument.

"I swear, Noah, if she doesn't stop talking to me like this, I'm going to hurt her," I warned in a near whisper, but I knew she heard me. I also knew I was better than this. I had to pull myself together.

Davina chuckled and moved toward me. "I get it. You're used to being the leader of everyone around you. Werewolves are also your allies; may I remind you? Not enemies. But this is the way it has always been. A wolf needs a pack, and our pack is a powerful one. There are twenty-five of us, and we're all like family. I promise I'll take care of him."

I threw my hands up. "So, what, Dorian moves out and lives here with you?" The stabbing pain in my chest burned with every word I spoke.

She rolled her eyes. "Well, that's a bit dramatic. But no. Dorian lives with *you*," she said, and my temper, for a moment, eased up. "You're his girlfriend, after all, right?"

I nodded and looked down, wondering if that really was the case now.

"It just means that if we ever need him, he must leave you and help the pack first. We're his family now."

I hated this, and her words crawled deeply under my skin. My temper flared back up. "Dorian has a family," I said. "Noah and me."

Davina frowned. "I understand, and I respect that. But if you don't accept this, you'll lose him."

My eyes met hers, but I couldn't find my words.

"Listen," she started again. This time, she carefully modulated her voice. "When Dorian showed up at my door and asked for this, I told him no. I don't turn just anyone. But then he told me about you and his life as a vampire and what it meant to him to have the strength and ability to protect you, even if you could protect yourself."

My heart skipped a beat, and the sickening feeling in the pit of my stomach returned. Dorian did this for *me*, regardless of the consequences. Even if it meant losing me forever.

"How did that change your mind?" I asked.

She smiled, taking a step closer to me. "Because most of the time, those who want to be turned do it for power. Dorian loathed being a vampire, but he also had no one else to live for ... besides you ... his mate."

Mate. Am I really Dorian's mate?

The shame and guilt burned me from the inside out, and the moment I looked up at Noah, I realized I shouldn't be here and that I didn't belong.

"I'm sorry," I said, feeling defeated. "Can I at least sit with him?"

She nodded and gestured toward Dorian.

When I sat on the bed, I leaned down, kissing him gently on the cheek, and when our skin touched, I inhaled deeply, taking in his scent. Dorian smelled different. Not bad, just ... different. He smelled like wet tree bark and dry autumn leaves.

I buried my face deeper into his neck and gently kissed him right below the ear. He didn't acknowledge my presence, and at that moment, I felt like Davina had won, even though this was never a competition. But I felt like I had lost the most important person in my life ... again.

CHAPTER 7

MERCY

Running. That had been my greatest escape these last couple of days. I'd taken a long run through downtown East Greenwich each night since I had left Davina's. I'd start at Dorian's house, sprint until I reached Main Street, then finish with a slow jog through Goddard Park.

The town was quiet tonight, with a light wind bringing in an icy chill. The only sounds were from a few boisterous customers tossing back drinks at the bar next to La Masseria.

I should join them.

Maybe a glass of wine would help ease this unbearable ache in my chest.

I sat on a bench in front of an adorable boutique dog shop and placed my hands over my cramped leg. I powered up just enough magic to ease the muscle tension, then leaned back on the bench, looking across the road.

My phone wasn't with me; I left it charging on the nightstand in the bedroom. To be honest, it felt nice being disconnected. I wanted desperately to take myself out of my world and take in everything else around me I had been too busy to notice lately. Like the dogs being walked every night down Main, while pedestrians stopped to admire the pet and compliment the owner on how cute it was. The local business owners were now locking up their shops or restaurants after a successful day of business. They'll most likely return to a safe home with their families, ready to prepare a warm meal for the night.

The coven and I took advantage of our powers and our mission, so much so that we had often forgotten we were also human. We lived in a human world where people went about their lives completely oblivious to the supernatural creatures around them. They were happy because they didn't have to fear that, at any moment, a monster would leap out of the shadows and kidnap or kill them. I put my hand over my chest, and the elements thumped gently against my hand in a strange, comforting gesture. I blew out a sigh and stood up.

Looking both ways on the road, I scampered across to La Masseria. I wouldn't be sharing a glass of wine with the patrons at the bar tonight, but I also didn't feel like going home and cooking anything, either.

It took me a little longer to get home since I had been speed walking instead of running the entire way to avoid dropping my dinner. I turned to the carport and spotted Noah's motorcycle. My heart kicked against my ribcage as excitement and anxiety surged up my insides.

I rushed inside and looked around the family room, spotting two backpacks on the couch. I hustled toward the kitchen. Dorian and Noah were sitting at the island, and Dorian had his cell gripped in his hand.

He turned to me, panic in his eyes. "Mercy," he said. "I've been calling—"

"I'm sorry," I said, cutting him off, and placed my dinner on the island. "I went for a run and left my phone here."

Dorian's face lit up as he stood from the kitchen barstool, and as he took a step toward me, I ran to him and leaped into his arms. I felt the warmth of his skin against my cheek as I squeezed him tightly to my chest. The temperature of his body was unbelievably hot. I had forgotten how warm werewolves could get during their first transition. Riley had been near boiling when he was bitten.

"Are you okay?" I asked, pressing my forehead to his. "Please tell me you're okay."

He nodded. "Davina said I should have my full strength by morning. I just couldn't be away from you any longer, though. I had to come home." His breath felt heavy on my lips.

I needed to hear that more than anything, but I didn't want to overreact as I had at Davina's, so I simply nodded. "I'm just happy the transition went smoothly and that you're okay." I lowered myself to the ground but didn't take my eyes off his.

He frowned. "I'm sorry I did this without you. I couldn't bear to watch the disappointment in your eyes that I knew I'd see if I told you what I was going to do. I'll regret that decision. I just ... I couldn't go any longer as a human. I couldn't bear that emptiness in my bones that I wasn't—and would never be—good enough to fight with you."

I pressed my hands against his broad chest. The dark circles under his eyes from the lack of sleep were more pronounced as tears glistened, slowly sliding down his cheeks.

I rubbed the pads of my thumbs under his eyes, wiping the tears dry. "Oh, Dorian, you were always good enough, but if this is what will make you happy, then I support this decision because I love you."

Dorian's smile was faint, but it still brought goosebumps to the back of my arms. My eyes left his mouth, and I examined the rest of his face, which looked slightly different from before. He was always strikingly handsome, but going from a vampire to a werewolf ... it *was* different. His skin was slightly tanned and rougher. His jaw wasn't as smooth as before. Now it was scruffy, and his hair was untamed. I placed my hand on his chest again, and even that feature was significantly different as my fingers traced the defined muscles that covered his stomach. I gulped. The faintest touch of his chest aroused me to my inner core and between my legs.

He leaned down, kissed me gently, grabbed my hand, and squeezed. "I'm going to go try to get some sleep," he said, his voice dropping to a whisper to keep his words from Noah. "I'd very much like to ravish your body in my bed, but my body isn't fully healed." He leaned back and smiled. "Do you want to head to bed now and lie with me instead?"

I smiled and winked. "What a silly question."

Noah passed us with a side smirk and a low chuckle, giving us our privacy, and Dorian escorted me to the bedroom.

Though Dorian was still healing, his hands roamed my naked body, as if, no matter what, he couldn't contain himself. Unfortunately, that was all he had the strength to do. His fingers found my breasts, circling outside my nipples before roaming down to my thighs. His other hand wrapped in my hair, giving it a gentle squeeze. "Once I'm healed, we should test out my stamina."

I couldn't hold back my wide grin.

"Okay, this transition may not be the worst thing that could have happened to you," I teased.

I laid my head on Dorian's chest once his hand returned to my stomach. He rested it there, closing his eyes, as if his body were aching again, and he could no longer move. The heat from his body wasn't as scorching as it had been earlier, but I still had to wipe the sweat off my cheek once I lifted my head from his chest. I brushed a stray hair away from his eyes and stroked his cheek gently.

The time was almost nine in the morning now. I slipped out of the room, secured my robe, and entered the kitchen. Noah sat at the dining table, sipping orange juice and reading something on his phone.

"Good morning," Noah said as I grabbed the brewed coffee from the kettle.

"Morning. Thanks for making coffee. I can't believe how long we slept," I admitted. "But it felt nice." Once I filled my mug, I looked back up. "I haven't been able to sleep since you guys left."

Noah placed his phone down on the island and offered me an apologetic smile. Then his attention diverted to Dorian, who staggered into the kitchen, stifling a yawn. He looked healthier than he had last night, though. The circles under his eyes weren't as dark, and his bloodshot eyes were regaining their natural, earthy brown. My attention didn't linger on his face for very long, though. My attention turned to his bare chest and his new werewolf physique.

Holy hell. I'll never get used to the change.

Dorian had always been well-built, but this new body was something else. I didn't realize my mouth had gaped open, and that I was staring stupidly at Dorian until I heard Noah chuckle behind me.

"You can see why he wanted to be a werewolf now, huh?" Noah said.

Dorian laughed but shook his head at Noah's comment, and I simply rolled my eyes. My cheeks warmed until they turned a visible red shade.

I then looked over at Dorian's hand, tightly gripping a book. "Here," he said, holding it out toward me. "I borrowed this for you to read."

On the cover, a pack of wolves gathered near a grove of trees. It was thick, heavy, and leather-bound. "What is this?"

"Davina gave it to me to help me understand where werewolves come from and what abilities I should expect with this new body. It has a lot of information about werewolf laws and politics."

"Oh," I said. "Werewolves have their own politics?"

I realized, once again, that there was a lot I didn't know.

"You don't have to read it, but since you researched so much about witches when you first learned you were one, I thought maybe you'd like to learn more about your partner."

God, I had questioned it a million times these last few days. Hearing Dorian say aloud that we were, indeed, still together brought a sense of pure relief washing over me. "I'd love to read it," I said.

I felt Dorian's hand on mine as I sat at the kitchen island. "You're my family, okay? And pack or no pack, you come first in my life."

My heart skipped.

He had heard everything Davina said that night while he lay curled up on that bed. Hearing him say those words brought the comfort I needed to stop dwelling on what had happened. He was mine, and no other bond would break that.

I gave him a warm smile and squeezed his hand tightly. "Thank you, Dorian. I ... I needed to hear that."

With my coffee in hand, I sat back in my chair at the kitchen island and opened the old book to chapter one.

CHAPTER 8

MAURICE

There were so many annoyingly cheerful people on Main Street. Every fucking human who passed me felt inclined to wave their hand in my face and smile, as if they knew me. I greeted every grin that came my way with a scowl.

I couldn't wait until the day when every single one of these powerless beings bowed before me and submitted. The day would come when every soul in this town and every other godforsaken city in this country would be mine for the taking, but I recognized it would take time. Rome surely wasn't built in a day.

My plan had to start somewhere, even though I'd already fleshed it out entirely in my mind. Julian suggested it was best to start at the location of our new lair: Providence. We'd work our way into Boston then back down to East Greenwich. Eventually, we'd take over the entire East Coast once we had enough followers, but for now, taking one city at a time was the best way to start. It would be a better way to control the expansion. It wasn't realistic to take the entire world as mine, but I could help restore balance and help create enough clans throughout each country, so we could become top of the food chain and not have to hide anymore.

They needed a leader. I would become that leader, the ruler of all the vampire clans across the globe.

Something I should have become centuries ago. I was meant to be a ruler, as my father was. He taught me that, without power your enemies would overthrow you. The wars fought when I entered adulthood taught me that life was precious and that I was close to tasting that status within the society my father reared me and my brother into.

That was, until my enemies attacked and killed my mother, but not before they stabbed me in the chest, making her watch. Once they believed I was dead, they slit her throat, and I could only lie there as her spilled blood mingled with mine. I was powerless, weak, and disgustingly human. I was on the brink of death before a vampire named Valentina found me and brought me back.

She was the first vampire created by Kylan, and she promised me a life of wealth, power, and respect. I would have the power to destroy the men who took everything from me. Then I could take whatever I wanted, never left vulnerable or exposed without being able to take my revenge. I could become a god.

I had been blessed with wealth and respect, but until I could subdue these humans and rule over the vampires who roamed this world, I would never have that power my maker had promised. She helped me see the world in a new light, and once she shared with me the prophecy of the Chosen Ones and why they were coming to this earth—to stop us—I knew I had to take what I wanted, no, *needed*. Power. There was no greater thing than absolute power.

The door pinged as I entered a small jewelry shop at the end of Main Street. I would have much rather been shopping at Tiffany Co., but I didn't have time to drive back to Providence.

"How can I help you?" a young, pretty redhead on the other side of the counter asked.

"Hello," I said, my voice calm and steady, so I would not make her nervous. "I'm looking for a necklace for my fiancé."

She blushed and averted her eyes. "Um, anything in particular?"

"Emeralds would be nice. To match her exquisite eyes." I looked down into the case, scanning the small selection of necklaces. Most looked antique, and I was certain none were real diamonds.

"Okay, hmm, let me see," she said, looking into the case with me. "How about this one, sir?"

She grabbed a silver-chained necklace with an emerald pendant, but there was a yellow line across the center of the vibrant gem like it'd been flawed. I didn't love it, but the selection wasn't what I had expected. "I'll take it. She's not particularly picky. She appreciates everything that I give to her."

The store clerk smiled and turned toward the cash register, ringing me up. She spun around and placed the necklace in my hand. Her smile reached her eyes. "She's going to love it," she said. "And that will be one hundred and forty-five dollars."

I handed her the payment and asked her to point me to the restroom.

"Oh, we don't have a public restroom, but there's one across the street inside the library."

I smirked. "Please. I'll be quick."

She shifted nervously and looked toward the back door of the shop. "I have to unlock it for you. Let me grab the key."

"You're so kind, thank you."

The hunger inside me pulled at my stomach. I hadn't eaten since yesterday, and if I were going anywhere near Mercy, I would need to feed now. When a vampire loses control, there's no turning back. I always had to be in control.

She led me to the back hall, and I followed closely behind. I scanned the back, and luckily, there were no security cameras. Once we reached the bathroom doors, she placed the key in and opened the door. She turned around right as I grabbed her by the throat and threw her across the bathroom. Her head slammed hard against the tile wall, but before she could move, I ran toward her at lightning speed and lifted her up, propping her body over my bent leg. I sunk my teeth into her neck as she screamed. The woman didn't put up much of a fight but continued to scream as I fed. Her taste was decadent, as if she had just eaten a handful of candy. I let the blood fill me to satisfaction then released her. Her eyes filled with horror as I pulled her up to look at me. It was impossible to use compulsion on any supernatural being but not a human. Not every vampire had that ability, either. But I did. Anyone who Valentina directly turned had been blessed with that gift.

I grabbed her jaw firmly in my hand and turned her face so I could look directly into her eyes.

"I'm trying to be a better man, so listen carefully. For the next few days, you will wear a silk scarf around your neck. You will not remember me or the necklace I bought today. You'll stay in the bathroom for five minutes before you come out. Clean every drop of blood. Do you understand?"

"Yes. I don't know who you are, and I'll cover my neck," she said, her tone ripe with compliance, like the good girl she was.

I released her, straightened out my shirt, and rubbed the remaining blood off my mouth with a paper towel.

She swayed slightly from the blood loss, but her feet wouldn't move. I then exited through the front door, the emerald necklace wrapped around my fingers.

———◦◦◦———

I stood outside Dorian and Noah's home, watching Mercy through the window as she flipped through a book at the kitchen table. She looked quite beautiful this morning. Her hair was flat against her back, and as she pulled it to the side, she twisted it into a loose braid. Dorian entered the kitchen and placed his hand on the center of her back.

A weird sense of jealousy hit me while I stood there, watching another man touch her, and there was no rational explanation as to why I felt that way. The human emotions I had been having lately were driving me mad. I fucking hated feeling anything for her, let alone compassion, need, want, desire.

Fuck! This is ridiculous!

Mercy *had* to die. I'd be a damn fool to let her live after everything she had done to me. She was a threat to my plans and to my empire.

My phone buzzed at my hip.

Julian.

"What the hell do you want?" I asked once I picked up.

"Why are you not back yet? Where are you?" he asked.

I chuckled to myself. "You know where I am."

I heard him sigh heavily. "You're going to get yourself killed. If Mercy sees you—"

"She won't. But there's something I need to do first before I head back."

"Don't do anything stupid—"

I hung up on him, made my way to Mercy's car, and placed my gift for her on the hood. I smiled to myself. I hoped she missed me as much as I missed her.

—ell—

Back at the club, Julian had a naked blonde woman propped up on the edge of the stage and was fucking her ruthlessly while another woman touched herself, watching them.

He turned his head after I cleared my throat, pulling himself out of her and tucking his cock back in his pants.

"You're missing out on the party, Maurice." He leaned forward, nibbling on the blonde's neck instead.

My lips curled at the corner of my mouth. "I don't see much of a party," I said, looking around. "Where's the liquor and human sacrifice?"

Julian snarled at me. "You need to learn to relax. Stay for a bit and," he added, gesturing to the brunette, "have a snack while you finish this one off." His brow rose a suggestive notch.

"I've already eaten," I said. The brunette winked at me, her hand still rubbing between her legs. "But perhaps ..." I sized up the beautiful woman, who, though stunning, wasn't who I really wanted. I shrugged.

Oh, well.

"There might be a little room for dessert."

I turned toward the brunette again, whose heart pounded heavily against her chest. The longer I glowered at her, the more nervous she became. These two women had no idea what kind of precarious situation they had gotten themselves into. If they were smart, they would run.

I kept my eyes locked on the brunette as I approached her, and I could hear her heart rate spike again. Humans never tasted as sweet as a witch, but feeling a human squirm and cry for help when they had no power to stop me was beyond exhilarating.

"Stand up," I ordered. "Now."

She was quickly on her feet and looked at Julian, who gestured toward me. "It's okay, Lidia. He doesn't bite."

I snickered at his joke and placed my hand on her neck, digging my fingers into her skin and pulling her toward me. "Are you afraid?" I asked. My fangs protruded, and she jumped. I dug my nails deeper into her skin, and my fingernails drew blood from her neck. "I asked you a question, beautiful. Are you afraid?"

She nodded quickly, tears welling up in her eyes. I couldn't help but notice the similarities in her features to Mercy's. I didn't think Julian planned that. In fact, he likely brought this girl to distract me from thinking about Mercy. It wasn't working as well as he had probably hoped. But she would do, for now.

"What are you going to do?" Her voice hitched.

My smile grew wider. "I'm going to drain you of your blood, and then I'm going to kill you."

And with those last words, I sank my teeth into her neck and sucked, savoring the taste of the sweet liquid on my tongue. My cock hardened as she writhed against me, trying to free herself from the pain. Her body relaxed after a moment, falling limply into my arms, and a moan escaped her.

Well, becoming a better man is more difficult than I thought.

I pulled her away, licked my bottom lip, and bit into my wrist. When I held it up to her mouth, she weakly squirmed in my grip to get away, but I kept it firmly to her mouth until she had no choice but to swallow my blood.

"That's a good girl," I said right before I snapped her neck.

The scream coming from the blonde girl pierced my ears.

"Julian, shut her the fuck up and bring her over," I commanded. He hustled to cover her mouth with his hand, yanked her up from the stage, and brought her to me.

He glared into my eyes. "This wasn't what I had in mind."

"Yes," I said, "but this is so much more fun, don't you think?"

He flared his nostrils at me and tossed me the girl. "Do you want to live forever?" I asked as I placed my hands loosely on her throat. Her brow furrowed, clearly confused by my question. I didn't wait for a response. I leaned down, placed my lips on her neck, and gave her a soft kiss before my teeth sank into my third victim today.

Once I had completed the process of turning my two new loyal subjects, I tossed their bodies on a chaise lounge and walked toward the bar. "Whisky?" I asked Julian.

He frowned. "You're a fucking psychopath. You know that?"

I flashed a grin. "Whisky?" I repeated, and he nodded, throwing up his hands in defeat. "Once they wake, feed them the blood from the cooler. I don't have time to go hunting for their first meal right now."

"You got it, boss," he said with a salute, using his middle finger.

"Is there something you'd like to say to me?" I asked, waiting for him to test me with his defiance.

He shook his head and tossed back his drink. "No, sir."

CHAPTER 9

MERCY

"What is it?" I asked Noah as he inhaled deeply, placing his coffee mug carefully on the kitchen island. I shut my book, and Dorian and I exchanged a glance. "Noah, what's wrong? What do you smell?"

Being a werewolf was new to Dorian, so I wondered if he hadn't quite learned what to look for, but whatever Noah smelled had caught his nose, too. He scanned the room, taking each inhale slowly.

"It's not what. It's who," Noah said. He turned to the window, peered out, and rushed toward the door. I followed, but Noah was already in front of me, blocking the exit. "It's Maurice."

"Good," I said, attempting to move by him, but he stepped in front of me, folding his arms over his chest. "Please move out of my way, so I can kill the son of a bitch."

"Not after he's kidnapped you," Noah said. "Twice now, might I add."

I scrunched up my nose, stepped to the side, and continued walking toward the door. Noah could try to block me all he wanted, but he knew I'd strike back.

Dorian rushed next to me as I stepped outside. Sitting on the front windshield of my car was a small, wrapped gift box with a yellow bow.

A gift? Really?

After grabbing the box from the car, we came back into the house, and I sat on the couch with the "gift" and opened it. Inside were several petals of ... wolfsbane.

Immediately, I tossed it back toward the front door, which Noah still had propped open.

"Dorian, back up," I ordered.

Noah and I rushed outside and shut the door behind us, keeping Dorian inside. I raised my hand, creating a force of power around the house, shielding any possibility of the scent of the wolfsbane flower entering the home. I wasn't sure exactly how much it took to affect a werewolf, but I didn't want to risk it.

Once the house was under my shield, I eyed the petals on the ground and noticed something silver and shiny sticking out of the box. "Wait, there's something else," I said to Noah.

I slowly approached the box and the unwelcome present, noticing a silver chain. I picked it up and pulled the rest of what I now saw was a necklace out of the box. A sparkling emerald charm dangled from the chain.

Maurice bought me jewelry? What the actual fuck?

Feeling disgusted, I placed the necklace in the box, gathered up the wolfsbane, closed the lid, and resealed it with what was left of the tape.

"Why the hell would Maurice give me that?" I asked Noah, but my eyes darted to Dorian, standing in the window with his arms folded, scowling at us. He was clearly upset that I was keeping him away from this.

Noah looked weary, and he, too, was welcomed with an irritated glower from Dorian.

"Maurice has a one twisted, fucked up mind," Noah said. "He has some delusion that you belong to him. Before any of us even met you, he obsessed over the fact that the one who slipped away all those years ago was finally coming back. You were his reward for all he had done for the vampires' cause. He was only waiting for the opportunity to finally take you after three hundred and thirty years. When you were born, you became the most powerful person ever to exist. You were *better* than him. It didn't just become a battle to be the best; he wanted to possess the best. Maurice wanted victory by taking the most valuable creature ever to be born on this planet. If he could have you, he could take anything he wanted."

I looked down at my hands, which were suddenly shaking. Death was not my greatest fear. The thought of being one of Maurice's possessions was. It frightened the fuck out of me.

"Maurice feels entitled to you," Noah continued. "When he lost and no longer had that control, it became like a game to him. I don't think he will stop until he has you again or kills you. In either scenario, he wins."

My stomach twisted into knots. He would kill those who ran and torture those who tried to protect me.

And that included Dorian.

By sending wolfsbane, he was sending a message that he was planning to destroy those I loved.

After Noah and I drove to an alleyway to dispose of the wolfsbane and the necklace, we hurried back home, and before we entered, I pulled down the barrier around the house. I walked in slowly, watching Dorian's face turn from anger to relief.

"Don't ever do that again!" Dorian barked. I blinked in shock at his tone. This was the first time he had ever raised his voice at me.

"Excuse me?" I hissed.

"I'll be in my room," Noah said, quickly moving toward the hallway.

Once I heard the door shut behind him, I threw my hands up. "There was wolfsbane in that box, Dorian. It could have hurt you!"

Dorian's eyes went wide, and he took a step back. After everything that had happened, I realized he never saw what was inside the box.

He sat down slowly on the couch, burying his face in his hands.

"Dorian?" I said, kneeling in front of him. "We protect each other. That's the agreement. Okay?"

He looked up and nodded.

I placed my hand on his cheek. "If there's a threat against you, I will do everything in my power to keep you safe. If there's a threat against me that *I* can't handle, then you be that hero for me. If you had gone near that box, I could have lost you because who knew what enemies were waiting to strike if the wolfsbane had crippled you?" I squeezed his knee. "I want a long, beautiful life with you, Dorian. I didn't sign up to lose you just when we finally found each other again."

Silence flickered between us before Dorian aggressively gripped my elbows and yanked me up from my knees, directing me onto the couch and over his body. His eyes swirled with heated arousal.

As my lips parted, my eyes challenging his resolve, he gripped my hips, tossing me on my back until he was pinning me to the couch, holding me firmly between his thighs.

Whoa. This is not how I thought Dorian would react to those words.

He relaxed his grip on my waist just slightly and bent down, kissing me gently on my soft lips.

"I will love you until I take my last breath," I promised.

"You'll never die," he said, arching a brow.

I smiled at him shyly, my cheeks turning pink. "Exactly."

With a wry smile, Dorian drifted lower, unbuttoning my pants and sliding them down my smooth legs with ease. It wasn't long before my underwear was gone, too—tossed away on the floor like the most irrelevant piece of fabric.

His lips inched to my lower stomach, kiss by kiss. His eyes locked with mine as he trailed his tongue over my tender skin, and I arched my back in response.

"I need you, Dorian ..." I murmured, his name blending with a soft moan that escaped my lips. As if the sound of my voice beckoned him lower, he didn't waste time teasing. I hated fighting with him. All I wanted was to ease any leftover tension between us, and Dorian knew exactly how to do that.

In one swift movement, his tongue found the spot that ached the most for him. I tipped my head back, tangling my fingers in his hair. The way his tongue flickered against the tender bundle of my nerves was effortless and smooth, and it pushed waves of tingling sensations through my body. I spread my legs wider for him, allowing Dorian full access to my heated core.

A subtle moan escaped his lips as two of his fingers found my entrance, prodding at it momentarily before they slid into me. My whole body tensed at the sensation, shuddering in sweet pleasure.

"Yes.... More," was all I mustered before Dorian's pace picked up. His tongue circled around my clit as his fingers moved at a curved angle. Thrust after thrust, they brought me closer to that peak I ached for.

It didn't take long. A few moments passed before he tipped me over the edge, shaking on the couch as I soaked his fingers with my release. My orgasm tore rapidly through my body, leaving a warm, tingling sensation in its wake.

Dorian pulled back with a smug expression.

"Personal record, I'd say," he teased me. I rolled my eyes in response, watching him stand up. Instead of allowing him to create distance between us, I reached for his pants, unbuttoning them.

Dorian stayed silent as I pulled out his hardened shaft, letting it spring free. I lowered myself from the couch to my knees, locking my gaze with his. He worshiped me with his dark eyes, though I was the one on my knees.

My tongue swirled around the tip of his cock, teasing him up and down as I watched pleasure flood his face. His eyebrows furrowed, and his lips parted as I started to suck him.

Inch by inch, I slid his cock deeper into my mouth until I could feel it hit the back of my throat. I gagged slightly, which caused him to tense as he wrapped his fingers around my hair, getting it out of the way.

I slowly bobbed my head back and forth, and my tongue lazily circled around his tip every time he was almost all the way out. I could taste him already.

"Slow down, Mercy ..." Dorian panted, his breathing heavy. I didn't. Instead, I took him deeper. Harder. Eager to have him come just as fast as I did. His eyes rolled back into his skull, and I could feel his grip tighten around my hair.

"Wait," he blurted out. I pulled back, visibly confused. He seemed to enjoy it so far, so I truly had no idea what the problem was.

"Is everything—"

I didn't even get to finish my words; Dorian grabbed me and lifted me back onto the couch, moving on top of me. His cock instantly found my entrance, lingering there momentarily as he leaned down and kissed me.

"Everything is more than fine," he assured me, his lips brushing against mine. He pushed his hips forward, allowing his cock to slip deeper inside of me. I tensed against him, making a slight sound that came out muffled against his lips. "I just wanted to be inside you."

With those words, he began to thrust, awakening each nerve of my body with his movements. His hands found mine and linked our fingers together as he pinned me down to the couch.

"Fuck." I moaned as his cock brushed against that sweet spot deep inside of me. The sound of my wetness, loud and prominent, accompanied each of his thrusts. His lips found my neck, showering my skin in soft, feather-like kisses that were an odd contrast to the pace getting wilder with each thrust. "Oh, God, yes."

My toes curled from the overwhelming pleasure that rampaged through me as I shook underneath his body. His grip tightened on my hands as he focused his eyes on the sight of his cock entering me.

"Mercy...." His forehead dropped on top of mine. We were both coated in a light sweat, lost in the shared, endless pleasure. "You feel so fucking good."

"I'm close ..." I murmured in response. I could feel the familiar tingling as Dorian drove me to that swirl of pleasure that I wanted to be forever lost in with him. My legs trembled violently, and I could feel his body tensing.

Two thrusts later, my orgasm exploded through me for the second time. Dizziness swallowed me momentarily as I buried my face in his neck, letting out a loud, broken moan. His peak followed mere seconds later; the sound he made mirrored my own as he released inside me.

We were both unable to speak afterward, needing a moment to wind down before either of us could gather the strength to move. I wrapped my arms around Dorian, pulling him down to lie next to me. His arms slid around my waist. Without a word, we drifted off into a sweet sleep where the world couldn't follow.

CHAPTER 10

MERCY

"Caleb only had time to give me a first name before we were ripped apart through the projection, Joel. He said the name, 'Dante.' Now, I did learn a few things this last year, though, that might be helpful. When Caleb couldn't find a way to bring me back," I explained, my arms folded across my chest, staring at Joel's computer desktop, "he visited this Dante ... a witch. This witch belonged to a bloodline who called themselves the Keepers of the Dead."

I turned my head and saw that Joel's eyes had gone wide.

"What is it?" I gasped. "What does that mean?"

"Exactly what the name sounds like," Joel said. "The magic they use is tied to the original covens before the Chosen Ones ever came to Earth. They have a special connection to the Upper World and Underworld. They can help lost souls find their way, summon the dead, you name it."

I rocked back into the office chair. "Cami's doctor, Doctor Harrison. He had the ability to communicate with souls that moved on. Leah had told me he was a 'Witch Doctor.' So, he must have been a descendant of that bloodline, just like this Dante guy." I pressed my lips together before adding, "Whoever Dante was, he helped Caleb bring me back to life by using the bark from the tree they hanged me from."

"What makes that tree so special?" Joel asked.

I shrugged my shoulder. "I've been trying to figure it out myself. Whenever I tried to pry more information from Caleb, he would dance around the question until something else distracted me."

Caleb was hiding something yet again, and I intended to find out what that was. I refused to believe that this was it. Especially since the second time they brought me back, all four had relinquished their elemental powers. *Not* the bark.

"We need to find Dante, since Caleb refused to give me any more information," I said.

"I find it odd that he'd keep a spell from you," Joel said.

"Caleb kept a lot of things from me. Perhaps it's dark magic, and he didn't want me dabbling in it," I suggested. "It's the only explanation I can think of."

"There's always a price to pay when using dark magic. It would explain the sacrifice. When the coven brought you back the second time, they had to sacrifice themselves to complete the spell." Joel leaned back in his chair. "True, they needed to siphon enough power from the elements, but they still had to die."

We both rubbed our faces simultaneously. "We need the witch's last name and where he could be now," I said, staring at the computer again. "During the time of my previous life, how many of the covens were part of the Keepers of the Dead?"

"Our history books mentioned two. The original coven came from Europe and was led by a witch named Elizabeth Chekov, whose ancestors came from Siberia. There were rumors that some even came from Barbados, but the stories about that coven were vague."

"That really expands our search, doesn't it? For all we know, they've spread out and live in completely different places these days. It's been centuries since then. Maybe they don't even exist anymore," I said.

I opened the search engine and typed in *Siberian covens, seventeenth century.* The webpage pulled up endless links to various Wiccan blog pages, the history of Siberia under Russian rule, and not much else.

I bit my lower lip, thinking about where to search next. "We can also try genealogy records. If we start with the covens in Siberia, including Elizabeth's bloodline, and track the lineages to those living today," I added, "we could find someone who uses the magic of the dead. Or, if no such person exists, we could visit Gallows Hill and see if our magic can find which tree was used to hang the coven that night. We can tweak the locator spell for that."

"We would definitely need to use magic to find it. No one really knows which tree was the actual one they used," Joel said. "They've barely been able to locate the exact coordinates of the execution until a few years ago."

"Or ..." I stopped. "Had the entire tree been cut down into small pieces?" I suggested. "Caleb mentioned that the witch told him it was the last remaining bark from the tree." I paused again. "But what if it wasn't the last of it? What if the witch tried to protect that power, and there's still more out there? The tree was enormous, Joel."

Joel narrowed his eyes at me and placed his elbows on the desk. "Here's what we *do* know. There are two ways to bring someone back from the dead. The bark from the tree on Gallows Hill, which we don't have, and the power of giving up the elements in order to bring back your coven, as they did with you."

"So, which one do we do?"

Joel smirked. "The one that doesn't require you to die by giving up your power."

I raised my brow. "So, the tree it is. We research every Siberian coven who migrated to Salem in the seventeenth century before the trials. Then we find out who is still alive today from those lineages and are using powers connected to the dead. Then search for each name for a man named Dante. That's all I've got."

"Then what? You want me to teleport you to Siberia, Europe, or wherever they are today?"

"Not yet. Dorian wants to go with me, and we are in the middle of something right now."

"No secrets," Joel warned.

"Maurice left me a gift. It was more of a threat in his twisted, sinister way."

"What did he leave you?"

"Wolfsbane and jewelry."

His lips tightened. "We need to gather the packs."

I nodded. "That's why we can't leave yet. We need all the packs to know what's coming. They need to be ready to defend themselves if there's an attack."

I shut down the computer and turned to Joel. "Will you update Lily and Desiree about what's going on? I'll call you tomorrow."

Joel ran his hand through his hair and shook his head. "Let's perhaps keep Lily out of this as much as possible. Okay? Things have been rough for her about everything that happened with Bradley."

I nodded in agreement and grabbed my keys to head back to Dorian's.

———*ell*———

Dorian was slipping his shoes on when I entered his room.

"Hey, you," I said as I approached.

His face lit up. "I was just about to call you."

"What's going on?" I asked.

He looked down, not meeting my eyes. "It's Davina. She wants me to meet the rest of my pack today and discuss a strategy against the vampires," he explained. He looked up, placed his finger on my chin, and pulled my head up to meet his gaze. "I have to go, Mercy," he finished as our eyes met.

"It's okay," I said truthfully. "Honest, I understand. It would be best if you asked Davina to reach out to Amber, though. Riley mentioned they were able to get commitments from several packs in the US. I think they're meeting the pack leaders this week in Salem."

He smiled, reached down, and pulled me onto his lap, wrapping my legs around his waist. I slid one of my arms around his shoulders and brushed a hair away from his face. He leaned forward and kissed me gently on top of my head then trailed his lips to my neck, sucking softly against my tender flesh. I could feel his length harden, pressing up between my legs.

I placed my hands on his shoulders, slow and gentle, pushing him down on the bed while my legs wrapped around his hips. I hovered over his body and kissed him softly on the neck. My hands traced the sensitive spots on the side of his hips, and he wiggled and squirmed between my thighs. I rolled my hips, already feeling the tingling in my core.

"Sorry," I said, but when I went to remove my hands, he grabbed my wrists, keeping them where they were.

"Don't move," Dorian said.

He raised my arms above my head, pulling his leg over mine and spinning us around as he had done on the couch, so I was now on my back with him hovering over me. He gripped my wrists, keeping them above my head, and traced his other hand down the back of my arm, sending a warm rush coursing through my body. My heartbeat raced as his lips touched mine. His kiss was deep and sensual, quite literally taking my breath away as that tingling sensation spread through my body.

My breathing was heavy as he ran his fingers through my hair, brushing a loose strand away from my eyes. Aside from the firm, possessive grip he still had on my wrist, the soft gesture was tender, causing a flutter in my stomach.

My desire for Dorian and the extreme need to give myself to him at every moment were clear within every fragment of my body as it sparked to life under his touch.

"I love you," Dorian said, and butterflies again pulled at the pit of my stomach. My breath momentarily hitched in my throat before I dared to say those words back.

"I love you, too."

He kissed me once more before releasing my wrists, allowing me to wiggle from his grasp. When I sat up, his hands rested on his head while turning from me.

"Noah's in the other room," he said. The look in his eyes showed it was likely a fact he was willing to ignore.

"He was last time, too," I retorted with a wink.

Dorian rolled his eyes and wrapped his arms around me, pulling me close to his warm body. His hand slipped under the fabric of my pants and underwear, inching its way closer to my aching clit. Once it reached my heat, he began moving his fingertips in a slow, circular motion that had my eyes rolling back.

"If you want to keep me quiet from Noah hearing, this isn't the way to do it," I said as I met his eyes, biting lightly on my lower lip.

He rubbed his thumb in circles, a torrent of pleasure skating through my body as he touched my nerves. His finger slipped down lower, finding my soaked entrance, and my hips rolled into his touch.

Dorian closed his eyes slightly and pressed his forehead to mine. It was as if my own pleasure brought him satisfaction, too. A lot of it, actually, judging by the bulge that was now prominent in his pants.

"Mercy ..." My name rolled off his tongue with a heavy breath. "You make me so fucking crazy," he said, panting in my ear. His warm breath tickled my skin, sending a shudder through my body. "I'll never get enough of you. I'll never get enough of your body reacting to mine."

"It's a good thing I'm immortal," I said. "I can do this forever, for as long as you'll have me."

He met my smile and buried his head into the crease of my neck, giving me a tiny bite behind my ear.

"Oh, God. Please don't stop doing that," I whispered. My fingers clutched his wrist, as if to ensure that he didn't pull back. I was so close already—I didn't know what power this man held over me. All I knew was that he knew *exactly* how to get me there. He quickened his pace, my back arching as I reached that blissful height, shaking underneath his firm touch. My eyes closed over, the pleasure dispersing within me and leaving no part of my body untouched.

There was a comfortable silence for a few minutes before I asked the question lingering in my mind. "What do you dream about, Dorian?" I don't know why I chose this moment to ask him that. All I really wanted was for him to finger fuck me until I came again, but I had to know. "Please don't tell me again that you don't remember."

His eyes narrowed in on mine, but he didn't look away. Instead, he removed his fingers from inside me and pulled back.

"Sarah," he said, and my heart stopped for an uncomfortable beat. My body immediately came down from my arousal.

Did I miss something?

"Jesus, Mercy, not in the way you're thinking right now," he explained, as if reading my thoughts. He lay on the bed, his eyes staring at the ceiling. He ran his hand through his hair and sucked in a breath. "I see her face in my nightmares and the day she was taken to Maurice's lair."

I slid toward Dorian and lay beside him, placing my hand on his. "It was you who took her, wasn't it? Then you gave her to Troy, who took possession of her."

"I'm surprised she didn't tell you."

I looked up at the ceiling with him. "You didn't kill her," I said, hoping my words would make him feel better, but I knew, deep down, they wouldn't.

"It feels like I did," he said. "Sarah was finally happy after escaping someone who nearly destroyed her in the past. I seduced her, made her feel safe, then took her to his lair because Maurice required that I prove my loyalty to him."

Dorian wasn't crying, but one ability that came with the gift of Spirit was feeling the subtle emotional energy shift from others around you. I felt it intensely with Dorian at that moment. His guilt was torturing him.

"I knew it was wrong, but as a vampire, it's a struggle to shut off that evil and ruthless side of you. But sometimes, you must in order to fulfill a certain task, or the guilt will eat you bit by bit. So, you have to shut off your humanity just like that," he said, snapping his fingers.

"And I took that ability from you when I turned you back into a human," I said.

He nodded. "Then I learned Sarah had died, and though it wasn't me who had done it, and her death wasn't at all related to Maurice, I still felt responsible. She would have never been involved in this life if I hadn't taken her in the first place."

"I blame myself, too. Bradley killed her because of me."

He turned to his side and frowned. "You were never a monster. I was—"

"Stop! Sarah cared about you, Dorian. She was your friend, regardless of what happened. She wouldn't want us to torture ourselves with guilt and the endless 'what-ifs.' We have to move forward and forgive ourselves. Both of us."

He looked back at the ceiling and sat upright, reaching out his hand to help me up.

"Tell Riley I'll call him later," Dorian said. "We're going to need as many wolf packs as possible. Not just in the States but everywhere. Maurice has had a year to recruit his army, and I've got a feeling we'll be outnumbered."

"I know Davina is your pack leader, but you can still train with Riley and his pack. They're strong, and Amber is fearless. She may look like she's in her twenties, but she's over sixty years old. Werewolves don't age like humans, which I read in your little history book," I said with a smile. "Though you're not immortal, you could still live to be five hundred years old." I tilted my head and pressed my lips together. "But I understand if she tells you no. They're your family now, too."

I wasn't giving up on him, though when the words left my mouth, I felt like I was admitting defeat. All I wanted was for Dorian to be safe.

He nodded in understanding and flashed me a forced smile, grabbing his phone off the nightstand and placing it in his pocket.

"Thanks for telling me about what's been really bothering you. We should be able to tell each other these things."

He pressed his lips against my forehead and let his kiss linger briefly before pulling back. "I have to go," he said softly. "But you and I will continue what we just did later tonight. Okay?"

I nodded with a playful smile and a wink. I didn't take offense at his sudden need to leave this conversation. It was a little out of his comfort zone, but I was happy enough that he had opened up to me.

"I'll see you tonight," I promised. "Naked."

CHAPTER 11

MERCY

Riley picked up speed before leaping high in the air, transitioning before hitting the ground. He touched his nose to Amber's hand before she stripped off her clothes, and her body transformed into a beautiful, midnight-black beast. The two ran into the forest until they were no longer in our line of sight.

I let out a low whistle of amazement. "Riley's a lot faster than he used to be," I said to Hannah and Aaron, who stood back with their arms folded across their chests, looking through the forest, waiting.

"They think we won't be able to catch them," Hannah said, looking over at me.

"They're both pretty fast," I said.

Aaron smirked. "I won't pretend to be as fast as them, but Hannah was a cross-country runner in high school."

Hannah glanced at Aaron and shrugged. "That's running on two legs, bro. This is different, but I'm getting better every time we train out here. The feeling of running through a forest in wolf form is unlike anything I've ever felt. It's exhilarating."

Two thundering howls echoed between the trees, and the werewolves beside me smiled at each other.

"Ah. Well, let's see what you've got then," I teased.

They both crouched down, and their coarse wolves' hair pulled through their skin. They glanced at each other once more before sprinting off into the forest and toward their prey.

Once they were out of sight, I grabbed my phone and dialed Dorian's number, but before he picked up, a firm hand gripped my wrist, causing my fingers to extend and drop my phone.

I jerked my arm away as I turned around and quickly held my hands up, palms forward, green light beaming from my fingertips. My powers blasted the attacker across the forest before they could do anything further. Once I eyed them, now sprawled out on the ground, I slowly crept in their direction, halting once I saw who it was.

Maurice.

"You're a fool," I seethed. "Get up!"

Maurice cackled at me and held up his hands in defeat. "Easy, Mercy. You're going to want to lower that magic if you want your friends to stay safe." His voice was eerily calm. So eerily calm that the hairs on my arms stood straight. Maurice looked around the forest. "You have ten silver-dipped arrows pointing at your chest right now, and they have orders to shoot you if you strike me."

I fought the urge to laugh in his face. "Unless one of those arrows is a magical dagger, it won't do shit to me."

A sinister grin appeared on his fair features. "Oh, I've not forgotten, but it will keep you down long enough for my clan to track down those wolves and put a silver bullet between each of their eyes."

My heart rate picked up. Maurice wouldn't hesitate to kill them, that was certain, but I also knew the pack wouldn't be far from heading back here. They would have picked up Maurice's scent by now. It surprised me they didn't smell him before he entered the forest. I wondered if a witch was masking his scent, like Joel had done with me.

"What the hell do you want?" I asked, letting out a sigh and allowing the green light to fade.

He smiled again and took a step closer. I didn't want to show him I was scared about what he'd do, but without thinking, I stepped back.

"I miss you, that's all," Maurice said.

"Bullshit."

He laughed at my response, brought his hand to my cheek, and brushed it lightly, but I smacked it away and gave him a cold, hard stare. "Mm," he hummed, "if only I could smell you and taste your sweet blood on my lips."

I smirked. "Please do," I said. "Here, I'll help you get started. Though I've heard it's not very pleasant for vampires." I bit down hard on my lip, drawing blood. His eyes turned black, and bright blue veins protruded under his eyes. "Isn't this what you really want?" I took a step closer to him. "To taste me in more ways than one."

Maurice hissed, his eyes drawing to the blood on my lips. As a smile pulled at the side of my mouth, he frowned, took a few deep breaths before his eyes looked normal again, and straightened his shirt. "I want to give you and your coven a chance to surrender."

I drew my brows together. "It's as if you've forgotten who we are. Very unlike your calculating and mastermind-like self."

"I'm not as evil as you believe I am," he said, and his face went flat.

He can't be serious. Is he delusional?

I waited, because I honestly had no idea what to expect from him or what could possibly be his next move.

"First, I'd like to offer protection to your coven, including Lily and Joel, and"—he paused, gesturing toward the forest—"Riley and his pack."

Protection?

"In exchange for what?" I asked.

"You never try to turn us human," he said, then paused again.

There was more. There was always more with Maurice.

"You want us to turn a blind eye?" I asked. "Let you abduct humans and witches again and make them your blood servants? Slaughter the other werewolf packs out there who may try to stop you? If you believe we're this stupid, then you might as well have your men turn those arrows at you and just end it for all of us. Believe me, it will be less brutal than what I have planned."

Maurice gritted his teeth. "I'm trying to negotiate with you."

"Where's the negotiation?"

"I let you live."

"Right. Did you forget I can't be killed?"

He frowned.

"You know what I think?" I started again, taking a step toward him. "I think you're a scared little shit. You're so terrified that this conniving yet mindless plan of yours isn't going to work, so you're trying to muster an idea to save yourself. That isn't how this works. You've killed innocent people. You've violated every part of my body in order to keep me from my coven." I felt my fists clench at that revolting memory. "I'm going to kill you, Maurice. I'm willing to save others in your clan if they stop slaughtering the innocent ... but not you. No. You had your chance at redemption, and you fucked it up. I'm going to cut off your head. So, you'd better start running." I glared at him intently, and his eyes turned back into that onyx black. I glanced down at his hands, which were balled into tight fists, and instead of taking a step back, I inched closer. "Do you really want to challenge me right now?"

He started to smile again, but his shoulders tensed. I looked to my right, and four angry wolves flashed their fangs in his direction. Maurice gulped and stepped back but lifted his hand, signaling to someone.

"No!" I screamed as I pulled my hands up, trying to pull up a barrier, but it was too late. A silver arrow shot through the forest and embedded in Amber's stomach. Riley jumped forward, but the barrier that was now up stopped him from getting to Maurice.

Maurice quickly picked up speed and ran out of the forest, along with whatever people had been surrounding us. I lowered the shield and ran toward Amber, pulling the silver arrow out of her side.

Riley, Hannah, and Aaron returned to their human form, and Amber lay half human, half wolf, blood pouring from her side. I kneeled, pulling warm green light into my fingertips. I pressed them to the wound and let the healing light flow into Amber. Injuries caused by silver slow the werewolf's rapid healing ability, so I lent my own to help Amber close the wound. Her transition back to human was slow, but eventually, she was back in her human skin, and the damage from the arrow was fading. Riley sighed heavily as the wound healed before our eyes, and Amber shed a tear, but her body never relaxed. She was angry. No, she was *pissed*. At all costs, the alpha swears to protect their pack, and Amber's pack had just been targeted.

Amber slowly sat up and looked at me. Her rage was palpable, like lightning flashing behind her eyes. She balled her bloody right hand into a fist and slammed it into the ground.

"No more waiting," Amber cried. "Kill that son of a bitch, and rip him limb from limb!"

"Trust me, I want him dead more than anything, but we can't attack without an army behind us. Right now, we are strengthening our powers while finding those who will follow us. I'm the only one left in my coven."

She shook her head. "No, you're not," Amber said. "You have the power of five elements inside you. You're stronger than you think. I know you've been afraid to use their powers, but you have to. Your coven would want you to. You can't keep being afraid or fucking cautious anymore!"

Tears formed in my eyes, but not from sadness. I was enraged with her. Angry with myself, angry that I wasn't anywhere closer to finding this witch who helped bring me back, and angry at my enemies, who were once again ten steps ahead of me.

CHAPTER 12

MERCY

It had been two days since Maurice attacked us. Amber had healed, and everyone was on high alert, knowing Maurice was back to his stalker-like ways. Because of that, our plan to find the bark became the number one priority.

"Mercy, great to see you again," Felix, the town's oldest librarian, said as Dorian, Noah, and I entered the front doors of the East Greenwich Library. Felix had been running the library since the 1950s. He and his wife once told me they had planned to retire once they were in the grave.

"Hey, Felix. How are things? How's Marie?" I asked while we filed into the front entrance of the library.

Felix shrugged. "She's helping Mayor Hathaway make streamers for tomorrow's fall parade."

He pushed his glasses higher on his nose and looked up at Dorian and Noah. "I don't know you young men. I'm Felix," he said, holding out his wrinkly, sun-spotted fingers.

After Dorian and Noah both shook his hand, Dorian stole a glance at me and gestured with his head to the back wall where the microfiche machines were set up. I nodded, throwing back a stern glare. I knew we were crunched on time, but Felix wasn't someone you could greet in haste and walk away from.

"I forgot about that," I said. "I'd help, but as I mentioned over the phone, we have a pretty big project today, and we need all the information we can get on it before we head out of town."

He eyed me suspiciously, tilting his head to the right and raising a brow. "You mentioned on the phone that you're researching ancestors of the original families in Salem, huh?" he said, turning from us and grabbing a microfilm from the front desk. "Here you go. This microfilm will give you better information than those web search engines."

Noah grabbed the microfilm from my hand and walked over to the microreader at the back. Dorian joined him, nodding a silent thank you to Felix.

"Yeah, my aunt Lily mentioned that since my mother died, doing some genealogy might be healing for us," I lied, staying behind to smooth things over with Felix. He seemed to ask more questions about what we were doing here than I had expected him to.

"I may be an old man, Mercy, but I'm not senile. The people you grew up with, me included, all know a bit more about you than you think we do."

I swallowed. "What does that mean?" I asked quickly.

A knowing grin appeared on his wrinkled face. "You know, I've been working at this library for sixty-six years. My grandfather also worked as a librarian since it opened in the early nineteen hundreds. He was good friends with the founder, Mr. Daniel Albert Peirce. They knew things about this town and its surroundings that you'd only read in fiction novels and bedtime stories your parents would tell. Or the stories your parents *wouldn't* tell you."

I studied him for a moment, cocking my head to the right. He folded his arms and inhaled a heavy breath. "I knew your grandfather, your mother, and everyone else in your family who came from a line of Salem witches. I know of the power that your family was blessed with. I've told no one your secret, and I don't plan to start now. If you need my help, I'll be in the back room sorting out the new sets of children's books that just arrived this morning."

My shoulders, which had been tense the entire time, finally relaxed. I hadn't seen that one coming. It did make me wonder how many people in town knew about the existence of witches, or even vampires, for that matter. Perhaps we had more allies than we thought.

"What's the point of secrets," I asked, "if we don't have people that we care about to keep them?"

Felix looked me over and nodded. "Life would be pretty boring then, wouldn't it?"

I gave him a slight smile. "Yeah, it sure would be. Please tell Marie I said hi."

Felix winked and headed toward the back of the library without speaking another word about witches and town secrets.

When I joined up with Dorian and Noah, the microreader was already up and running. On the screen was a news clipping from the local Salem newspaper, marked October 5th, 2000.

"Joel got lucky with his research and pulled up some genealogy records last night, tying a few families who came to Salem from Europe and Siberia long before I was born the first time," I said. "These specific families settled in Salem after the trials, though. We followed the records to today, and we came up with three families who still live in Massachusetts and practice or have practiced witchcraft. There was only one Dante, well two, if you include his father, but he passed away before I was reborn."

"That seems too easy," Dorian said.

"Unless Caleb wanted me to know this all along, planting clues that if anything were to happen to him, I'd someday get my answers as to what the hell happened to me."

Dorian rested his hand on my shoulder, giving it a comforting squeeze. "He sure fought pretty hard to keep his name from you."

"Until a darkness ripped through the astral plane we were in and tore us apart. Caleb seems a little desperate now." I shook the mouse, waking the computer up. "The town referred to these families as Shamans since they worked with the dead. Dante and his wife ran a business in Salem for years. They would have been there when Caleb was searching for magic to help bring me back."

"They communicated with spirits?" Noah asked, leaning over my other shoulder.

"More or less, they claimed to see beyond the veil of our world," I said. "I had Felix gather any news articles of anything out of the ordinary around the year I would have been conceived. There wasn't a lot of information we could find online since, most likely, the Keepers of the Dead tried to keep it a secret, but this library has pretty much every article you can find along the East Coast, specifically the ones that contained strange and unusual events."

"Like this one," Noah said, gesturing to the screen.

"I guess we'll see," I said, moving the mouse to the top of the article and scrolling it down. "Caleb mentioned the witch lived in Salem. Dante was born in the US, but his ancestors came from Siberia, the same ones who settled in Salem in the late seventeenth century. The same family who was known to use magic linked to the dead. It has to be him. Felix was familiar with those families. At least that's what he said over the phone before we arrived today. This particular story happened exactly nine months before I was born. He said we might find what we're looking for." I narrowed my eyes at the screen.

"Alright," Dorian said. "Let's check it out."

THE SALEM DAILY NEWS:

Local Woman Found Murdered in Her Hospital Room. Suspect at Large

Salem, Massachusetts. October 5, 2000

Molly Boyce, age forty-two, and famous local healer, was found dead Wednesday night, at approximately 11:16 p.m., in her hospital room at Salem General Hospital. Molly had been battling multiple sclerosis, but police investigators state Molly did not die from her disease. They are treating this case as a homicide.

Dante, Molly's husband, arrived earlier that day and hasn't been seen since. Dante is the prime suspect, and police have warned the public that he could be armed and dangerous.

Annie Clayborn, a nurse attending to Molly, never saw anyone else go in or out of her room after Mr. Boyce left.

Molly was loved by many locals and has run a healer shop in downtown Salem since 1975.

Police have asked that anyone with any information regarding her death to please contact local law enforcement.

I looked up at Dorian and then at Noah. Dorian leaned forward and clicked the mouse, moving on to the next article on the slide.

THE SALEM DAILY NEWS

Autopsy Report for Molly Boyce Released

Salem, Massachusetts. November 10, 2000

Police investigators have released the cause of death to the public but will not be answering questions regarding the cause of death until they can complete a further investigation. The preliminary autopsy report revealed that Molly's body appeared over one hundred years old when she was discovered. Every part of her body, including her hair, skin, brain, and bones, indicated that she had aged over sixty years between the hours of 9 p.m., when she was last monitored, and 11:16 p.m., at her time of death.

"It's impossible," Chief Richards told the press. "But we are still looking at all possibilities."

Investigators have revealed that her room had been wiped clean of fingerprints, and surveillance monitors were shut off minutes before her death.

Police have not released any further findings, and her death has become a mystery to the residents of Salem.

THE SALEM DAILY NEWS

The Mysterious Case of
Molly Boyce

Salem, Massachusetts. June 15, 2001

The case of Molly Boyce has officially been closed, and the people of Salem are still scratching their heads.

Annie Clayborn, the hospital nurse who found Molly's body, refuses to speak to the public regarding what she saw that day. Investigators have now closed the case.

Mr. Boyce, though no longer a person of interest, was never found, and the town mourns the loss of a local favorite.

How Molly aged quickly has become a mystery to everyone in this town. Is she the first? Will she be the last?

I leaned back, running my hand through my hair. "That *is* impossible," I said aloud.

I heard a creak behind me, and all three of us turned around to see Felix standing, body slumped over, with two children's books gripped under his armpit. "After that, it was as if the town had forgotten about her," Felix said. "Maybe there are answers out there. We just haven't been looking hard enough or in the right place."

"What do you think happened?" I asked. "Do you think it was magic?"

I heard a collective gasp come from Dorian and Noah.

"Felix knows," I explained.

Dorian pressed his lips together, giving me a stern stare, as if he was unsure if that was a good or bad thing.

"Could be." Felix shrugged. "We are talking about someone aging sixty years within hours. It's easy for the public, who aren't aware of the existence of magic, to speculate, but why waste all our energy when you'd most likely come out with nothing?"

"Why do I get a feeling you know more than what you're telling us?" I asked.

A touch of a smile reached his lips. "I've spent my entire life in East Greenwich, but I've always made a point to understand the culture and politics of other towns, especially Salem. That city has many secrets, Mercy, and I made sure I knew what was hidden under its bed." Felix pulled the microfilm out of the reader and tucked it under his other armpit. "If you want your answers, you need to go to the source."

I raised an eyebrow. "The hospital?"

"No, dear. That hospital shut down ten years ago. You can start by finding Annie, the nurse who worked the unit and took care of Molly."

"And do you happen to have her address?" I asked.

Felix had a gleam in his eye. "I seem to have the answer to everything today, don't I?"

All I could do at that moment was let out a deep breath of utter relief. Because, for the first time, we were finally getting the answers we needed. We had another clue.

"Thank you," I said.

After he grabbed the address for us, we hurried to the car.

"Now we just have to hope she speaks with us," I said, turning to the guys.

"If she doesn't, then we might be stuck," Noah said. "If Dante hadn't been seen in the last twenty-two years, what's saying he even wants to be found?"

"A little locator spell always does the trick," I said. "But he could be dangerous for all we know. Before we do anything else, I need to find out what this nurse knows. I need to find out exactly what she saw happen to Molly." I shook my head. "Whatever Anne knows, it's something Caleb's been trying to keep from me my entire life."

Dorian held firmly to Annie's address and opened the door for me. "Let's go find out, then."

CHAPTER 13

MERCY

We waited patiently on the doorstep after ringing the bell twice. Nothing but silence greeted us from the house. I tucked my hands into my pockets and looked back at Dorian and Noah.

"Maybe she's not home," I said.

Noah closed his eyes and stiffed the air. "Naw, someone's here. I can smell a powerful aroma of freshly baked cookies, and a scented candle is lit near the front entryway."

I looked through the window to the right of the door, and right then, the door cracked open a few inches.

"Can I help you?" a woman said quietly through the narrow opening.

"Hey, um. My name's Mercy Brawling and these are my friends, Dorian Hale and Noah Kaai. We're looking for Annie Clayborn."

She shook her head. "Annie doesn't live here. Go away."

The woman tried to shut the door, but Dorian stuck his foot in the entryway, and she quickly backed up and ran down the hallway.

"I'm on it," Noah said.

He rushed into the house, grabbed her by the waist, and hoisted her up, keeping Annie secure in his firm grip. She let out a terrified wail and tried to pry Noah's arm from her body.

"Easy, Noah," I said, holding up my hand. "Let her go."

He relaxed his arms, allowing her to slip down to her feet, but she bolted toward the back door again. That time, I held up my hands and placed a barrier around the house. She slammed right into it, falling back on her rear, then scrambling toward the hall bathroom. She slipped into the bathroom, slamming the door, and we heard the lock click.

Great.

"Maybe we should have called first," Dorian said while letting out a low snicker. "Well, at least we know she most likely knows something."

"Annie, please. We aren't here to hurt you," I said through the door, ignoring Dorian. This woman was clearly terrified. "I swear to you. We only need to ask you a few questions about Molly Boyce's death."

It was silent on the other side of the door. Noah stepped toward the bathroom with his fist in the air, ready to pound on it until it cracked open. I held my hand up to stop him. "Maybe the two of you can step back for a minute. Wait by the foyer."

I turned back and pressed my ear and cheek against the door. "Listen, Annie. If I really wanted to break this door down and pull you out, I could. But I won't do that to you. Please, I just want to talk to you about Molly."

It was quiet for a moment, but then the door opened slowly. Annie's pale face peered from behind the door and met my gaze.

A look of pure terror crossed her face. Her breath caught, and her mouth opened slightly.

"I've seen you before," she said.

I looked her in the eyes quizzically. "Do you want to come out here to sit and talk about it, or do you want to have this chat in the bathroom?"

She looked past me and eyed Dorian and Noah, leaning against the wall next to the foyer. "I want them to leave."

I smiled at her kindly, attempting to hide my growing frustration. "Fine. Whatever makes you feel safer." I turned to Dorian and Noah. "Guys?"

They exchanged glances, then nodded, and once they reached the door, I lowered the shield at the entrance so they could leave and then sealed it back up.

"It's just us now. No one can get past my barrier. You're safe. Let's go sit and talk," I said. "Okay?"

She nodded, wrapping her arms around her waist, and I followed closely behind her as we made our way to her family room.

Annie was shorter than me, with medium-length red hair that reached just above her shoulders. She appeared to be in her early fifties with a thin build. She wore no makeup, showing off her dark freckles over her nose and under her eyes, and she wore a long, green, strapless dress that reached her ankles.

While Annie sat on the loveseat, I sat on the couch across from her, creating a space between us. I took a few deep breaths, trying to think of the right questions to ask. I hadn't thought about what I would say when I arrived at her home.

"You were a nurse at the Salem General Hospital around the year 2000, correct?"

She nodded, but her lips formed a straight line. I couldn't read her expression clearly. It was a mix of fear, sadness, and confusion.

"And you took care of Molly Boyce?" I continued.

"Yes."

I paused, gathering my thoughts again. "And you know who I am?"

She nodded slowly this time. "Yes ... and no."

"How?"

Annie looked around the room then out the window, as if making sure we were, indeed, alone.

"I ... I saw y-you d-die," she stuttered.

My mind raced, my palms felt slick with sweat, and my heart rate sped up. "What?"

"The wooden horse," she said. "I saw you die when I touched the wooden horse."

"What horse? What are you talking about?"

I wondered if we should have researched Annie before we came to her home. I now wondered if she was actually sane and if she really did have any answers to the endless mysteries regarding my rebirth. If not, we were wasting our time.

"It belonged to Molly," she said. "Her husband, Dante, left a carved wooden horse in her room shortly before she died. We honored his wish to leave it by her bedside. But when my hands accidentally touched it, I had a vision."

My eyes went wide. "Please tell me about this vision."

She shifted in her seat and rubbed her legs nervously. "I was transported to a different time. It was there that I saw this beautiful oak tree. It was so bright, I had to shield my eyes, but it was also haunting as if it held a power that—"

She placed her hand on her head and rubbed it vigorously.

"Annie, what is it?"

"Sorry. I get these headaches. I've had them for over twenty-two years. Ever since—"

"What do you need?"

"No, you're my guest. I'll—"

"Don't move. What do you need?"

She glanced toward the kitchen. "Water, and there's aspirin in a small vase near the kitchen stove."

Odd place to keep aspirin.

In the kitchen, I reached above the stove and retrieved the vase. Inside were a few bottles of medication. Most were prescription pills, including heavy painkillers and medicine for anxiety. I found the aspirin, grabbed three, and searched for a cup.

When I returned to the living room, Annie had laid her head down on a pillow but sat upright when I handed her the cup of water and medicine. She swallowed the pills and placed the cup on the table.

"Continue, please," I said.

Her leg twitched again, and she tapped her heels against the wooden floor. "At first, the tree was inside a cave, but then it wasn't. The scenery suddenly shifted, and I was then transported to Salem during the witch trials. Mercy, I saw you hanging from a tree before I woke up. The vision flashed in front of my eyes. Then it was gone. But I recognized your face as if it happened yesterday."

So, the answer is in the wooden horse.

"Do you know what happened to that horse?"

"I don't know. I obsessed about it for several days, but I told no one. The night Molly died, I felt a sharp sting in my neck as if someone had injected me with something. It was around nine p.m. that night. I awoke, called 911, then checked on the patients. When I made it to Molly's room, I discovered her shriveled, aged body and the wooden horse was gone."

"You didn't see anyone come or go before you were knocked out?"

She shook her head. "Just—"

"What is it?"

She averted her eyes and wrapped her arms around herself tightly. "I'm afraid."

I inched toward her and placed my hand on her shoulder. "No one can hurt you," I said. "But I need to know if there's anything else you remember?"

Her eyes met mine. "When the investigators showed up and questioned me, one of them was this very handsome man. I remember every detail of his face as if it had happened yesterday. I found his questioning to be a bit odd, and after he left, the other investigators who arrived asked me who I was talking to. I told them I spoke with their colleague, but they said that no one else was with them. It seemed like maybe he wasn't who he'd said he was."

"Did you share that information with the police?"

She lowered her head. "I was too afraid to. For all I knew, it was that man who hurt Molly, and I would be next if I talked."

"Can you remember what that man looked like?"

Anne nodded. "Shoulder-length, wavy brown hair, beautiful face, flame tattoo on his forearm ... and his eyes were a golden, bright amber."

I couldn't breathe. I couldn't think. I ran out of Annie's house without looking back and rushed past Dorian and Noah on the sidewalk.

"Mercy, what's wrong?" I heard Dorian ask from behind me as I hurried to the car.

I whipped around as I felt his firm hands on my shoulders, gripping me tightly, trying to keep me from fleeing. "It was Caleb. Caleb killed Molly."

His eyes narrowed, and he placed his palms against my cheeks, lifting my face so my eyes met his. "How do you know? She saw him?"

"Yes! He was there!"

"She saw him kill her?"

I shook my head. "No, but he was there."

"Mercy, breathe, baby." Dorian wrapped his arms around me and pulled me into his chest. His hand ran down my hair, attempting to soothe away my fears. "We don't know everything, okay? We don't even know if this woman knows anything."

I pulled back a step and glared at him. "Dorian, she knew enough."

"What now?" Noah asked, stepping toward us. "What else did you find out?"

I opened the car door. "I need to ask him about a wooden horse."

"Who? Dante?" Dorian asked.

"No. Caleb."

"Mercy," Dorian said my name sharply. "Are you out of your mind?"

I shook my head. "I've never thought more clearly than I have right now in my entire life." Heat flushed through my body as

I found my words. "I'm going back to Purgatory, and I'm not leaving until Caleb tells me what I want to know. Even if I have to rip the entire realm apart."

CHAPTER 14

MAURICE

Every movement from Clara's body seemed to drag at a leisurely pace ever since Kylan possessed her body and mind. It was fucking pathetic. All Kylan did was drink, sweat, and rot. He had done nothing since the possession to help further my plans.

"We should kill him now," I told Julian. "He's worthless to us and what we have planned."

Julian snickered under his breath, as if what I had said amused him. A muscle in my jaw flickered at the sound, but I kept myself calm. He was the only one from whom I tolerated that kind of behavior.

He sipped his whisky and set the glass down with a delicate motion on the table in front of him. "Maurice, we need his knowledge about the other side, and besides"—Julian paused and glanced up at Kylan then back at me before lowering his voice—"I'm almost done with my exorcism spell, but we're going to need a witch who can read his mind before we remove him. I can replace the real memories with false ones, but reading those thoughts is an entirely different power."

"I know a witch," I said, raising an eyebrow.

"Oh, fuck. Please, for the love of God, don't drag her into this," he whined.

I rolled my eyes at such childish protests.

"We may not have a choice. Once Kris retrieves those memories, we can kill him. We'll know everything about Kylan's king and the Underworld, and we can use that knowledge to our advantage." I couldn't help but smile at the thought.

Julian smirked with me, and we both looked over at Kylan-Clara, who was hacking up a lung in the back corner.

We walked over to him. "Kylan ... Master," I said, internally cringing at my choice of words. "Is there anything we can do for you to make your time—" He looked up at me and panted, his shoulders heaving. Clara's body was almost skeletal at this point, and no trace of her personality seemed to remain. Kylan's physical features were showing through, but they appeared rotted. Kylan's repulsive breath smelled of cheap rum and bile. He had difficulty keeping blood down since possessing a witch's body. The vampire spent most of his days drinking liquor and trying to learn how to harness Clara's magical abilities and function in her form. "More ... enjoyable," I finished. I swallowed my disgust and added, "Perhaps I can bring in one of my female colleagues to help you learn how to manage a woman's body?"

"I know how to manage a woman's body, you pathetic fucking excuse for a vampire!" Kylan snapped back, rasping in Clara's feminine voice.

His head wobbled as he slowly brought the glass of rum to his lips. More sweat poured from the matted blonde hairline. I couldn't stomach much more of this thing's presence any further.

We moved out of earshot, and I turned to Julian again. "Why is it that when he took over a weakling of a human like Cami, he did just fine? But with Clara, he's a complete embarrassment."

"The natural transference of demon power possessed Cami," Julian explained. "That isn't new in the demon world. Those who are from the Underworld have been possessing humans for centuries. With Clara, we used a spell. She permitted him to control not only her body but also her mind and powers. Kylan isn't used to that kind of power, let alone having complete control over her body and soul. Cami could still do things for herself because he didn't take her mind completely. She fought him the entire time he had control over her, which allowed her to maintain a normal body. It wasn't until the last few weeks before we removed him that he finally had control, but at that point, he wasn't sure what to do with himself. Kylan has no power and no way of accessing his own magic to gain his body. He has to rely on witch magic which is proving difficult to tap into. He's like a foreign organ inside Clara, and her body is outright rejecting it."

I sniffed the air and scrunched up my nose. "Hurry up with the exorcism spell. I can't take this vile stench any longer."

CHAPTER 15

MERCY

I called Joel to let him know what we had discovered from our visit to the library, which led to the meeting at Annie's home. Sharing with him what I now needed to do was a little harder. Joel understood the gravity of our situation, so thankfully, he didn't fight me on it.

After we finished dinner, we drove to Joel's, because I would need both his and Lily's power to do it. We gathered in the living room, where an array of stones and herbs were arranged to facilitate the spell. Derek, thankfully, was out of town on business, so there was no risk of dragging him into whatever blowback may happen.

Dorian tucked a loose strand of hair behind my ear, a nervous smile adorning his perfectly handsome face. "Why won't she help you?"

He was referring to Patricia, the psychic witch shop owner. When that evil, dark force entered my mind and tried to break through the walls of Purgatory and enter our world, it terrified her. I didn't blame her one bit for refusing to help us any further, so I had to do it myself. The power of five universal elements was now a part of me. I should have been able to do this without a guide to take me there and bring me back.

"She's afraid," I said softly, stepping toward Lily, who placed her hand in mine. She gripped Joel's hand until we formed a triangle.

"I've never done this before," Lily said, "so you must lead the entire time. All you're doing is using our magic. That's it. Everything else is up to you."

Joel squeezed my fingers. "The truth of the matter is that even normal humans can do astral projection. Once you understand it, you won't need a spell. And if humans can do it, imagine what *you* can do."

Easier said than done.

Lily and Joel had years to learn their powers, using them as they did. Though I was meant to be this all-powerful anomaly, I had barely scratched the surface of what my magic could do. I knew it was strong, because I felt the powers of all five elements, but parts of me hesitated to use them to their fullest potential. I was scared because, despite being immortal, I was still human. There was still a chance I could break.

"I'm not just separating my spirit from my body, Joel. I'm traveling to another realm," I said, thinking about the last time Patricia had sent me there. "It was terrifying. At one point, I felt like I was going to be trapped there."

"You're the Fifth Element, kiddo. Don't just picture yourself being there. Imagine yourself being able to control that world, just like you do with your powers. Be one with it," Joel said.

"Have you ever been dreaming and suddenly realized you could control it however you want?" Lily asked.

I nodded.

"That's what you're doing," she affirmed. "Use your elements, and control them to pull you away from that world when you're ready."

I closed my eyes and felt Dorian's hand reach under my hair and rub between my shoulders.

My skin prickled as I felt a sharp pinch.

"Ouch!" I squealed and rubbed the back of my neck.

"It's just a needle," Dorian explained. "If you feel that, come back to us."

"A little warning would have been nice, babe," I said, but I gave him a warm smile and closed my eyes. "Alright, I'm ready, Joel."

Lily was the first to release her power and didn't hold back. The force of her magic shot up my arm and out the other, flowing through Joel and squeezing us together like a tightly knit rope. Joel then released his magic, and it surged through my other arm and continued throughout our chain-linked connection.

As my nerve endings bounced off each other, it felt like bugs were crawling under my eyes. I searched within me, reaching out to the coven's power. I touched the elements and released them into my magic. A thrilling wave of power welled up inside, breaking free.

The swirling power of all five elements consumed me, and my body lit up with a force I had yet to feel since their magic entered me. I chanted a spell from Joel's spell book, which I had memorized earlier that evening, and felt my eyes roll to the back of my head. There was a strenuous pull tugging at my chest, and my mind drifted with it. As Dorian's hands left my skin, I realized he hadn't truly let go of my shoulders but that I had left my body, unable to feel the sensation of touch.

I looked down at myself, still joining hands with Lily and Joel, and Dorian's grip on my shoulders to keep me steady.

I glided across the floor, floating gracefully through the family room, and it was then that I ascended upward. My spirit was taking me on a journey that I had no control over. I climbed higher toward the ceiling, my eyes taking in the detail of the fibers of the wooden boards on the second floor as I moved through it. Once I exited the roof, I blinked once, and a light shone over my eyes. When I looked up, I felt myself being pulled quickly through a vortex. Once I was in the vortex, I felt like I was being teleported through time itself; the energy was chaotic. This was a very different feeling than when I was with Patricia.

When the force of the energy stopped, I stood before a massive tree surrounded by a bright, luminescent light. I walked closely toward the tree, like my last venture to Purgatory. Caleb sat with his back against the trunk, looking straight ahead. I didn't see the other coven members again, and a slight panic rushed through me until I heard Simon's voice in the distance. They were there, and they looked ... happy.

I turned my attention toward Ezra and Leah. They were lying down next to each other, looking up above at the sky. Simon was picking roses from a bush blooming in the clearing to the right. They looked peaceful and comfortable in this world.

I crept closer to Caleb and touched his arm. "Caleb," I whispered, trying not to draw attention to us. I didn't want the others to see me. As much as I wanted to embrace each one of them, the last time I was here, something had heard me and tried to attack us. I had to get my answers quickly and then get the hell back home.

He turned around, and his eyes widened. I held up my finger to my lips and gestured to him to come around the tree. "Shhh, I don't have much time."

Caleb looked at the rest of the coven and back at me before quickly standing and moving toward me. "Did what happened last time not scare you enough that you had to be foolish to come back here?" he asked in a hushed tone.

I looked at our surroundings but didn't see that black mist from before.

"Caleb, I need to hear your side of what happened to Molly?" I asked.

His eyebrows pulled together. "Just from his name?" he asked. "You figured it all out from a name?"

I shrugged. "Something tells me you wanted me to."

Caleb pressed his lips together. "It's more complicated than that. Yes, I had hoped someday you would know the truth. It's been eating me inside to keep it from you, but knowing the truth also opens you to a haunting history of power that I even struggle to think about, let alone speak of it."

The ground suddenly shook beneath us, but I planted my feet to keep from falling down. "Did you kill Molly?" I asked quickly, ignoring the fact that whatever that mist was, it had sensed my arrival and was coming for me. "Tell me it's a lie. That you didn't do it."

He nodded, and if I had been with my physical body, I wouldn't have been able to stop the tears.

"Why?" I asked. "How could you do something like that?"

Caleb knitted his eyebrows together and glared at me. "It's not black and white."

"Yes, it is! You took an innocent woman's life!"

There was another tremble on the ground beneath my feet. It didn't matter how quiet I was. Whatever darkness was lurking in the Underworld below or around us had known the moment I entered this realm.

"I want to know about the wooden horse and what happened that night," I said.

He inched closer to me, and I felt the power of fire ignite inside my soul as if trying to pull toward the vessel it was meant to inhabit—Caleb.

"I may have left out a few details about how I brought you back," he confessed.

"You wouldn't be Caleb if you didn't." I couldn't conceal my annoyance. "You always did keep your secrets."

His lips tightened. "I tried to bring you back repeatedly with different ancestors in your bloodline using my own spell. It was true that it never worked. I was missing the key power to make it happen. I was trying to protect you from knowing the truth, because if you knew what I had done—"

"Tell me what really happened, and I'll leave," I said, feeling panic rising in my chest.

"After we buried you, I returned to Gallows Hill," he started. "I wanted to pay my respects for what had happened to our fellow witch allies who died that day, including you, but what I saw there stunned me," Caleb explained.

My shoulders heaved, and though I wasn't with my physical body, I felt anxiety fill every bone inside me as if I were.

"There was another group of witches there," he continued, "but they weren't using the elements. They were casting an entirely different type of magic. That was when I remembered what Roland had taught me. They were the Keepers of the Dead. They gathered in a circle around the tree, holding hands. Suddenly, the tree vanished before my eyes. I didn't know the others, but I recognized one witch: Tituba."

"I vaguely remember her," I said. "What else?"

"I don't believe she was one of them, but she helped, at least, keeping the villagers from finding the Keepers and stopping whatever spell they were doing. Tituba told me the tree had gone to an island, where it would stay protected until you returned. Well, *if* you ever returned. I may not have understood that coven's motives, but to them, they were protecting your power."

"What was so special about that tree, Caleb? How were they protecting my power by moving the tree that killed me?" The ground rumbled again beneath us.

"Mercy, go."

I knew whatever was coming into Purgatory was close. "What is so special about that tree?" I asked again, not turning around but feeling the tingling sensation of a needle prick in my neck.

No!

I wasn't ready to leave this place. I didn't have my answer. I dug deep into my projection, forcing myself to stay rooted to my spot.

"Tituba told me it held the power to bring someone back from the dead. They all felt it the moment you left Earth. Tituba disappeared shortly after, so I couldn't learn more. For over three hundred years, I searched for that tree and was always met with a dead end. I tried on my own to create a spell I thought would work on several of your ancestors, but the spell I created didn't have the kind of power I needed. I moved to Salem in 1999 and stayed close to where your mom lived. She and Lily were the last women in your bloodline with direct ties to the power of Spirit. They were the last hope of linking you to them."

"How did you even find the magic to do it?" I asked.

"A year later, I felt the power right there in Salem." He ran his fingers through his hair. "It wasn't until that night in the hospital that I finally had the magic I needed to make it work. It was Molly who told me what to do."

"She told you how to kill her?" My mind raced.

Caleb bit his bottom lip. "Yes, because Molly understood why we had to do it. Her husband, Dante; he was afraid, but this was my last chance to get it right. I knew the universe was lining itself up for what happened that night to bring you back, but the price that had to be paid wasn't what I had expected. I didn't want to kill her, Mercy." Caleb closed his eyes and looked away from me.

The ground shook angrily beneath us.

"Mercy," Caleb cried, "please, go."

"Not yet. What happened that night?"

Caleb rubbed his upper thighs and began pacing. "As soon as I entered her hospital room, a light glowed from a small wooden sculpture of a horse sitting on the table by her bed, but ..." He stopped moving and averted his eyes from mine. "Dante had planned to use its power to bring back his wife once she passed from her illness."

"From a sculpture?"

He nodded. "It's made from the oak tree from Gallows Hill."

The floor between us split, and black smoke crept through the ground. I closed my eyes tightly and pulled myself back with the elemental power, yanking me away from the vortex that led into

Purgatory. But as I tore through the veil, red eyes glared at me within a dark, cloudy mist. Every hair on my body was raised, and the fear I experienced stunned me. The moment my spirit thrust back into my body; I couldn't move. I must have collapsed, because I was no longer standing and holding hands with Lily and Joel. My head rested in Dorian's lap, and my entire body felt stiff as a board.

Dorian pulled me up and held me tightly, but I still couldn't move my limbs.

"What was that?" Dorian asked, panic rising in his throat. "I've never experienced anything like that, and I've seen a lot of creatures in the centuries I've lived."

They had seen what Patricia and Riley had. My head spun from what Caleb had revealed to me.

"What's wrong with her?" Lily asked. She grabbed my arms, rubbing them aggressively. The sensation managed to ground me, and the room stopped shifting in my vision. I inhaled deeply and looked up, my body finally molding into Dorian's hold.

"Do you believe in the Devil, Lily?" I finally asked.

Lily shook her head. "I don't know what I believe. But whatever *that* was, it was darker than anything I had ever felt. Your body was trembling, and black smoke filled this room. Whatever *that* was, it wasn't *here*. It was watching us from another realm, as if it were connected to you by a rope, and you had pulled it toward us."

The room spun as I recalled something Kyoko had told me.

"Remember the story I told you of the Devil who sent Misha to create an army of vampires?" They nodded. "I think he's still out there, trying to stop me. Somehow, it has control over Purgatory, where the coven is. It's terrifying to think that something that evil is able to reach our world."

"You aren't going back there," Joel said.

"I know," I said. "I don't need to go back there. I have what we need."

"What did Caleb tell you?" Dorian asked.

"We need to find Dante and a wooden horse."

CHAPTER 16

MERCY

After a quick Google search on Molly's husband, Dante, there were more than enough articles to help us pull up photos of him and create a locator spell. If I could envision his face and his name, finding him wouldn't be a problem.

We were able to pinpoint his location at the top of a hill in Victoria, Canada, right outside of Mount Douglas Park. It was isolated, surrounded by dense forest, and only one access road.

Noah decided to stay behind to help Riley gather the remaining wolf packs who wanted to join forces with us. A few werewolves were willing to leave their packs to come here and fight, but the majority were afraid to leave what they knew and loved—their families.

Patricia, though no longer helping me with spells to take me to the other side, did provide us with literature to learn about the original covens—the Keepers of the Dead.

The original covens were nothing like ours. They respected the elements but didn't use elemental power to harness their magic. They connected with spirits from the other side and used their powers to heal others through herbs and magical potions.

I tried to recall what limited knowledge I had of Tituba from my previous life. Slavers had stolen Tituba from her homeland and sold her to a plantation in Barbados a year prior, and after Tituba was brought to Massachusetts, she began to use her magic, as well as voodoo, to call to her coven for help. Thankfully, Tituba's coven found and rescued her from the village shortly after she was released from the trials. No one saw her ever again.

I had vague memories of her, mostly a few encounters when we'd visited the home of Samuel Parris during the final months before I died. Though we had very different ways of practicing magic, I never felt threatened by her. If anything, Tituba seemed rather kind and even showed me a few simple spells when no one was looking.

Joel recounted stories that my grandfather, William, had told him, which had been passed down through the family for centuries. The other covens didn't think kindly of the Chosen Ones. We were, according to them, an abomination that created an imbalance in this world—the opposite of our purpose. Speculation was that the covens surrounding Tituba had influenced the village girls to crucify us, so we could not be conduits for other witches to use. If anything, they believed they were protecting our kind.

I couldn't understand it, though. Had they not known about the vampire threat? What made them think that what they were doing was any better than what my coven was sent here to do?

Joel explained the coven believed in the elements and their purpose to balance the universe, but that the magic should never be used for selfish power or superiority. When the universal elements came to this earth and received a body, to them, it was a blasphemous act toward the higher power, even though an angel created us.

Luckily, Joel's research was just enough to help me prepare to meet Dante. After finding where Dante was living, we went into the family room, so I could begin practicing teleportation magic.

"Can't be too hard, right?" I asked Joel.

Joel smirked, shaking his head. "The power of teleportation is harder than you think, but I was only five when I learned, and I'm not as powerful as you."

"Yes, but you have had years of practice and experience. This is brand new for me."

Despite being told how powerful I was, I still doubted my ability to create new magic. I rubbed my palms over my thighs, trying to get rid of the anxiety building up.

What if I can't do this?

Dorian pulled me aside and cradled my chin in his palm. "My love, you can do this," he assured me, as if he read my mind. "You doubt yourself more than you should."

"I'm trying not to," I said.

He cupped my chin tighter, tilted it upward, closed his eyes, and kissed me gently. My stomach did a flip, and when he released me, his lips curved into a smile that almost reached his eyes. "Mercy, you were the first person I ever fell in love with. Since then, I have never loved another. There is no one in the world that I believe in more than you. See yourself as I see you. Please."

My jaw dropped. Had Dorian really not loved another since I died? "The only one? You've never—"

"Fated mates. If that truly is a thing in our world, then you are mine." He placed his hand on my temple and traced his finger over my skin until I felt the tiny hairs on the back of my neck stand straight. "It wasn't just because you saved me that day. It wasn't just your beauty or powers that drew me to you. It was your ability to believe in yourself. The witches in the village doubted you and your coven. They had difficulty accepting that one witch could save them from monsters like me." Dorian removed his hand from my cheek but didn't step back. I felt the heat from his breath on my face. "You didn't always have allies around you. But you didn't care. You knew your purpose. You didn't need someone to tell you that. You don't need *us* to tell you that, either."

I gazed past him as I thought about what he had just said. He and everyone else had so much confidence in me, and I wished I had believed what they did. I *needed* to believe it. I glanced at Lily and Joel and then placed my fingers around Dorian's palm, giving it a squeeze. "I'll try," I said, turning toward Joel. "Show me how to do this."

He grabbed my hand and escorted me to the center of the room.

"Our bloodline," Joel started, "represented the element of Spirit." He grabbed my hands and inched me closer to him. "But you *are* the actual element in human form."

He implied that this should be simple. Nothing about my powers was simple. But I had to allow myself to let go and trust in my power.

"Hold your hands out and close your eyes," Joel instructed.

With my arms outstretched, I shut my eyes. The breeze from outside picked up and entered the room, causing my hair to dance. My powers were already igniting around me, but it wasn't just that. The powerful gust of wind hadn't come from outside. It had come from within me. The powers that stirred within felt warm but also like water rushing through my veins, like a mighty river.

Simon.

Leah.

When I opened my eyes, I saw the tree branches outstretched and swaying from my magic through the window in front of me. The ground beneath me moved gently, like it was lulling me to sleep.

Ezra.

"Easy, Mercy. Take a breath. We haven't started yet," Joel said, likely feeling the heavy energy vibrating in the room.

"I'm ... I'm not doing it," I told him. Dorian grabbed my hand but quickly released his grip as sparks shot through my fingers. I looked down and saw the faint glow of firelight in my fingertips.

Caleb.

Tears welled in my eyes and dripped down until they touched my lips. "I can feel them," I said, wiping my lips dry. "The coven is here."

It wasn't just my coven's power; I felt *them*. They were in the room, helping and guiding me through this spell. Goosebumps trailed up my arms, and I closed my eyes again, breathing in and out, their presence guiding me into the calm state of meditation I needed to achieve.

Joel grabbed my hands, which were outstretched again, and moved them from side to side. "Visualize that you're opening a wormhole. The portal won't open until you can envision the location. Pinpoint exactly where you're going to go, then focus on that. Then use your powers to pull the energy around you and command it to open. Your powers alone will do it. You just have to ask the other elements inside you to obey your command."

"That simple, huh?" I asked.

"In theory," Joel said.

We weren't traveling far tonight through the portal, so I only focused on Joel's backyard. I pictured his rocking bench swinging forward and back and the maple tree directly to the right. I narrowed in on the tree, moving my hands from side to side as he had instructed, and I felt the five elemental powers pulling until they became one at my fingertips. As the portal opened before me, I opened my eyes and stepped inside. I zipped quickly through the energy, appearing in front of the maple tree. I landed hard, feeling a sting of pain in my knee, but the pain only lasted a few seconds. A light flashed around me, and I wondered if that was the coven leaving me again.

My heartbeat picked up, and tears burned my eyes. I didn't want them to go, but they were there when I needed them. I wished so badly they could have stayed. I didn't want to feel so lost without them.

I felt Dorian's soft fingertips trace the back of my arms, drawing me back to reality. I turned around to face him and fell into his arms. As I mourned my coven, I felt the pain in my chest crushing my heart.

I'm so close, guys. I'm going to get you out of there.

CHAPTER 17

MAURICE

I paced the floor, watching the clock as it ticked away each second. It had been over an hour since Kris was supposed to arrive at the club, and my patience was running thin. I felt like I was the only person on this fucking planet who believed in punctuality.

"Relax, Maurice. Tonight, we celebrate. She'll be here," Julian said, trying to calm my irritation at Kris's tardiness.

He placed a bottle of wine on the counter in front of us and poured me a glass, filling it to the brim.

The door chimed as I took my first sip, feeling the cool liquid of chardonnay go down my throat and tasting a hint of vanilla and oak. The sweetness of the wine took the edge away from my agitation. I turned toward the door and the tardy guest of honor.

"Maurice, darling, how are you?" Kris said, sauntering her way over to me, but she paused when she spotted Julian.

Fuck. I was afraid of this.

"Oh, what the fuck? Hell no, I'm leaving," she snapped, but I sped toward her, slamming the door shut and stepping in her path to prevent her from leaving.

"Julian says he's sorry," I told her, keeping my eyes locked on hers. "Right, Julian?"

Julian chuckled under his breath and shrugged. "Sure."

"Move out of my way, Maurice," Kris said. "I don't want to be anywhere near that asshole. I'm also a bit surprised you'd deceive me this way. So, you can fuck off, too."

Kris was among the few women I knew who didn't fear me. In normal circumstances, this would irritate the hell out of me. If they didn't fear me, they'd disrespect me. Kris, on the other hand, I had known for over ten years, and she had never turned on me. That's why, a few months ago, I set her up on a date with Julian, but things didn't go quite as well as I had hoped between my two friends. They were the only ones I considered *actual* friends.

"Julian, make this right," I fumed. "Now."

"Because you need me?" Kris asked, folding her arms across her chest. Then she cursed under her breath. "Is that the only reason I'm here? You can't even greet me with a hug?"

I grinned and pulled her in for the hug she was bitching about. "I've missed you. But also, yes, I need your help." She slapped me hard against the arm. The slap only created a soft vibration against my skin. I chuckled softly as I gestured to Julian to get the hell over here.

I heard Julian sigh deeply behind me and slowly approach us both. His head hung low, and he stared at the ground.

"If you're going to apologize, you better look me in the eye," she snapped.

Julian clenched a fist and bit his lower lip. He wasn't used to women talking to him like that, which obviously infuriated him.

He lifted his head, and his eyes met hers. "Sorry that I fucked you like an animal and then ghosted you until you gave up."

Kris's lips slowly stretched into a wide grin. "Wow. You must be exhausted. How many times did you practice that pathetic attempt of an apology?"

Julian finally relaxed and smiled back. "A lot, actually. I've thought perhaps I can make it up to you with round two beneath the sheets."

Kris slapped Julian hard against the cheek. He winced, and she quickly spun around toward the door, but I caught her by the collar of her blouse and pulled her back. "A genuine apology, Julian," I said, releasing Kris.

"Fine." He threw his hands up. "I'm sorry I was a dick. I didn't realize how much that would hurt you. Let's put the past few months behind us and move forward, shall we? You're already dating someone new, Maurice tells me, and I'm—"

"Still single and a pathetic man-whore who couldn't keep a relationship if you even tried ... so I've heard," she said, amusement in her voice, as if that discovery brought her the utmost joy. "What do you need from me, Maurice?"

Good. We were finally making progress. "I need you to pull some information from a witch's mind. She's incredibly powerful, though, so I need to know that if I drug her, you'd still be able to reach certain parts of her memory."

"Why can't you just have Julian do it?" She looked at me quizzically.

"His power is a bit ... different from yours."

She glowered at him. "That's a pity. It's quite an amazing gift."

Julian rolled his eyes and folded his arms as if pouting like a small child.

"Yes. I can, but it's harder because her mind will be distorted. If you can hold on to her for at least ten seconds, I should be able to get what you need."

I turned to Julian. "And there you go. We're getting somewhere."

Kris moved past us and walked behind the bar, pouring herself a glass of vodka, topping it with a squeeze of lemon, and throwing back her shot. "Who exactly am I reading?"

I walked toward the bar to join her. "Her name is Mercy Brawling."

Her eyes narrowed. "And what is she to you?"

Julian chuckled under his breath, and I frowned, turning back to Kris. "You're reading my mind right now, aren't you?" I asked.

Kris smirked. "I've had several people who I thought were friends turn on me through the years. Of course, I'm reading your mind."

"Well, stop, or you can forget I asked you for any favors," I said, rage burning inside me. "Because I know you've been bored out of your fucking mind without me."

She shrugged, tossing back another shot. "True. We always did have fun together."

Julian reached out, grabbing the third shot Kris was about to drink. "Thanks," he said.

"It's *your* mind that's more fascinating, Julian," she said to him.

Julian didn't look pleased. "If you read my mind again, I'll make you forget about your sweet little boy toy and make you believe you're in love with me. Don't think I won't."

She cackled, throwing her head back. "Oh, I know you will, but you know it's nearly impossible for me to stop once I've started."

Julian shifted, looking uncomfortable, and wouldn't meet her eyes.

"Interesting," she said, tilting her head toward Julian.

I slammed my hand on the counter. "Will the two of you knock it off and tell me what you're talking about?"

"Julian is sharing his thoughts with me about you, Maurice, and this ... Mercy. Are you, Maurice Tomassi, having feelings for a witch? Let alone a nice one?" She grinned, turned back to face the liquor shelf behind her, and grabbed another bottle of vodka. "I don't think there's enough alcohol in this world to allow me to forget this moment."

I gritted my teeth and yanked the bottle from her. "You think I want to feel this way? I'd rather be ripping her head off and feeding it to the goddamn wolves."

I wasn't lying. I wanted to hate Mercy. I *needed* to hate her.

Kris leaned back against the bar and folded her arms across her chest. "But she can't die, can she? She's a Chosen."

I shook my head. "Well, there's a dagger."

She stared at me for a long moment and then said, "Oh, that's even more interesting." She turned to Julian. "Maurice doesn't intend to use the dagger to kill her."

I wasn't ready to tell Julian about my plans yet, but of course, I couldn't control Kris's need to read every damn thought from every person she came across, let alone keep it to herself.

Julian shot me a curious glance. "What else would you need the dagger for, Maurice?"

Kris pressed her elbows against the counter and leaned forward, her chin resting on her palms. "It's for us, Julian. He wants it for us."

CHAPTER 18

MERCY

I spent the next three days practicing the teleportation spell. Every time I'd jump through the portal, I'd take us further from our home. Dorian stayed behind at the portal entrance each time, just in case anything went wrong. I didn't think I needed him at that point; the spell was coming naturally for me, and for that, I was relieved.

Dorian had just finished cooking me a meal he had been practicing since becoming human again. He found he enjoyed cooking and could stomach home-cooked meals, as opposed to anything from a restaurant. Everything was too salty or greasy for his palate. Not that he really remembered what food had once tasted like. Still, it was much different from drinking blood.

Tonight, he made us each a sweet potato chickpea buddha bowl, and I dove in the moment it hit the table. Whatever he had put in it satisfied all my senses.

"I think this was the one thing my mom never taught me," I said, taking another bite and swallowing before I spoke again. "We pretty much ate at Lily's home every night or at her café, because she was the one in our family who actually knew how to cook. And she was good at it. If she wasn't around, I lived off frozen dinners and fast food."

After he swallowed his bite, he reached out and touched my fingers with his. "I enjoy cooking for you. I can't do the whole fast-food thing."

I couldn't help but smile at this. "Well, as long as we agree I will never cook for you, then we're good. My cooking would probably kill you, anyway."

"Deal," Dorian said with a wink before taking another bite of food.

Once we cleared our plates, I leaned back against the kitchen island directly in front of him. "What were you like back then?" I asked. "I mean, before I met you for the first time."

We hadn't talked much about the past since he came back into my life, at least not on a personal level. Everything was still very new to us. I remember parts of our relationship before we died, but it was all very vague and mostly centered on our relationship and future, not the past.

"In what sense?"

I shrugged. "I don't know. Like, did you enjoy cooking before becoming a vampire? Were you a hunter? Did you have any hobbies?"

His eyes narrowed. "What's this about?"

I wasn't sure how to explain that I still loved him but that most of my love was tied to my other life. I didn't remember every conversation, and I didn't know how much he might have changed.

"We don't ever talk like this," I admitted. "I think we should."

He pulled a chair around the kitchen island and leaned against the back of it, stretching his legs out. "I wasn't a hunter. I joined my father from time to time in the field to help bring food to the table for our family, but I enjoyed other things."

"Like what?"

"Reading," he answered quickly.

I suppressed a smile. "From what I remember, reading anything other than the Bible back then was forbidden."

"I was very religious back then," he said.

"And now?"

Dorian hung his head and looked down at his hands. "When you've seen what I've seen, Mercy, you struggle to believe in God. I'm not saying gods don't exist, but if they do, they don't care much for the undead."

Before getting too much into religion, which I tried to avoid in my everyday conversations, I studied him for a moment before changing the subject. "Okay, what did you do aside from reading the Bible?"

"Like most men back then, I worked in the field. Helped my mom with the daily chores, including caring for my little sister, Rebecca. We didn't have as much time to develop hobbies as we can today. We were always working on the property, and when we weren't, we either slept or were in church."

"And now?"

"Now, I paint, I learn different languages, and I have the chance to start over with the woman I love." He gave me a weak smile. "I know it's not how we thought our future was going to go, and your coven is a priority before we move forward, but I'm here for the long run. I want to travel with you and take you anywhere you want to go. I want to take care of you, even if you don't need it, and fight with you when you don't get your way." He winked at me, and I felt my cheeks warm.

As he looked into my eyes, my mind drifted to my coven. As much as I wanted to start over with Dorian and move forward in our relationship, I had to bring them back. The longer they were there, the more at risk they were from whatever darkness was trying to enter that realm.

Dorian stood directly in front of me when my thoughts returned to the present. He leaned forward, and before he touched my lips with his, he lightly licked his bottom lip. I glued my gaze to his lips, eager to feel them against mine. Everything Dorian did caused my core to react; I found myself wondering how I could live all these years without him ... Without experiencing this kind of attraction. So unholy, yet so pure at the same time.

His palms rested on each side of my neck, titling my head upwards as he kissed me. Instantly, something was triggered within me, and I was hungry for more of him. A small shudder shook through my body as I desperately leaned closer, grabbing the back of his neck to draw him in.

I never wanted to be away from him.

One of his hands instinctively dropped lower, clutching my hip before it dared to venture upward underneath the fabric of my shirt. Goosebumps rose over my skin as he touched me, his hand drifting toward my breast. I whimpered quietly, my breathing heavy and uneven.

"Dorian ..." I murmured against his lips. My hands found his pants, unbuttoning them in a rush. I needed him right here and right now.

"I know, Mercy ... I know," he responded, as if he could read my mind and all the filthy thoughts that roamed around. All I could think about was his cock ramming deep inside of me, with his fingers circling around my tender clit.

A moment later, we were both startled by a loud crash from the family room. Our lips separated from each other, shock visible on our faces. His arm immediately shot out in front of me, keeping me from moving.

"What? Are you crazy?" I barked. "I'm a witch, Dorian."

"And I'm a werewolf now, remember?"

"You can still die."

I brushed his hand aside but gently. Dorian couldn't help his need to protect me, but *he* was the one who could die. Not me.

As much as I expected him to stand behind me, he wouldn't be Dorian if he did. I heard a loud growl come from his chest. He wanted to transition, but I gripped his hand. "We don't know what that was. Try to stay calm."

"I'm stronger in my wolf form, Mercy. I'm changing whether or not you try to stop it."

Dorian huffed, and his eyes grew dark. His wolf's hair pushed through his clothes, ripping them apart. We heard another sound of broken glass, that time in front of us, and purple smoke filled the air. I coughed and backed up, and Dorian released my hand as he collapsed to the floor mid-transition.

"Shit! Dorian!" I screamed as a hand gripped the back of my hair firmly and shoved me toward the wall. My face cracked against the drywall, and my nose broke, blood spurting everywhere.

I swung around with my hands out, and I saw Maurice. He flashed his white fangs, his dark eyes drawing me into flashbacks of torture and pain. He reached his hand out and gripped my throat, cutting off my oxygen, and I fought for every breath. Wiggling to break free wasn't going to work, and my strength was evenly matched with his. I concentrated a magic pulse into my hands and slammed it into his body, throwing him across the room. I was able to catch my breath and look around at what was happening.

My heart raced wildly as I stood there, unable to move. Maurice didn't come alone. A woman stood by the couch with her hand out toward Dorian, and as she extended her fingers, Dorian screeched in pain. Julian stood quietly in the corner with a devilish smirk and walked toward Maurice to help him off the floor. Maurice slapped his hand away and got to his feet without help. When I looked back at Dorian, the woman had gripped him by the back of his neck to make him look up at her. I didn't move. I was too afraid she'd kill him.

"Maurice, stop! Please don't hurt him. I'll do whatever you want. Just let him go."

Julian walked quickly to Dorian, and the woman dropped her hands, but Julian replaced them with his own. He wasn't touching Dorian, but his palms faced Dorian's temple, and Dorian's eyes were bloodshot. The wolfsbane in the air had crippled him from transitioning, but whatever Julian was doing was much worse.

"Now that everyone is where they need to be," Maurice said, his voice rough and sharp, "let's get down to business."

His movements were swift as he rushed at me again, grabbed my throat, and slammed me hard against the back wall of the family room. I heard a low growl come from Dorian, but whatever was happening to him, he couldn't move to help me.

I tried to pry Maurice's hands from my throat, but it only caused him to squeeze harder, cutting off my air supply. The lack of oxygen alone was crippling me from using my magic. I pulled my hands up again, hoping something would come out of my fingertips, but a needle pricked my hip, and I heard something plastic hit the floor. My head immediately started spinning, and my vision blurred. Maurice leaned forward, pressing his cheek against mine, and whispered, "How does it make you feel that I have all the power now ... yet again?"

He looked at my damaged lip and nose that knitted themselves back together, but the blood from the injuries was still smeared across my skin. Veins protruded under Maurice's eyes, and his breathing hitched.

Was this it? Was he going to taste my blood out of pure temptation?

But he didn't.

Maurice only ran his finger over the blood, wiping my lips clean, and then used his shirt to clean his finger. Then he caressed my cheek as if silently cursing himself for hurting me. Like he genuinely cared.

"You're a sick bastard. You know that?" My voice cracked, and fear and anger fueled every part of my being. "I'm going to fucking kill you."

Maurice's solemn gaze turned venomous, as if the still moment we had just experienced never existed. I turned my head from him as he inched closer; the coldness of his breath chilled my skin. The only thing I could do was focus on my energy, that tiny, dim light hovering over my fingertips. I tried to channel as much as I could to combat whatever drug the psycho had injected into me.

The lights in the room flickered, and Maurice looked around, suddenly frowning.

"Is that you, darling?" he asked.

I didn't answer. I knew the power I was pulling up wouldn't be enough to do anything that would keep Maurice down, and I'd be too weak to stop Julian from taking Dorian's life.

Maurice squeezed my throat again, inching so close I felt his erection pressed up against me. "If you do anything to kill me, Julian will kill your *boyfriend*."

The way he emphasized the word "boyfriend" didn't sit well with me. It was as if he were upset that Dorian and I were together. Why would Maurice care?

I felt his icy-cold breath again, that time on the side of my neck. His lips parted slightly as he moved closer. Once again, I thought he was going to bite down into my flesh, but Maurice would never trade his immortality to be human again. As he came closer to my throat, he loosened his grip, and his lips touched my neck. What Maurice did next puzzled me. He kissed me gently, his lips gliding up to my ear.

This isn't happening. This cannot be happening.

He released the kiss, and a sinister smile reached his lips. "Your uncle still has that spell lingering inside your body to mask your scent, but I remember clearly what you smelled like, and I'll never get that out of my mind."

"Go fuck yourself," I said. "Then burn in hell. You have several friends waiting for you there."

Maurice laughed aloud, placing his fingers around my wrist, and pulling my arm up, then the other, until he had both my wrists above my head in his tight hold. His grip tightened as he pinned me firmly between his body and the wall.

"We're almost done with the new bracelets that your dead angel destroyed when she took down my lair. And once that's done, you'll be mine again."

What the hell was he talking about? I'd be *his?*

"Why do you want someone who plans to kill you? That's not much of a relationship now, is it?" I asked sluggishly. "I have never been, nor ever will be, yours. I hate you, Maurice."

He smiled. "Hate. I don't think so. Detest, maybe, but you're incapable of hate, love. How many times have you had the opportunity to kill me, and yet, you haven't?"

I winced at his question. I was disgusted with myself that I hadn't yet, and if this poison in my body wasn't crippling me, and if they didn't have Dorian's life in their hands, then yes, I would. Maurice was delusional to think I'd hesitate to end his life.

"Kris," Maurice called to the woman, and she stepped toward me. "Do it now."

Her eyes squinted, and I felt an overpowering pressure at my temples, as if she were pulling my blood toward the surface of my skin.

What was she doing?"

"It's destroyed, Maurice," she said. "They destroyed the dagger."

His grip on my wrists tightened. "Destroyed?"

I glared at him with a look that could kill. "Oh, yes," I said with a slightly slurred laugh. "The one thing that could kill me is now powerless at the bottom of the ocean ... oops."

CHAPTER 19

MERCY

"That's impossible. The dagger *can't* be destroyed," Maurice said.

I laughed to myself, my head swaying with the effort. "Wrong. My coven created the dagger to perform the immortal spell in 1692. Part of that spell gave this dagger the ability to kill us. It was the price to pay for using dark magic, which immortality is. It creates an off-balance in the universe, regardless of its *good* intentions. When they died, so did the spell they used to bewitch it." A slow smirk pulled at my lips. "You can't ever kill me."

His eyes grew dark, and he inched closer to me until our foreheads almost touched, his hips rolling into mine. "Who said anything about me wanting to kill you?"

I looked at him curiously.

What else would they use the dagger for?

I glanced over at Julian and Kris. "Oh, you think you can use the dagger to make *them* immortal?"

Abigail had once told me that the Chosen Ones were the only ones allowed to cast the immortal spell, not that we were the only ones who could.

Thank God it was powerless now.

I smiled at that thought. "Is it because I killed your brother, Colin, and your little friend, Kyoko? And now you're lonely?" As my grin grew wider, he tightened the grip on my wrists. "What's your plan, Maurice? Are you going to keep showing up here, threatening me, threatening the people I care about, and acting like you give two shits about me while you run your rapey hands all over my body and press your vile lips on my skin? You're so pathetic that it makes me sick."

Maurice breathed heavily. His shoulders heaved, and his eyes turned red. I may have pushed him too far.

Oh shit.

Maurice turned to Julian. "You can kill him now."

"No!" I screamed.

He held up his hand to stop Julian, who was already pulling his hands closer to Dorian's temples. Julian paused but kept his fingers a few inches away from Dorian's skin.

"What will you do for me if I spare his life?" Maurice asked.

I blinked. "What?"

"To save Dorian's life, would you sacrifice yourself to be mine?"

"What the fuck are you talking about? I hate you!" I swallowed. "Have you forgotten that I'm your greatest enemy? You should hate me, too!"

Maurice shook his head. "I don't hate you." His words made my head spin a million miles per hour. He looked me over, and a deviant grin spread across his face.

How did I miss this? I thought everything he had done since being held captive at his lair was all to hurt and torture me because he loathed my very existence. But he almost seemed to care or have some weird obsession with me. It was exactly what Jade had described. At the time, I didn't understand it. It confused me, but mainly, it was terrifying. He was out of his goddamn mind.

I felt a tingle at my fingertips, and warmth filled my body from head to toe. As my body fought off the drugs that he injected me with, I felt my powers grab me. I was so much stronger now; a little syringe of drugs wasn't going to cut it. "Yes, I'll go with you if you spare Dorian's life."

Maurice's eyes lit up, and he let go of my wrists, allowing my arms to drop to my sides. He brushed my cheeks with the back of his fingers and licked his bottom lip. "Good answer," he said. "Release him." But Julian didn't budge. "I said release him, Julian."

"Don't trust her. I read Mercy's thoughts. She lied," Kris interrupted, but before Maurice turned back to me, I threw my hands out, knocking Maurice back a few feet. I turned toward the two witches and threw out another surge of magic. My power took hold of Julian, and using my telekinetic power, I began to squeeze. Blood leached out of his eyes and ears in rivulets. As a screech left Julian's mouth, I flung his body toward the wall with incredible force, and he slammed against a wooden table, crumbling upon impact. He didn't rise again.

Dorian fell to his knees and looked up as Maurice grabbed me again, twisting me around so my back was against him. He seized my wrists, pulling my arms behind my back and pressing my face into the wall. Dorian yelled, but the witch, Kris, yanked him back.

Maurice was a fool to think I needed my hands to use my magic. I've learned a few things since the lair. As Kris's magic lingered in my thoughts, I turned my head and stared at her, using my powers to shoot back in her direction. My telepathic abilities distorted her own mind, causing her to wail and grip her head, freeing Dorian. I pictured seizing her magic from my mind, twisting it into sharp blades, and sending them back into her, taking her to her knees. Maurice screamed in my ear, but I only moved my focus on the table that had broken under Julian's fall and used my powers to conjure a green rope of light to pull a shard of wood toward Maurice. I yanked my arms free, spun myself around, and dropped to the floor as the sharp piece of wood flew toward Maurice and directly at his chest.

The wood pierced through Maurice's skin, and he screeched in agony. I quickly stood and planted my feet, using all the strength I could muster. I kicked Maurice's flailing body away from me while putting my other hand out and opening a new portal, then bolted toward Dorian, grabbed his arm, and pushed us through.

CHAPTER 20

MERCY

"I missed his heart!" I cried after we plummeted to Joel's family room floor, jumping to my feet and pacing across the room. "Fuck!"

Joel ran into the room, looking panicked. "What the hell happened? Are you two okay, at least?"

"I missed. That's what happened. I had Maurice and Julian in the same room, along with this psychopath female witch, and I missed his heart!"

I placed my hands on my head, gripping my hair. "We leave tomorrow for Canada. We can't do anything without Dante's help to bring the coven back. It's not safe for us here anymore."

Joel nodded. "Dorian, call Noah and make sure he doesn't return to the house. I'll head to the market to grab what you guys need for your trip and put a protective spell over the house. No one leaves here until you're going through a portal and out of the country."

I felt Dorian's hands catch me and cover my arms, stroking my skin until I relaxed.

I turned around and placed my hand on his cheek. "I need to take a shower. All I feel are Maurice's grubby hands all over me."

Dorian frowned and backed up, slightly lowering his head. I knew this was torturing him to no end, because he wanted to rip Maurice's head off just as much as I did. That damn purple smoke, which had to have been wolfsbane, rendered him helpless. Dorian was unable to help me, and that would eat him up inside.

"I'll call Noah and then pour us a glass of wine," Dorian said.

I gave him a weak smile. "Thank you."

I heard Joel's keys rattle in the kitchen. "Mercy, once I head out the door, the shield will go up around the house. Call me if you guys need anything."

"I will," I said. "Promise you'll be extra careful out there. He's coming after everyone."

I turned back to Dorian and stepped toward him, reaching out my hand and pulling him to me slowly. I wanted to comfort him, reassure him, but I was at a loss for words. I kissed his cheek gently, removed my hand, and padded to the guest bathroom.

The water hit my skin hotter than usual, and I let it burn my backside. I inhaled the steam around me, letting the warmth flood my lungs. I squeezed the soap in the luffa and scrubbed my skin until it felt raw. Then I rinsed off the dried blood from my face, feeling my lip and nose. Not that it mattered since I had healed the physical wounds of the attack. Getting Maurice out of my head was another injury altogether. How did this happen?

Why do I keep failing and letting him beat me over and over again?

Time slowed down for a moment, and I plugged my foot over the drain, letting the water build up in the tub, and sank into the hot bath. I closed my eyes and spoke to my powers, reaching out to the elements. I called on the water, which grew hotter than it had been when it came from the showerhead. This would burn any human to the point of second-degree burns, but not me. It hurt like hell, but I endured it. I didn't know why I wanted to feel this kind of pain, but I did.

Was I punishing myself? Did I deserve this?

I slowed my powers down as I grimaced at the pain. I cooled the water down slightly and opened my eyes. The room was so steamy now that I couldn't see in front of me.

Was I sick and twisted like Maurice?

I recoiled at that thought. No, I had to be better than that monster. Because if he drew me to that level of evil and hate, I would be no better than him.

I wasn't sure how long I had been in the shower, but a tap at the door pulled my attention back to the present.

"Yes?" I called.

"Joel's home, and the shield is back up. I'll have dinner and wine ready when you are," I heard Dorian shout through the door.

I sat upright and reached for my towel. "Give me ten minutes."

Dorian had a light meal on the table since we had just eaten only a few hours ago. I joined him, took a few bites of the salad he had made, and sipped the dark wine.

"I think Lily has rubbed off on me," I said. "Not like I can ever really indulge in this bitter taste, but right now, it's all I want ... all I need."

Dorian smiled, leaning back in his chair. "For good reason."

"I know what this drink will do to my powers, but—" I stopped, looking in the distance through the window at the trees swaying in the heavy wind. "We're safe tonight?"

Dorian nodded. "No one can get through the doors or windows of the house. We're safe, according to Joel. I spoke with Noah and gave him the heads-up about what happened at the house. He's going to stay with Riley and Amber until we get back from Canada."

I raised the glass to my lips, taking a slow sip.

My smile was weak, but it was hard to stay upset around Dorian, especially since he was the kindest person I had ever met. I couldn't bear to hurt him, and my self-loathing would do just that.

After twenty minutes and two glasses later, I was relaxed enough to truly smile and enjoy our conversation.

I heard a thump in the hallway as Joel dropped two bags on the floor.

"I picked you both up toiletries, undergarments, and a few items of clothing. I put the two of you in the guest bedroom upstairs."

I smiled but kept my eyes on my glass.

"Thanks, Joel," Dorian said for the both of us.

I glanced up at the time, realizing we needed to get to bed now since we had a long journey ahead of us in the morning.

After brushing my teeth, I slipped on thick sweatpants and a long T-shirt Joel had bought for me.

Dorian sat upright against the headboard as I crawled in next to him. He was bare-chested, but I had seen him put on light sweatpants that hung loosely on his hips before he slipped under the covers.

"You look cute," he teased as I inched closer to him. He playfully grabbed me and threw me on my back, running his fingers down the sides of my arms.

I lifted my head, greeting his lips with mine, and kissed him gently. Our tongues swirled around in a slow, seductive dance. My fingers ran through his hair, and I gripped tighter, causing him to moan. His hands trailed down my arms again, and I caught my breath, my chest heaving with every breath I took.

"Dorian," I paused, collecting my thoughts. "I want you to fuck me."

It wasn't that I didn't want him inside me, but he and I both knew, at that moment, I was only trying to mask the pain I was feeling.

"I know," he said, running his fingers gently down the curve of my neck until his hand stopped at my chest.

Dorian moved to my side and rested his hip against the mattress, his arm curling around his pillow, his other hand still resting over my heart.

"I want to take it all away," he said. "You know I do."

Right then, we heard Joel walking down the hall, talking to Derek, who was still in New York. Joel wasn't ready for him to come back until our enemies were defeated. I hated that they were separated like this, but our number one priority was keeping our friends and family safe.

Dorian removed his hand from my chest and brushed his fingers through my hair, tucking my long brown strands behind my ear. He leaned in, kissed me again, and pulled me close to his chest in a firm bear hug, then kissed my neck and whispered in my ear that he loved me.

That night, we only rested, as tomorrow we would start the longest journey of our lives.

CHAPTER 21

MERCY

"Here are a couple of portable cell chargers," Joel said as we pulled on our backpacks.

I sipped the last of my coffee and handed the tumbler back to Joel, exchanging it for the chargers. We were standing out in front of the house, where the driveway met the road.

Dorian secured the backpack's clips, so it didn't fall off when we zipped through the portal, and I pulled out the map of the surrounding area of Victoria.

"The portal will take us here." I pointed to a small dot on the tip of a hill near the property.

"Got it," Dorian said as he grabbed the map from me and placed it in the back pocket of my bag. "What's the plan if our reception is less than friendly?"

I tightened the last strap and turned to face him. "We'll tell him the truth about who we are and hope for the best. If he attacks us for any reason, you get down and let me take the hit."

He frowned. "Mercy."

"This is non-negotiable, and you know it. If you aren't okay with that, then you need to stay."

He glared at me, deadpan. "Fine, I'm okay with you being shot," he said sarcastically.

"If you get injured, your werewolf side will heal you, or if you're on the brink of death, I'll heal you with my own magic."

"Noted," he said, avoiding eye contact with me.

"Bottled water?" Joel asked.

"Check," I affirmed.

"Alright, kiddo. I think you two have everything you need. I'll be waiting when you come back through." He paused before adding, "And be cautious, okay? We know little to nothing about this man."

I winked at him. "I promise."

Joel backed up, and I turned toward the road ahead, pulled my hands up, and moved them around until the portal opened.

Dorian grabbed my hand, and together we jumped into the vortex and flew through space.

It was the beginning of fall, and the leaves were changing into shades of chestnut and amber, the first signs that autumn was approaching. However, the tall trees surrounding us were already losing their leaves, and the ones that still hung from the trees were dried, cracked, and hanging loosely from the branches. As each gust of wind picked up, the tree branches waved in a graceful dance, dropping more of their leaves onto the grass.

As we neared the top of the hill that led to Dante's house, I inhaled the crisp air mixed with burning cedar wood. Smoke rose from the chimney of the property we'd identified as belonging to

Dante. If the locator spell was accurate, he was home. We cautiously made our way down a long pathway, but we stopped before we reached his gate, which appeared to be unlocked.

"Are you sure about this?" Dorian asked.

"No, but what other option do we have?"

The all-brick, one-story cabin's door was painted bright red, and five concrete steps ascended to the porch. There was a speaker outside the door and a camera above us in the corner of the doorway. My hands felt clammy, and I sucked in a breath and pressed the call button. It rang three times before a man's voice spoke on the other end of the speaker.

"What do you want?" a low, gravelly voice answered.

"Are you Dante Boyce?" I asked.

"You have the wrong house. Get off my property."

I looked up at Dorian and shrugged.

"Just tell him," Dorian said, but I knew the truth would probably not matter at this point.

I turned back to the speaker, but the man's voice called back. "You're Caleb's Mercy, aren't you?"

My stomach lurched as I looked up at the camera and nodded.

A knot twisted in my stomach as we waited for him to respond. A minute later, the door opened. He looked exactly like he had in the pictures we'd seen while researching him, just over twenty-two years older.

The middle-aged man was wearing a thick red robe and flannel pajama bottoms. His hair was dark brown, streaked with silver, and fell above his shoulders, and his messy beard looked as if he hadn't trimmed or cleaned it in months.

"Dante?" I asked.

He silently gestured toward the front hallway. "Come on in," he said.

I looked up at Dorian, and he nodded, so we stepped inside.

I felt the warmth from the living room fireplace burning, and the overhead lights were dimly lit.

Bookshelves lined the walls, filled with old, leather-bound books and what looked like ancient artifacts. Several wooden sculptures and tiny figures lined the walls and shelves. Stacks of magazines, newspaper clippings, and a few half-empty coffee mugs covered the coffee table, sitting right at the center of the family room.

"Would you like some coffee? I just put on a pot." He gestured toward the kitchen.

"No, thank you," I answered for the both of us.

He grunted. "My coffee is getting cold. Have a seat."

When Dante exited, I looked around again, taking in the room. All the drapes had been pulled up, and he'd cracked each window to allow a slight breeze. It was chilly this morning, but the cool air mixed with the warmth of the fireplace created a serene balance, which made the room feel cozy and inviting. As we walked further into the family room, a powerful aroma of musky cologne burned my nostrils.

Dante returned a minute later, moved toward a thick velvet chair near the corner of the room, and gestured toward the couch. "What is it you want, Mercy?" he asked flatly when we sat down.

I eyed Dorian nervously, then looked at Dante. "My coven is dead. I ... I need your help to bring them back."

He frowned. "No."

I squirmed uncomfortably in my chair. "Please. We traveled a long way to get here, and not to mention, I traveled to Purgatory

... twice," I emphasized, holding up two fingers, "to find answers. So, please, will you at least hear us out?"

He narrowed his round eyes and rubbed his hand down his beard. His face was unreadable as he tilted his head slightly. After a couple of seconds, a slow grin appeared, revealing his yellow, stained teeth.

Dante arched a brow. "Interesting. *You* traveled to Purgatory?" His voice was pitched with amusement.

"Yeah, it was a great time. Have you heard of it?" I asked, matching his tone. It was clear he had no intention of speeding this visit along, and by the looks of the grin on his face, he didn't care that my coven was dead.

He leaned back in his rocking chair, placed his coffee mug to his lips, and sipped, but he never took his eyes off mine. "My answer is still no."

I let out a frustrated sigh. "Dante, the future of—"

"You think bringing someone back from the dead is as simple as a mediocre spell with a damn piece of bark?" he snapped. His right hand tapped rhythmically on his knee as if he were nervous about something. "When you bring someone back from the dead, *witch* ..." The way he said "witch" was almost as if the word disgusted him. "You have to take the life of another, and you're too young to be put in the position Caleb put *me* in when I helped him twenty-two years ago." He gestured around the room. "I'm trapped here because of Caleb. My coven disavowed and banished me after helping the Chosen Ones, which was forbidden, *by the way!*" He tossed his hands up. "You came a long way for nothing."

"You've been a prisoner in your home for twenty-two years?" I asked him, completely astonished.

He didn't answer me, but my question *was* rhetorical.

Dante waved his hand as if to dismiss my comment and strolled toward a bookshelf against the back wall. Sitting by two stacked books was a beautifully carved wooden horse. I hadn't noticed it until now. My mouth gaped open slightly, and I felt Dorian's hand on my knee. It was right in front of us the entire time.

Dante pulled the horse off the shelf and carried it back our way with such care, as if this were the most priceless piece of art in the world.

He placed it on the coffee table in front of Dorian and me and returned to his rocking chair. "I used to be a carpenter," he started. "My ancestors were of the original covens in Siberia, but we were persecuted, and several of the surviving witches were driven out, so my great-grandfather joined the coven in Salem." He huffed. "He had to belong somewhere, and he wanted his bloodline to be raised by our own kind. The Keepers of the Dead weren't just a form of practice in my family. It was our culture and way of life. Just like being a carpenter had been. The trade that was passed down through the men in our family wasn't a job or an after-school hobby. It was who we were."

He paused and eyed the sculpture again on the table, so Dorian and I looked, too. I wasn't sure where he was going with his story, but we sat patiently, waiting for him to speak again.

"When I was barely twenty," he said, pulling our eyes back to meet his, "I met my wife, Molly. She was a talented herbalist and potion maker. But ten years after we were married, she got sick. It took a turn for the worse that fall, and the disease attacked her lungs, then she developed pneumonia. Her body slowly shut down, and at that point, they had to admit her to ICU. I knew it wouldn't be long before I'd lose her."

"I'm so sorry," I said, glancing over at Dorian, who squeezed my knee tightly.

He leaned forward and scooted the sculpture toward us. "Molly loved horses. We owned several throughout our years together. This was my last gift to her."

"May I?" I asked.

He nodded. I reached out and gently lifted the horse. It was heavy, and the wood felt smooth, polished to a beautiful sheen.

"It's exquisite," Dorian said.

My fingers traced the curves of the horse's neck and down the legs. The artwork was stunning, with ornate details around the edge.

If this figure contained the power to bring someone back from the dead, I couldn't feel it.

"This is from the tree I hanged from?" I asked.

He stared at me blankly, his silence answering my question.

"How did you even get it?"

"I stole a piece of a branch from that tree the last time I visited the island the Keepers took it to, so I could use it to bring my wife back once she passed. I had to find a way to hide it from the witches who lived there, so I carved it into a wooden horse."

My heart was pounding hard against my chest as I looked back down. "Caleb mentioned that the bark had a power that drew him to find it in the first place. I don't feel that power from it. Why is that?"

"It's not enchanted anymore," he explained. "Not after he used it on you."

"But how?"

He smirked and sat upright in his chair. "You want to know how you were brought back?" He paused, and the room suddenly felt significantly smaller as his smirk changed into a scowl. "Or how he aged my wife sixty years right before my eyes to sacrifice her, so that you could live?"

My mouth gaped open. "Is that really how it happened?" I asked, feeling defensive for Caleb's sake.

"You don't know Caleb as well as you think. And yes, that's exactly how it happened. But Molly let him," he explained. "Molly called me saying she needed me to come to the hospital, so she could say goodbye. I thought the pneumonia was about to take her, but that's not what happened."

When I visited Purgatory, Caleb admitted he had taken her life, but hearing how she died from her own husband's account was an entirely different kind of pain and guilt.

"Molly had already decided. She had taught Caleb the spell and told me she was going to help bring back Spirit." Tears glistened in Dante's eyes. He rubbed his hand over his face to wipe it dry. "Nothing I could have said would have changed what happened next."

My eyes widened. "She—"

"Sacrificed herself," Dorian finished.

Dante frowned again and nodded softly. "Molly believed in this idea of saving the world because why save one person when you could save billions? She had faith that bringing you back, no matter what sacrifices had to be made, was the only way to end the torment the future held."

"I'm sorry about your wife, Dante."

"What's done is done, so let it not be in vain."

The energy in the room shifted again. All I knew was that time was ticking away, and we still didn't know exactly how to bring the coven back.

"Then don't let it. Tell me how to get to this island, so I can bring my coven back. Darkness is coming, Dante, and I can't do this without them," I begged. "Please."

"The witches on that island will kill you."

"I can't die."

"No, but he can," he said, lifting a finger and pointing at Dorian.

I turned to Dorian, who nodded. We'd had this conversation a million times, and I couldn't convince him to stay behind, even if I begged him to. So now, we had to move forward with our plan. "I have to," I said.

His lips pulled into a straight line. "Are you willing to sacrifice someone to do it? It's not just one life you'd have to sacrifice. From my understanding, there are five of you. So, if you bring back four, you must kill four."

I have to do it. No matter the cost.

Dark magic always had a fine print and human sacrifice was the only thing that would help prevent an imbalance in the universe.

I thought about his question longer than I should have. The correct and moral answer should have been "no."

"How much of the tree is left?" I asked, trying to steer the conversation back to our reason for being here.

"All of it," he said.

I gasped. "W-what?"

"You see, the tree is hidden away in a cave, enchanted by a power none of us understands. When I stole a piece of the bark to help my wife, the moment it broke from the tree, a branch grew back. This power keeps the tree alive and thriving ... and ... never-ending."

"Do the Keepers use it?" I asked. "I find it hard to believe there's a power to bring back the dead hidden away on their island, and no one is tempted to use it."

Again, he stared at me blankly, which told me I was right.

The sickening feeling in the pit of my stomach was back. Yes, I knew I would be doing the same thing. I had to justify over and over again that the Chosen Ones had to be here, or the future of humanity would cease to exist. But I had to sacrifice four lives to do it. But perhaps those lives weren't worth living on this earth. Perhaps there was so much evil out there I would be doing the world a favor by taking them out.

But you'd be a murderer.

It was back, that torturing voice I kept hearing after I was resurrected again.

I wasn't killing a vampire who was technically already dead, but I'd be killing a witch. A human.

Was I wrong to assume that what I thought was evil was actually all part of Tatyana's plan and there wouldn't be repercussions? Or was I more concerned about the consequences of my mind and not the law? Would it really change me?

My thoughts returned to the present. "Are they murdering the innocent on that island?" I asked. That time, my words weren't filled with nerves but anger. Just the question itself made me nauseous.

"Sacrificing the innocent," he stated. "That's what you call it, anyway, because it makes your coven feel better about what they're doing. The Keepers of the Dead changed our traditions. Murder or sacrifice is not the way, but the coven from that island, well, the moment they got a hold of that tree, it changed them.

"When the tree first arrived on the island, the inhabitants were convinced the Keepers of the Dead brought it there to protect it. I honestly believed it, too, until I saw what was being done," Dante explained. "The new coven leader had orchestrated a yearly gathering on the island. They would use the tree to bring someone back, but our coven leader would pick who she would sacrifice for that to happen. It was usually the elderly or someone who had broken their law. There was always someone more important than the other, of course." He drummed his fingers against the arm of the chair. "She made sure of that. She made sure that everyone on that island was someone who would obey her and not question what she did. If anyone questioned her authority, they had to flee that island, or they'd be used as the next sacrifice when someone she loved passed."

"But you were going to use it for your wife," I said, gesturing to the sculpture.

"Damn straight I was. And I planned to sacrifice the leader, Anahi, for my wife to return once she died. She was who I had chosen to sacrifice, because Anahi didn't care enough to help anyone but herself or her family."

Dante kicked back in his rocking chair. "After the doctors informed us that my wife's organs were starting to shut down, I went to the island. It just happened to be the time of year when we'd have our annual celebration of life ... or death. I guess it depends on how you look at it. This was my opportunity to take what I wanted and bring my wife back when she died.

"But I was afraid they'd find it, so I carved it into a wooden horse and placed it in her hospital room. But it wasn't the witches who tracked it down. It was Caleb. Some kind of power enabled him to find it." He frowned, flared his nostrils, and rubbed his hands over his face. I could see that sharing this memory was torturing him. "What you will have to do to bring your coven back is going to change you. It changed Caleb."

"Did she ... suffer?" I asked.

He nodded once. "Caleb didn't want her to suffer. Molly sort of left that part out of it when she shared the spell with him. We both knew about vampires and what our future looked like, so I think she figured she'd take one for the team."

He looked like he was in a daze as he rocked back and forth, gripping the chair's armrest. "Caleb told me to leave the room. He didn't want me to watch, but I couldn't leave her side. So, I witnessed in horror the spell snuffing out my wife's last breath."

It wasn't until Dorian touched the bridge of my back that I realized I had been crying. No. I was sobbing.

I wiped my tears dry and looked back at Dante. "I—"

"Don't apologize, Mercy. You may have been the reason she died, but you didn't kill her."

His words didn't make me feel any less sick to my stomach.

Dante stood, picking up the sculpture. "It's the thing that took her life away, but it's also the one thing that helps me remember her and how important she was to me." He walked back to the bookshelf and placed it back in its spot.

"Caleb didn't look like the same man after what he did to my wife. It changed him, too. He turned to me before he left and asked if there was any other way to bring you back, just in case they lost you again because he wasn't going to take another innocent life."

"Magic from the tree wasn't used to bring me back a second time," I told him. "How did the coven do it? If I choose not to end four lives to bring them back, would I have to give up all these elements inside me and die again, as they did?"

He planted his hands on his hips. "For the Chosen Ones to bring each other back, the coven member you bring back would need to consume all the elements, as they did with you, and yes, you'd die again, because—"

"If you give up your power, you die," I finished.

"Yes, but you're still only bringing back one member of your coven. In order to bring back all four, you will have to use the power from the tree and sacrifice four lives." He paused and took a step toward me. "You have a little bit of that magic in you from when you were brought back the first time."

I raised an eyebrow at him. "The power stayed with me?"

He grinned. "Of course. It's your power."

"I don't understand," I said, my mind racing.

"Because you don't remember."

"Remember what?!" I asked, my voice elevated as frustration filled my entire body.

"When you died centuries ago, right before the rope hanged you, Tituba and the Keepers of the Dead watched the execution. When your light went out, they used their magic to pull that power from you and put it into the tree. It had to go somewhere, and because your power was the source of life, it went into nature. Then they stole the tree to protect that magic."

A sickening chill ran up my spine. "What?"

"The power from that tree is yours, Mercy. That's why Caleb sensed it and was led to the hospital. Caleb simply pulled that power out of the bark and put it into your mother to bring you back, so the power of Spirit was put into her baby. It's not the bark that's magical. It's you."

I held my breath, and I blinked once. Was he saying ...

"Spirit doesn't just heal people," he interrupted my thoughts. "You were born with the power to bring someone back from the dead."

CHAPTER 22

MERCY

I probably paced the floor ten times before I looked up. My hands trembled, and I tried desperately to settle my nerves by taking a few deep breaths, but nothing was going to help me stop freaking out about what Dante had just told me. Having the ability to heal someone felt crazy enough, but bringing someone back from the dead?

"Hey, are you okay?" Dorian asked.

I spun around and looked him in the eyes. "No, Dorian. I'm not okay."

He walked up to me and hesitated before placing his hand on my cheek. "Just because you have this power doesn't mean you have to use it."

"She's going to need a hell of a lot more than what's inside her from the branch I stole if she's going to use it for anything, really," Dante explained. "You're going to need all of it." He smirked and looked past me, as if conjuring up an idea. "Perhaps I can help you find that island, and you help bring down the spell they put on this house."

I frowned. "I ... I don't know how."

"It's just a protection spell, but *they* cast the spell on me, which means I can't remove it."

"Oh."

I wasn't going to tell him no, even if he chose not to tell us where the island was. He didn't deserve to be here, especially since I was technically the reason he was here to begin with, but if I could use this as leverage, then yes, I would play along.

"You tell us how to find the island, and I'll free you from this prison."

A smile reached his eyes. "We have a deal."

———

For the next hour, Dante explained that the Island of Turi was hidden within the Sargasso Sea, and the tree was safe inside a completely off-grid cave on the island.

The more he shared about the island and how I'd have to transfer the power back inside me, like what I had done with my mom, the more terrified I became. But I didn't let Dante or Dorian know I was dubious about my plan and, frankly, everything I had thought about doing after I got my power back.

"Listen. Going to that island is dangerous. The moment you enter their territory, they're going to attack." He nodded toward Dorian, insinuating that he'd be the target.

"We understand, and Dorian," I warned as I turned to him, "now is your chance to back out. I'm going, regardless of the danger that will come our way, and I understand if you choose not to go."

Dorian gave me a wry smile. "We still have a lot to learn about each other, don't we? You honestly believe I'd let you go without me?"

I raised an eyebrow.

"Mercy, you're mine. And there's no road so dangerous that I wouldn't follow you down."

I smirked. "You're as stubborn as I am, aren't you?"

"I think I might be worse."

"Okay, you two. You can do this later. Now, your end of the bargain, Mercy," Dante said.

I winked at Dorian and stepped to the center of the room.

"Thank you," Dante said as I raised my hands above my head.

"You can thank me after I actually do it. I have no idea how powerful the spell is until I try to reverse it."

Dante gestured to the walls. "My home is all yours."

I closed my eyes, focusing on my magic.

A blast of subtle energy pushed at my fingertips, forcing me to focus harder on my power. The magic used to create the barrier was resisting my own, like two angry currents moving in opposite directions. No matter how hard I pushed toward it, it pushed back, causing my arm muscles to grow heavy and tired. I felt Dorian's hands on my shoulder. He lightly brushed my skin, and the heat of his breath tickled my ear. "Push harder, Mercy. You've got this."

I did. I pushed harder and harder until sweat seeped from my pores, but my strength picked up and called for the power of the five elements. Once I reached each point of the universe's driving force, a wave of magic flooded through my hands and into the protection spell. I felt my power weave into the barrier and pull it apart, causing the spell to rupture, and a blast of energy shot me off my feet. I stumbled, fell back over to Dorian, and winced as my head cracked on the hard wooden floor. When I sat up, I eyed the room around me. Every piece of furniture and every object in the room had been blasted away from the center and slammed up against the walls. I saw that Dante had been knocked over and was lying prone near the bookshelf.

I quickly ran toward Dante and placed my hand on his forehead, which bore a three-inch laceration, and I used my power to heal him. The rest of his body appeared to be undamaged.

"Dante, wake up. Are you okay?" I asked. His eyes slowly opened, and he immediately scanned the room.

"Well, I'll be damned," he said. "You fucking did it!"

I wasn't sure exactly what I had done. For all I knew, I'd just destroyed a room. Did the spell actually work?

"Try walking out your front door," Dorian said from behind me.

I helped Dante to his feet, and he staggered to the door, opening it slowly. He took his first step onto the porch, and once the sun beamed down, warming his cheeks, he dropped to his knees, letting out an audible sob.

He kneeled there, soaking in the sweet taste of freedom for the first time in twenty-two years. The overwhelming emotion on his face was the same expression Abigail had made when I turned her human again.

I felt an ache in my chest, thinking about how we had lost her and everyone else this last year.

I peeked over Dorian's shoulder and into the living room. It was a complete disaster. "Let's help clean this up."

"Don't worry about it," Dante called back, staggering to his feet. "I need to sort through it, anyway. Especially since I'll be traveling from here on out. I won't need all this shit."

He reached out his hand, and I shook it, giving him one more look of gratitude. "Thank you, Dante. And good luck to you."

"Godspeed to you, too, Mercy," he said as he turned to Dorian. "Take care of her. Take care of each other."

One minor detail dawned on me before we walked out the door.

"Oh, Dante, you said Molly taught Caleb the spell to bring back life. We're going to need that."

He smirked. "You won't need me to write the spell down. Once you touch the tree and get your powers back, you're going to remember it."

I sighed. "I created the spell, didn't I?"

He nodded with a small smile.

"Move forward with forgiveness and courage, because that is what Molly taught me and everyone else around her. Now, go save the world."

CHAPTER 23

MERCY

I brushed off the dirt and the leaves that stuck to my legs during the landing, and we both immediately felt the extreme humidity in the air.

It was a relief that we didn't see anyone; the island appeared uninhabited. For every action we took from here on out, we'd have to be careful not to run into any surprises. According to Dante, the coven had lived on this island in secret for the last three hundred years, and it didn't welcome unknown visitors.

"Over there," I said, pointing to a shadowy pathway. It appeared to be a game trail; by the looks of it, it was still used frequently.

Dorian clasped his fingers around mine. "We walk on foot from here."

He led me down the trail, which was rich with foliage. The air was thick and smelled sweet. The thick palm trees kept us shaded from the intense heat of the sun, but the humid air started to make me sweat profusely. After walking about two miles, we spotted several mango trees, and Dorian reached up to pick a few.

"We need to make it look like we came here looking for food," he explained.

"Good idea," I said, looking straight ahead. "Looks like a coconut tree over there. Grab at least one."

We continued down the trail near the coconut tree and were poked and scraped by every branch and twig along the way, pushing overgrown tree branches and leaves from our faces. The vegetation was bright green and leafy, and given the beauty of the island, it felt like we had ended up in a tropical resort rather than a hidden island full of powerful witches.

Stunning blue and red flowers blossomed along the trail, with vines and shrubbery along the ground. The canopy of trees was so thick that it cast a dark shadow over most of the forest floor. The humidity was intense, though, and getting thicker by the minute.

Before we reached the coconut tree, we heard a commotion in a clearing ahead, so we took cover below a large, leafy branch at the end of the trail. A group of inhabitants appeared, carrying large baskets of freshly picked fruit. Dorian set his foot down, and a branch cracked underneath. The cracking sound was loud enough that the person closest to us carrying a basket halted and turned toward us. Our eyes met, and he dropped the basket, speaking in a language I didn't recognize and took off. The rest of the group quickly vanished into the forest after the man.

I cursed, placing a hand against the nearby tree trunk. I reached out through my magic and into the connecting roots, asking the trees to strike out and protect us if the islanders attacked. We didn't want to run. That would defeat the entire purpose of coming.

A rustling alerted us to the man reappearing, now armed. He must have raised the alarm and brought others to our location. My heart pounded heavily against my chest, and Dorian stood behind me like I had asked him to. After a few minutes, three to four more men joined him and walked toward us. Two men held bows and arrows pointed directly at our heads and the other two gripped axes.

Great.

"What are you doing here?" one of them asked us. They spoke English, as Dante had informed us, but his accent was thick.

I held up my hands, showing the men we had no weapons. "We're unarmed. Our boat sank a few miles from here. We would have drowned if we didn't sail our life raft to the shore. Please, we only need food and water," I explained, hoping it was enough for these men to lower their weapons.

"Your clothes are dry," one man carrying an axe pointed out.

Dorian stepped in their direction, and they quickly raised their weapons higher. Dorian stopped abruptly. "We'd been on the shore for a few hours before we decided to explore the island for food."

"Name," another demanded.

"Mercy, and this is Dorian."

The man who asked for our names looked at me, and his eyes narrowed in on mine as if contemplating if he should trust us.

The man slowly lowered his bow and signaled with his head to the older man next to him, and he walked toward us with an arrow pointing at Dorian's head.

I sucked in a breath, and the trees encircling us began to shake. I instructed them with my mind to stand down because if these men were going to kill us, they would have attacked us by now.

"Open your bags," the older man instructed, and we did just that.

I turned to Dorian, and he nodded. They searched our bags and saw they only contained a few clothing items, the fruit we had taken from the island, and emergency supplies. Thank God we had thought to remove the map and our cell phones and leave them near the portal entrance.

The man holding a bow nodded to the one holding an axe, and they each grabbed us by the arm, escorting us out of the forest and toward a large encampment away from the shore. Ahead of us, and off to the right of the beach, were a few tents and a couple of wooden cabins. The leader of the group shouted toward the encampment, causing several of the inhabitants to raise their heads and look at us.

A beautiful woman wearing a long, blue cotton dress that reached her ankles exited one cabin. Around her neck was a necklace made from wooden beads. Her white-silver hair was pulled into a tall, red wrap, and her warm beige skin was bare of any makeup. "Place your bags down next to you, and let me see your hands," she said, her accent thicker than our captors'.

We did as she instructed, and when she approached us, I asked, "What's your name?"

She smiled. "Anahi. I govern the people on this island. But you're in my home, so you will answer *my* questions."

The moment her name left her lips, butterflies fluttered a million miles per hour in my stomach. I couldn't show her I was afraid or knew anything about her, so I nodded and held my hands out. She looked at my palms carefully, then at Dorian's hands. She retracted when she touched his skin but placed her fingers back on his palm. "How long have you been a werewolf?"

My stomach lurched.

"Just a few weeks," he answered honestly. "I won't hurt you."

A huge grin reached her eyes. "You wouldn't be able to, even if you tried, young man."

I bowed my head, and Dorian followed my lead. "We aren't here to hurt you or your people. I promise you," I assured her, and she smiled wanly.

I knew full well how she'd react if she knew who I was, but knowing I was with a werewolf, I suspected she'd know we didn't just accidentally end up here.

"Sit down and remove everything from your bag. We can't be too careful when someone trespasses on our land. I want to ensure you're not bringing anything onto our soil that could harm us."

I nodded, and Dorian and I unzipped our backpacks and pulled everything out, spreading the items on the sand. She signaled to her men to search our things once again, but more thoroughly. After carefully examining our bags, Anahi grinned at us.

"What brings you to our island, Mercy? It was not because of some shipwreck or some getaway," she asked with a sideways smirk. I tensed for a moment, but my face remained poised.

She knows my name.

"Sorry I lied, but given your coven's history of killing witches all those years ago, you can understand my reluctance to divulge our secrets."

"Hmm, interesting choice of words ... that you believe it was us who killed other witches."

I narrowed my eyes at her comment.

"The Keepers of the Dead may have handled things a bit differently than I would have back then, but our ancestors were fools to have come after the Chosen Ones," she said.

"But not the tree," I said. "That part of the history you do agree with, don't you?"

She narrowed her eyes and snuck in a glance at Dorian. "How did you find our island, though?" she asked, ignoring my remark. "Our magic conceals it to the outside world unless you use location magic. But even then—"

"Dante," I answered. "You kind of pissed him off when you imprisoned him behind his own walls for the last two decades."

Anahi chuckled. "A thief and a traitor can never go unpunished."

"He helped restore a prophecy. Is he really all that you claimed him to be?" I asked. "That's not even your magic in that tree. If anything, Dante stole from *me*. Just as you have."

She frowned. "You cannot steal from the dead. If my ancestors hadn't done what they did, who knows what vessel your magic could have gone into? By the Keepers of the Dead placing it into that tree and preserving it here, we've kept that power safe and away from our enemies."

"So, you can use it," I said. "How self-righteous of you."

"You, Mercy, were never supposed to be born."

I shrugged my shoulder. "Maybe. Or perhaps abusing a power you know nothing about has become your downfall. My mother used my magic that was never meant for her, and she suffered because of it. The only place the magic from that tree belongs is inside me. It didn't matter what the Keepers of the Dead did in those last moments. I still died, and many innocent women and men who weren't even real witches died that day, too. Now I'm back, and I need to restore my powers, and I'm not leaving until I do."

Anahi gave me a slight smile, but something was off about her demeanor. It wasn't real.

Dorian stayed silent. Nothing he could say could help this situation, but Anahi approached him slowly. "And who is this handsome American werewolf?"

"This is Dorian. He's—" *My boyfriend?* Would that put him in more danger, as if they could use him as leverage, as Maurice had done? "He's my travel guide."

She laughed even harder that time. So hard she grabbed her belly and looked around the camp at the crowd of people that had gathered to observe. Everyone joined in with her. "Travel guide, eh? No. Unless you two have fallen in love during your travels, no one looks at a woman the way he looks at you and you at him."

I glanced at Dorian and grabbed his hand. "Fine, he's my boyfriend."

A smile crept across Dorian's face, and his eyes lit up. Despite the dangerous situation we had put ourselves in, this was the first time I had referred to him as my boyfriend out loud, and he found pleasure in that.

"No need to lie to me, though I need to ensure he's free of disease."

I looked at her quizzically. "Dorian's not sick."

"You may be able to heal quickly or prevent disease in your own body, but he does not."

I held up my hand as she approached him. "I assure you. He's not sick. He's been a vampire for over three hundred years, and I turned him human only a few weeks ago. So, unless he contracted polio since then, he is clean of disease."

She frowned. "Philip," she called to one of her men, and he grabbed Dorian's arm, yanking him up from the log where we sat.

I stiffened, but I didn't attack. Anahi placed her hands on his head, then down the rest of Dorian's body. She closed her eyes, and light smoke left her fingertips. It looked as if she were covering him with white clouds.

Dorian panted heavily the more her hands lingered on his head, and I inched closer to stop her if he became too distressed. But when she finally removed her hands from his body, she smiled. "He's clean."

I released the breath I was holding in.

She looked at me and nodded. "The two of you have come at an inconvenient time. We are a few hours away from celebrating my daughter's union with her fiancé. Consider this an invitation."

"You want us to attend a wedding?" I asked, perplexed by the sudden hospitality.

Anahi gave a quick nod. "We have a lot to learn from each other. Just because our covens were enemies long ago doesn't mean we cannot teach each other our ways. Today, you are among friends." She gestured around the shore, pointing to each home along the shore, many having groups of other witches gathering outside on their porches. "Look around, Mercy. Everyone here comes from somewhere else. Some were born on this island, but many have come and gone to different parts of the world. None of us are the same, yet we came here for one purpose—to find safety in magic and a family that would welcome each other with open arms." Anahi turned to her men. "They can stay in the Mason Cabin." She looked back at us. "You stay one night, and come morning, I'll take you to your tree so you can claim what is rightfully yours."

Anahi turned and gestured to a woman carrying a copper mug in each hand. "You'll dehydrate within hours, so drink this. It will provide more than what water can."

"What is this?" I asked, taking the mug and looking down at the purple liquid inside."

"It's tea. The herbs on this island are quite remarkable. It will keep you from sweating out what will eventually kill you if you don't."

None of this is what I had expected when we showed up today. Nothing could be this easy. It was as if they had expected us to show up.

Something is wrong here.

The covens had been protecting that tree since the seventeenth century for a reason. Anahi wasn't about to give that up now. Even to its rightful place within the vessel of Spirit. And I certainly didn't expect to be served cold tea, shelter, and an invitation to a wedding.

I'll play along, though ... for now.

"Okay." I looked at our surroundings and was suddenly aware of the scent coming off my body, created by the scorching heat. "Is there a place we can bathe before the wedding?"

"Of course," she said. "There's a waterfall at the bottom of the trail that leads to the other side of the island. You'll run right into it if you follow the path. I'll show you where to start."

Anahi entered a cabin and came out with a couple of towels a minute later. We hesitantly followed, as we knew we'd be branching out from the main village and into unfamiliar territory where we were not one hundred percent welcomed.

Anahi gestured toward a flattened path and handed us the towels and a jar of what looked like thick, black liquid, almost like tar.

"What is this?" I asked.

"Soap," Anahi said.

She smiled, and without another word, she left us to walk from there.

"Soap," I repeated while eyeing the tar-like substance.

"We're on an island, and by the looks of it, they've used what resources they have to make that soap by hand," Dorian said with a side smirk. "I don't think it's poison. I can usually sniff that out."

I smirked at his joke, and we continued down the path, sipping the cool tea and feeling a slight shudder as it went down. The strong, earthy mint taste made my tongue feel numb.

It took us about fifteen minutes to reach the waterfall, and it was one of the most beautiful sights I had ever seen.

A tall cliff reached at least fifty feet into the air with white, frothing water tumbling over, and the entire lake at the center glistened with crystal blue water. I could see vapors of steam rising from the surface of the water. Surrounding the lake were rounded, smoothed-out boulders as if they had been placed there to keep the water in a perfect circle. It was breathtaking.

There was also an energy shift, as if the water and surrounding environment alone had been cast with magic. A blissful state of awareness made my skin tingle and the hairs of my body stand straight, not from fear, but almost as if the energy was alive, speaking to me.

"I've never seen something so beautiful in my entire life," I told him. "It's as if this island was created by magic."

"Maybe it was?" he said.

Dorian pulled his shirt over his head and threw it to the ground beside him, followed by his pants, then boxer briefs. No matter how many times I had seen him naked, I was always taken aback by how perfectly beautiful he was.

"I don't know if I trust Anahi," I told him as he stepped into the water, steam rising over the surface. From a distance, the sound of the waterfall created a soothing effect over the lake.

"Not everyone is your enemy, you know? For now, enjoy this moment between us. A secret island. A magical waterfall, or at least, it feels that way. We may only ever do this once."

He disappeared behind the water, and I followed, stripping my clothes off and swimming in his direction.

I felt the sand at the bottom squish between my toes. The water was warm and inviting, like a heated bath, though it would have been nice to have cold water all over my body to cool me off. I breast-stroked toward the waterfall and let myself enjoy the feeling of the colder water against my skin. With my eyes closed, I held my breath as I dunked under the waterfall. When I resurfaced, Dorian was there with a hint of a smile on his lips.

"What if they try to kill us?"

"What if they don't?" he remarked. "What if tomorrow you touch that tree, reclaim your power, and we live another day?"

We stared at each other in silence for a moment, and my body grew hungry with anticipation. The sight of Dorian standing in the water, naked, ignited a fire within me. It didn't matter that we were on an unknown island surrounded by strangers. Being with him like this made me feel safe. Everything else disappeared around us.

He swam even closer, closing the gap between us until I felt his hips press against mine. He leaned in closer and kissed my lips until my body relaxed from that single touch.

The awareness of his hardened cock caused me to blush as he brushed up against me. Our chests touched, and I melted into his embrace. The kiss deepened, and Dorian's hands trailed hungrily up my back, creating a mountain of goosebumps in its wake.

He released the kiss but not the embrace. Instead, he moved his lips to my cheek, then my ear, behind my earlobe, and down my neck. One hand touched my chest, and nothing else mattered anymore at that moment, as his other hand reached up and wove into my wet hair.

"Enjoying yourself?" I murmured. The soft lull of the current brought us closer to the shore.

"With you? Always," he responded. We ended up on the rocks on the side of the lake, still intertwined in each other's embrace. Being in his arms made the concept of heaven a little more believable for a witch like me.

Dorian's lips swiftly moved over the top of my head, my cheek, and my lips, kissing me wherever he could reach. Neither of us could get enough of the other; this magnetic pull we shared only left us yearning for more.

After a moment of hesitation, I tapped into my powers, drawing out the vines from the tree behind us. It was for a selfish reason, I supposed, but after everything we had gone through, it felt well-deserved.

This island ... this island was doing something to me ... to us.

"Mercy?" Dorian blinked in surprise but was quick to catch up as the vines wrapped around his wrists, holding him in place.

I moved on top of him, bracketing him in with my knees.

"I bet it drives you crazy that I'm in control now," I teased him, his cock resting in between my heated folds. My hips moved back and forth slowly, stimulating both of us.

"On the contrary ..." he said, his breath hitching as he watched me settle on top of him. His cock lingered at my entrance, but I didn't let him slip in just yet, only rubbing his length up and down my folds but not inside. "I'm quite enjoying it."

A small smile curved my lips before I lowered myself on his cock, feeling my pussy stretch around his size. My eyebrows furrowed in sheer pleasure while my forehead dropped on his.

"Mercy ..." Dorian moaned, his muscles tensing as I began moving my hips. He pulled on the vines instinctively, but they were firm and unbreakable in the way they held him down. The elements of Earth did as I told, and I relished the fact that I had all the power then.

My tongue trailed over my lips as I watched the sight of his cock disappear inside of me as I lowered myself down. Dorian's gaze was glued to the very same sight, as if we were both hypnotized by it. My hand reached down, finding my clit, and I began to rub it. Slow. Teasing. Just the way he touched me.

"Jesus, Mercy," he protested breathlessly, his cock tensing inside me. "Sweetheart, let me go ... I want to touch you. Let me touch you." The way he looked at me was something else; it was as if I was the only thing that mattered in existence.

Love.

That was what it was. Pure, untouched, and perfect.

Instead of letting him go, I leaned forward, my lips eagerly crushing against his as I picked up my pace, now bouncing on his lap. My fingers moved faster again on my clit as I began my chase.

"Mercy, fuck ..." he panted against my lips, leaning back against the rock, still in the vines' firm hold. His entire body was trembling from the sensation that roamed through us both while his cock buried deep inside me. "Baby, slow down. I don't want to come before you do."

His words had the opposite effect of the one that he had expected. I didn't want to tease, nor did I want to take it slow. I needed him in the most primal way there was ... And I was going to take him.

"Fuck, Dorian..." I exhaled sharply against his mouth, feeling my legs tremble. I was going to get to that point of no return soon. I could feel it. All of my fingers joined together to rub my clit now, frantic and relentless in their motion, as I slammed myself on his cock. Over and over and over again until I buried my face into his shoulder, my teeth sinking into his muscle to muffle a scream that built up in the back of my throat. My orgasm rocked through me hard, momentarily leaving me lightheaded as I shook on top of Dorian.

Just a moment later, he reached his release, too, with a loud grunt as he shot himself inside me. Tipping his head back, he struggled to catch his breath. It was then that the vines finally released their hold on his wrists. Instantly, his arms wrapped around me, holding me close. We stayed in each other's arms for a little while, recovering, before Dorian broke the silence that surrounded us.

He placed his hand on my cheek, his gaze locking on mine. "I will *never* hurt you, Mercy. I chose you, and you will be *mine* for as long as you'll have me." The possessiveness in his voice caused my heart to thump harder than it had been just minutes earlier.

I smiled shyly. "I know."

He brushed his hand over my wet hair and rubbed my cheek with the back of his fingers. He leaned in again and kissed my forehead, then down to my lips, pulling his hands back around my waist and pressing against me.

Being on an island surrounded by a coven we didn't know, trusting that our lives were in their hands, felt scary, but being in Dorian's arms took that fear and melted it away until all we had were each other. And that was enough.

CHAPTER 24

MERCY

We quickly bathed with the tar-like soap, which felt grainy and rough on the skin but formed thick, bubbly suds once lathered up. It smelled like pineapples and oranges. After rinsing off the soap in the warm lake water, I felt rejuvenated, albeit a little lightheaded. I chalked it up to the humidity and the island's heat.

We dried off, and I knew without a hair dryer, my hair would air dry into a frizzy wave, so I braided it over my shoulder and tied it off with a small piece of vine. Once we reached the village, we were greeted by a crowd of both men and women, who dragged Dorian and me to a tent to get ready for the wedding ceremony.

Whatever herb was in the tea had made its properties known by now. I felt a slight wave of euphoria run through me, and it seemed like my mind opened to awareness. It was an incredible feeling. It didn't feel like I was drunk or dizzy; more like every detail around me was seen through fresh eyes. The colors were more vibrant, so vivid in hue that I could almost taste them. The grainy sand felt sharper against the heels of my feet. Even as little as the air tickling my skin was like tiny, delicate butterfly wings brushing up against me.

I also felt the comfort of love, desire, and the need to be closer to Dorian. To be touched, relished, right then and there, and not care if anyone watched us. I no longer felt threatened by the islanders. I didn't fear retaliation for coming to their island unannounced and plotting to take back my magic. They felt like family. They felt like home.

As we neared the tent, I looked up and heard rolling thunder booming through the clouds. The breeze picked up, and I could see distant flashes of lightning several miles off the shore.

A storm was rolling in, and the sky had grown darker, but it wasn't going to stop the festivities from taking place. I saw that the islanders were beginning to take their places along the shoreline, around a massive bonfire. Some sat upon woven tapestries, and others sat on homemade wooden chairs. The group of women instructed us to change into different attire that was customary to the island's traditions, which they had provided. Two women with sun-tanned skin and dark brown hair sat me down and pulled my hair up into a stunning design that was required to be worn during formal festivities. They wove the rest of my hair into two braids and wrapped them tightly on top of my head. As they were finishing up, someone handed me a small cup of the same purple tea. I took a large swallow and watched as a third woman placed a tortoiseshell necklace over my head.

A man with silver hair and rich brown skin then applied black and white paint on my arms in a detailed vine-like design from my shoulders to my fingertips. My dress was a beautiful shade of aquamarine, and so long it reached my toes that had now slipped into white wicker sandals.

When I left the tent, I eyed Dorian standing next to a fire pit, which hadn't been lit yet. They dressed him in long brown pants and sandals, and he was shirtless, but he wasn't bare-skinned. Like the art on my arms, they covered him from neck to torso with similar ink patterns.

Dorian smiled when I walked toward him. "My God, you look stunning." He leaned forward and kissed me gently on the cheek, and then a smile curved upon his lips. "I think we might be high."

I giggled at his comment, and then it turned into laughter that I couldn't stop. I tried to control it, but I couldn't until the tears were streaming down my face, and Dorian reached out, pulling me in.

"Alright. No more tea for you, love," he said. "Can you feel your powers?"

I looked up and shook my head because all I felt was silence when I tried to reach them.

Fuck.

I held my hand outstretched, intertwining my fingers with his, and we joined the others around the fire.

"Deep breath. It'll be okay," he said.

I nodded, squeezed his hand, and sat comfortably on a red blanket along the sand. From where we were seated, we were in front of a small wooden stage by the bonfire. Anahi soon arrived, and the crowd erupted into cheers and applause.

Anahi held her hands high in the air to silence the crowd of guests. I didn't realize how many people lived on the island until now. At least a hundred had joined the festivities, and I wondered if everyone here had the same kind of magic as Anahi.

"Thank you for coming to Nadia and my future son-in-law, Malachi's, union today," Anahi started, turning to Malachi. "From here forward, Malachi, you will refer to me as Mother. I will love you like my own child. Do not hurt your wife. Do not dominate her, for you are equals in our eyes. You are one."

After she addressed the engaged couple, she turned to face me. "We are a people of love and trust. Those who come into our lives, we treat them like family."

She raised her hands again, but that time, white smoke left her hands and encircled her. The smoke pulled to the right and formed a silhouette.

Am I really seeing this, or am I hallucinating from the tea?

An older man, translucent and beautiful, stood next to Anahi. He was made of grey smoke, but I could still make out his facial features. She held out her hand, and he motioned his hand toward hers as if she were touching him, but they weren't. They couldn't.

He was a ghost summoned by his wife, one of the Keepers of the Dead.

"When our loved ones pass to the other side, they are simply going home. This world is only a tiny puzzle piece on our journey to the other side. My husband died when Nadia was only eight years old, but his memory and life will never be forgotten. He vowed to always watch over her, and he always has, even though we do not see him like this most of the time."

Nadia's father smiled down at his daughter and then at Anahi.

Nadia stood, walked toward the ghostly figure before us, and held her hand to his. Although she wasn't touching him, their spiritual energy bounced off each other, similar to what happened with Caleb in Purgatory. Anahi grabbed her daughter's other hand, and the three of them formed a triangle. After that moment of silence, the apparition disappeared like a cloud caught in the breeze, losing shape and blending into the night sky. Nadia fell to her knees, and Anahi kneeled with her, placing her hand on her daughter's back as she wept.

"Nadia's father gives his blessing on this glorious day," Anahi said, rising, and Malachi bowed his head to her.

Dorian squeezed my hand, and a warm smile crossed his face when I turned to look at him. We had just witnessed one of the most beautiful moments I had ever seen, and tears left my eyes and dripped down my cheeks.

Why the hell am I crying again?

Malachi stepped closer to Nadia, grabbed her hand, and helped her to her feet. They both walked over to Anahi and kneeled before her. She placed her hands on their heads and uttered a short vow of trust, love, union, and honor.

When Nadia looked back at Malachi, she said, "I will be your equal. Forever and always."

Malachi repeated those simple yet eternal words. Once they shared their first kiss as husband and wife, the shouts and celebratory laughter echoed through the crowd.

elle

The reception which followed differed from what I was used to. Clothes were optional; people mostly danced around the fire and threw their hands toward the sky as if they were calling upon the gods.

Nadia and her mother offered us more tea immediately following the ceremony. Of course, we wanted to say no, but the tea we had earlier took away all responsible choices and tossed them away. Even though I didn't want to drink anymore, my body moved of its own accord.

When I finished the tea, a man I had noticed watching me earlier in the evening grabbed my hand and yanked me toward the fire and away from Dorian. Dorian tried to reach out in protest, but words failed him, and when the man said, "Dance," I did.

I swayed my body with the music and looked at Dorian, who was now in the arms of a half-naked woman we had seen earlier with the man I was dancing with. Sweat beaded down my face from both the fire and the island climate.

The tea wasn't helping with the humidity. If anything, it made it worse.

My dress flowed with my moves, and though nothing was coordinated, I danced. It didn't matter if they had rhythm or knew what they were doing; everyone danced. Four women who used drums, deer hoof rattles, and striking sticks conducted the music. I closed my eyes and felt like I was being transported into another world.

Perhaps I was.

The stranger released me, and Dorian leaped at the chance to pull me closer. My hair was slowly falling from my updo, and Dorian pushed it away from my eyes and leaned in, kissing right below my ear and causing my heated core to spark. We danced together and continued to get lost in the beautiful music. And though I felt myself getting carried away with the music and dancing, my instinct focused on what I knew for certain: they drugged us on purpose, and our lives were in danger.

Suddenly, a bright light flashed across the sky, followed by a loud boom that seemed to shake the ground. I was startled, and my heart pounded heavily against my chest. The music stopped right as I felt thick raindrops hit my face. The guests hurried away from the fire and took shelter inside the tents and cabins nearby. Dorian tried to pull me out of the rain, but I wouldn't go with him. I continued to stare at the ominous, dark clouds hovering in the sky, and heavy raindrops pounded against my cheeks.

"Mercy?" I heard Dorian's voice call out. "Mercy!" That time, I whipped around in his direction, my eyes wide with confusion. "We need to take cover. The storm rolling in looks bad, plus I think the tea they gave us has hallucinogens. You're zoning out."

I looked down at my hands, and everything seemed to slow down a bit like my head was in a daze and the storm was speaking to me. I thought I needed to connect with it in some way. I knew it didn't make sense, and maybe the tea made me think I could. No matter how dangerous the storm was around me, I couldn't quite get my feet to move out of harm's way.

I felt Dorian's hands grip my waist and hoist me over his broad shoulder, and he carried me into the main cabin. Once inside, Dorian placed me on the floor. I closed my eyes and leaned back against the wall. It felt like the ground was spinning, and my tongue felt thick.

"Anahi, what the fuck did you give us?" I heard Dorian ask.

"The same as everyone else, of course. It's just tradition during a wedding to drink our herbs," Anahi explained. "Nakaya Batuto!"

Anahi ordered one of the men. It wasn't a name but a command in a different language.

From what I remembered from my research before we came here, most of the coven spoke English or Russian, so I wasn't quite sure what she was saying. It sounded very different than what the man in the forest had shouted when they first discovered us.

"What did you say to him?" I asked with a shaky breath. Confusion muddled my thoughts, and I could barely form a sentence.

I also weirdly wanted to hug her and everyone else in the cabin.

This is bad. I can't get a hold of myself.

"It's an ancient tongue my ancestors created when they settled here over three hundred years ago. We don't use it often anymore," she explained. "I asked him to bring you some water."

My eyes narrowed at her. "Is that really what that means?" Though the herbs took away most of my fear, they didn't remove my conscious mind from knowing danger when I saw it. She was lying.

She smirked. "No ... not really."

Those were her last words before I heard Dorian let out a feral growl, and the world went dark.

CHAPTER 25

MERCY

Once my blurry vision cleared, I looked around. I must have been unconscious for a while, as the cabin was dark, and I couldn't hear any voices outside. Dorian was sitting in a corner, in his wolf form, secured with chains around his four ankles. My wrists were handcuffed and tightly locked, the metal pressing hard against my skin.

"Fuck!" I cursed aloud, trying to wrench free of the clamps, but I couldn't break the metal.

One thing was certain and a relief: the drugs they had given us through the tea had worn off. I could feel the power flowing through me, and the elements hummed in my chest.

Dorian was awake but panting heavily. Light smoke came off the chains, and I realized what the clamps were made of—pure silver.

"Dorian," I called. "Speak to me with your mind if you can."

He glanced up. *"Hey, beautiful."*

I felt relieved that my telepathy abilities were intact. I pressed my fingers against the lock of the handcuffs and tried using my powers to unlock it, but nothing happened. Power radiated from my hands, but I never heard the click of the lock. Opening locks was always easy when I first got my powers back, but this time, even that didn't work.

"Listen. I'm going to be in a lot of pain, but know I will heal immediately, okay?" I said. "Don't react or make a sound."

"I don't like this. But do what you have to do," Dorian projected.

I knew the agony I was about to endure was something I could handle, but I also knew it was something Dorian couldn't. I had to do my best not to show it on my face.

I needed to break my thumbs.

I held my breath and used my other hand to snap my right thumb. As the pain shot up my arm, I kept my breath steady and pulled my hand through. The snapped bone quickly knitted together, and the pain abated. The cuffs were much tighter, on the other hand, so I knew I had to break my hand entirely to pull it through the clamp. My face scrunched up, and I bit my tongue to keep from screaming. I looked up, and Dorian was pulling at his chains, instinctively trying to reach me, but it was useless.

Once I was free, I held my hands out as the rest of the bones repaired themselves, and the aching sensation in my hands settled.

I rubbed my skin and looked at Dorian again.

"Why aren't you turning back? Is it because of the silver?"

"I think so. I keep trying, but it's not working. I turned like this to fight them after they knocked you out, but they stopped me with these chains before I could attack."

I cast my eyes around the room, wondering if they had carelessly left a key. The last thing I wanted to do was break Dorian's limbs. Yes, he'd heal quicker than a human, or I could help heal him, but I didn't want him to go through that pain.

I placed my hand on his lock, hoping the magic would work once I was no longer shackled, but it didn't work on his chains, either. The silver interfered with the spell, completely nullifying it.

"Break my wrists and ankles."

I shook my head.

"Shit. Shit. Shit," I cursed. "We aren't dealing with the kind of magic I use, Dorian. They aren't using elementals. I don't know what the hell this is. This is something I should be able to do. I need the actual key, or yes, I have to break your bones."

"Do it, then. It'll heal."

I shook my head. "I don't want to hurt you."

There were footsteps on the dirt path outside the cabin. I held my hands out, preparing to fight off whoever was coming in. I thought it was Anahi or her bodyguards, who had barely left her side since we'd arrived, but I was surprised at who came through the door.

It was Nadia.

"Okay, first, I want to say I'm so sorry for what happened to you two," Nadia said as she hurried toward us. "Partially, this is my fault for sharing my vision with my mother this morning that you were heading here. God, she's going to kill me for helping you, but you can't be here."

"What?" I asked. But she was already pulling up Dorian's chains as she pulled out a key from her pocket, unlatching the lock. She backed up as Dorian transitioned back into his human form. He was completely naked, so I quickly grabbed clothes, which were hanging in the corner closet of the cabin.

"Why are you helping us?" I asked as I tossed someone else's pants and a T-shirt to Dorian.

Nadia glanced behind her at the cabin's opening and turned back, speaking in a near whisper.

"My mother isn't a bad person. She knows you're here for the power in the tree, which means the moment it's off this island, she risks losing me someday. It's the revival power she'll never let go of. The power that keeps our family together. You take that power; you take everything from her."

She looked at the opening again. She was very paranoid that she'd get caught and was afraid of what the coven would do to her.

Nadia pulled my hands in and gripped my fingers tightly. "I died ten years ago and again last year," she said. My mouth gaped open. "Your power from that tree has brought me back twice, and both times, a sacrifice had to be made. Before Malachi, I loved another, and that man was murdered last year so I could live and marry Malachi. My mother will never give up that kind of power. It's the one thing she can control. She will not gamble with the chance that she could lose me forever. Or anyone else she cares about, for that matter. And Mother doesn't love easily. She will sacrifice someone else. That's a promise. But in her heart, she is only doing what she believes is right."

"But you don't agree?" I asked.

"We have no right to choose who lives or dies, Mercy."

As those words left her mouth, my mind drifted to my coven. Yes, I would be playing with magic that goes against the laws of nature, but wasn't that the reason I was created in the first place? To save the world from evil? To protect humanity? Having the power to bring someone back from the dead wasn't a power I wanted. I didn't want to know that I had the power to bring someone back to life but then live with the decision of who deserved to live, who didn't, and who I would have to sacrifice for it to happen.

I wasn't the same woman I was a year ago. I only thought about myself and my own selfish needs. God, even just two weeks ago, I had been ignoring everything my coven wanted and doing what *I* felt was right.

Caleb wasn't wrong to call me out on being selfish when I took away my love for him and Dorian. I *am* selfish. And I don't deserve them or these powers.

She grabbed the chains and tossed them to the side, and the sound of silver clattering to the floor pulled me from my thoughts. "You need to go. Take the path that took you to the waterfall, turn right before you get to the water, and then scale the wall along the lake. Walk about a hundred yards across the path, and then you'll come to another cave. The tree is inside."

She spoke with rapid fire. Time was ticking, and we had to hurry.

"Thank you," I said, "but what's going to happen to you?"

She gently shoved me forward. "Don't worry about me. Go."

I wanted to take her with us. Take her off this island. But Nadia didn't come off as someone who would abandon her family, no matter how much she disagreed with them.

Dorian grabbed my hand, and we ran toward the cave as directed. Once we reached the lake, a tall man I recognized as one of Anahi's bodyguards stood there with his arms crossed over his chest. I heard a low growl come from Dorian, and I released his hand, raising mine over my head.

The power came immediately, with no hesitation or resistance. The power of all five elements left my hands and swirled around us. It was forceful, but I held tight to its strength.

Like before, when I used all five elements, I felt that pull from my coven, but having it inside me, and my body being that vessel, my human weaknesses and strength battled with how much I could control without my body being torn apart.

I focused on the storm brewing in the west. When I pulled my hands closer to my body, a roaring crash of thunder pounded through the sky, and lightning jolted across the clouds and down to where we stood. I threw my hand down to the ground, feeling the surge of lightning respond to my command. I didn't want to kill the man, but the force of the bolt hitting the ground near us blasted him across the lake. We heard a heavy thump and a loud groan from the man. I was sure he had broken something, but he didn't raise any alarm, nor did he get back up.

Dorian gripped my hand again, and we quickly climbed the lake wall, hurrying to the cave. Once inside, we rushed toward the back, as Nadia had instructed. It was pitch dark, but the closer we got to the back of the cave, the lighter it became. A bright glow nearly blinded us as we entered an open space with a tall stone ceiling within the cave.

Once my toes hit the wet walking stones that led down to a small flowing river, I saw it: the tree of Gallows Hill.

It wasn't like anything I had imagined. The tree looked like any oak tree in Salem. Its leafless brown branches were outstretched, like arms reaching out. But the light that radiated from the bark was not what I remembered from my time in the seventeenth century. That kind of power was not known to me, and I hadn't seen it when I was hanged.

No, the power from that tree was beyond anything I had ever imagined. It was intimidating, even just to look at, but beautiful at the same time. This tree contained the last of the powers that had been taken from me. The ultimate gift Tatyana had bestowed so I could save humanity.

"Oh my God. Dorian...."

"Holy shit," was all Dorian could say.

Even under the pressing circumstances to regain my power and get the hell off this island, I approached with trepidation, stopping just close enough to feel the light radiating down on my skin. I slowly crossed the raised stepping stones that covered the flowing water that was pulling from the lake and surrounding the tree. The closer we got to the tree, the taller the hairs stood on my arms, and my heart raced faster and faster. It was as if the light itself created an electric charge that was reaching toward us. I held my breath and stepped back. I looked at Dorian, and his eyes went wide.

"Mercy, are you okay?" he asked.

I shook my head. "The power is calling to me. I've never felt anything like it."

My hands were trembling as I looked back at the tree. I mustered what courage I could and moved forward. As I focused on my breathing, I felt like I was in a state of meditation. I closed my eyes, leading myself blindly toward the tree until my fingers were mere inches from the trunk. I turned to Dorian, and he nodded, permitting me to touch it. I turned back, reached my hand out again, and gripped my fingers around the trunk, digging my nails deep into the bark until I felt one of my fingernails break off. As

I felt the sting of pain, I shouted to Dorian, "Dorian, step back. Now!"

I didn't need to cast any retrieval spells. The mere touch of my hand on the tree ignited the power trapped within it.

The sudden jolt of energy that blasted through my body almost threw me back, but I planted my feet firmly to the ground, holding onto the tree with all my power and strength. I heard movement behind me, and I assumed it was Dorian being tossed across the cave. I tried to turn and check on him, but I was unable to remove my hand. Even if I wanted to save him, I couldn't. My powers were rushing back inside me from the tree, and my grip on the wood was the only thing keeping my limbs from being ripped apart.

I felt the power flow down to my toes and back up my back, but once it reached my head, my eyes rolled back, and it threw me into a vision from my past. As images from my past paraded my mind, so did the emotions that were tied to them. But they weren't just visions. They were memories ... moments I knew I'd experienced but were long forgotten.

The memories slowed to a point in time where I was walking through a field until I reached a hilltop. I spotted where Roland stood next to a thirteen-year-old me. I came closer to the figures, turned to face my younger self, and kneeled to look into my own eyes. It was an eerie and surreal moment. The younger, former version of myself was clearly afraid.

I remember this moment as if it was yesterday.

I wished I could reach out, embrace the young, frightened me, and comfort her. But instead, I watched as Roland rested a hand on her shoulder and spoke gently to her. "I know it's hard to accept, but you have a power inside you that can save humankind.

Tatyana showed me all this in a vision. It's not just vampires who will destroy us; it's witches, as well. Too many have gone to dark magic and evil intentions. She gave you a gift that will allow you to save humanity from destruction."

Tears poured down the cheeks of my younger self. "But I'll have to kill some of my own kind." It was a statement, not a question. "I'll have to kill witches."

Roland looked intently into her eyes and gave a curt nod. "Yes, you will. But you'll also be saving millions."

As I replayed the memory of the first time Roland had shared this power with me, a sense of nostalgia and horror collided inside me. I had been so terrified about what I would be forced to do, but I knew I had to use this power to save the world, no matter the cost.

"But you can never tell the coven. They must never know what we're doing or why. Do you understand, Mercy?"

"Yes," the younger me said, the weight of this revelation weighing heavily on her soul. "I understand."

My memories sped up again, but to the day my village had hanged me for being a witch.

I looked off into the distance as a crowd of angry villagers marched through the forest with lit torches.

I looked down, and my hand was wrapped around Martha Good's throat. She was a witch who had worked with others to betray us. They gave our names to the village elders, marking me and my coven for death.

Next to us lay a girl from the Blackwell coven—one of Caleb's cousins, Betty—who Martha had just killed. I closed my eyes and chanted the words of a spell. Martha's body went from that of a young, beautiful teenager to that of a crippled old lady. I watched as light faded from Martha's eyes and flowed down to Betty's corpse. Tituba emerged from behind a tree and blasted her powers at me. I deflected the magic, and Martha's frail body flew against a tree, dropping dead to the ground. I held up my hand and flung Tituba across the forest. She slammed into the ground, coughing as she pushed up to her knees.

Tituba looked at me with horror in her eyes. "You know what you're doing isn't right, Mercy. We can help you with this kind of power. We can help you use it for good. This isn't the way." Her hands stretched outward, and I wasn't sure what she was going to do. I looked back and saw Betty clamoring to her feet, her eyes wide with shock.

"Get out of here, Betty," I shouted. The young girl quickly fled through the brush, vanishing into the night.

I looked back at Tituba, and panic coursed through my veins. I knew the villagers would be arriving soon, and I needed to get to my coven as soon as possible. I ran as quickly as my feet would carry me toward my home, and there, in the kitchen, was Caleb, coming to take me to the barn where we would go through our Awakening and perform the immortality ritual.

My eyes opened to the quiet trickle of water flowing around the tree inside the cave. The tree no longer glowed with white light. It looked dead, the branches cracking under their weight.

I now remembered everything from my past life. The memory gaps that were once shrouded by a dark veil to hide the truth were now opened, revealing my secrets. The secrets I kept from my coven.

All of it. Even the memories I once had of Caleb holding me in his arms when we were growing up. The feeling of love for him had faded, but the images would never leave my mind.

I let out a heavy breath, but it wasn't from relief at having recovered all my memories; it was from shame. I hadn't just been a vampire hunter, but I'd been a witch hunter, too.

The Mercy of the seventeenth century and who I was today had always been two separate women. These memories would now change me, and I had to decide which version of that woman I wanted to be.

At that moment, I knew my answer. I *was* a hunter, and as horrific as that sounded, the salvation of the witches and humans on Earth depended on me accepting that I would have to kill my own kind.

I looked back at Dorian, and he was already on his feet. The room was still brightly illuminated, but the light wasn't coming from the tree anymore. It was coming from me.

I shut off my powers and locked my eyes with Dorian's. "Now, *this* is power."

CHAPTER 26

MERCY

Dorian sprinted toward me, but I held my hands up to stop him. "Give me a minute. My body is still shaking, and I don't know if this power is going to hurt you."

He threw his hands up. "I don't fucking care." A smile touched his lips that looked like he was both happy and relieved I was alive. He wrapped his arms around me and squeezed, burying his face into my hair. After our embrace, I gently pushed him back. "What is it?"

"I remember everything. All my memories came back once the powers consumed me. I did things that may cause you to look at me differently."

"You're not that person anymore," he said.

"But I am. I killed witches to bring back the dead because if I didn't, those witches would use their power to destroy us."

Right now, the Mercy in the twenty-first century hated the Mercy of the seventeenth century. Two minds, two memories, and two hearts were now sharing a space in my head, and I had to find a way to balance them.

"You can choose not to use that power," Dorian said, gently tucking a stray strand of hair behind my ear.

Tears burned my eyes. "What if I can't?"

He cupped my chin gently with his fingers. "Ever since you discovered you were a witch, you've always done what was best for humanity, regardless of what anyone else thought. Do what you need to do. I'm in your corner, no matter what you choose."

"Even if it means that I'm okay taking a life? A human life? Killing Bradley still weighs heavily on me, Dorian."

He took one step closer to me and placed both hands on my shoulders. "I know you. I know you now, and I knew you back then. Do what you have to, then let it go. If you need to sacrifice a witch to bring back the coven, then do it." He took another step closer to me. "We know at least two witches working for Maurice who deserve that fate."

He was referring to Julian and Kris, and something told me there were more traitors of our kind in Maurice's circle. I had to be willing to kill them.

To slay a monster, I would have to become a monster.

"Shh. I hear someone," Dorian said as he gently pushed me back against the stone wall that encircled the village.

The sound of crushing leaves echoed louder and louder until a tall, burly man stood directly in front of us, his eyes looking more frightened than angry.

Without saying a word, I raised my hand and used the power of air to suck out his breath. But I pulled the magic back the moment he was on the brink of suffocating. Once he collapsed to the ground, we headed for the beach.

Once we reached the shore, I raised my hands again and waved them back and forth until the portal opened. We heard more movement from behind us, and when I turned around, I stepped in front of Dorian. I heard him sigh behind me.

"Not now, Dorian," I said. He'd have to get used to me standing on the front line of danger.

"Stop!" Anahi shouted as she emerged from the forest. Her face contorted into a hard, fierce stare. "Please don't take it from me. Please!" The desperation in her voice caused a sharp sting in my heart,, because I knew why she wanted it. I understood the love she had for her daughter and her willingness to do anything she could, so she'd never lose her, but it wouldn't change anything. This was wrong.

"Please stand down, Anahi. It's over," I said. "The tree is useless now. This was never your power to take."

Anahi gritted her teeth. "Says the witch who's slaughtered her kind."

I winced. Her words hit their mark, but I didn't let my shame show. "You think I want this power? It's more like a fucking curse, but I'm not leaving that power in the hands of someone who would kill an *innocent* without a second thought to save their daughter. It has to stop!"

Anahi's face went still. "You know that feeling all too well, don't you?" she said. "Your love for whomever it is you need to save overpowers your moral code. You are willing to do whatever it takes, just as I have done all these years and every coven leader who has used that tree before me."

She stepped closer to me, but I didn't budge. I positioned myself, ready to strike.

"And what will *you* do with it?" she asked.

"I'm ..." I turned to face Dorian, who stood behind me, and I reached out my hand. As soon as he took it, I turned to Anahi again. "I'm going to bring back the elemental powers that bring us light, because if I don't, the darkness will consume us all. Then maybe, someday, our covens can stop turning against each other and fight as one."

As I stepped backward, I slammed into Dorian's chest, pushing both of us through the wormhole.

CHAPTER 27

MAURICE

"Do you have it?" I asked Kris as soon as her hands left Clara's temples. The spirit of Kylan dwelling inside of her spat in my face.

Disgusting.

I gripped Clara's jaw and squeezed her cheeks together, holding her head in place. The flesh felt too soft under my fingers, like rotted meat. I looked into what used to be Clara's eyes, and disdain roiled in my gut. We needed to get this over with.

"Kris!"

Kris turned to me, and a wide grin reached her eyes. "Yes. I have it. You can kill him now."

I leaned down and bit into Clara's neck. The screams that followed were a mix of Kylan's low, demonic voice and Clara's screeching female vocals. They had been battling for control for weeks now, and I was sure the screams from Clara weren't from me biting her, but from her disgust and fuming rage over what Kylan had done to her body.

I continued to drink, even though the odor coming from her skin was almost unbearable. Once I felt satisfied enough to stop,

I bit harder into her flesh, digging my fangs deep until they broke through the cords of muscle and tendons, then ripped open her neck, spitting a mouthful of her flesh onto the ground.

While Clara's body lay lifeless on the floor, I stepped back as Kylan's spirit exited his now-deceased vessel and swirled around the room, enveloping us.

"Hello, Kylan. Feeling a little exposed, are you?" I sneered at him.

Without a body to control, he was just a mist-like demon with nowhere to go. He would have to possess another body quickly, but I wouldn't allow that to happen.

"You've been nothing but a hindrance to my plans, and now it's time to end our partnership. We're done here."

I gave a nod to the others. Julian, Kris, Marcus, and my other witch ally, Courtney, held their hands high and uttered a spell that sounded like gibberish to me.

I heard a loud screech, and the smoky mist picked up speed, whipping through the room, a howling cyclone of demonic energy. Courtney held her hands out to her side, creating a portal to the Underworld below us. The smoke demon tried to resist the magic, but as Courtney's eyes lit up with an ethereal glow, a strong, invisible force sucked Kylan into Hell. With a loud snap, the portal closed, leaving the room empty of that bastard's insufferable presence.

The thought of what lay beyond that portal sent a shiver down my spine. The Underworld was a place that none of us quite understood, but whatever it was, it was not somewhere I planned to go.

I looked down at Clara's corpse, smiled, and without feeling an inkling of remorse for her loss, I turned to my witch allies. "I need a minute with Kris."

Julian scowled, not happy I was leaving him out, but he didn't argue with me as he and the others filed outside of the club.

I turned to Kris and smirked. "So, tell me about the Underworld."

She padded over to the bar and pulled out two glasses. "We're going to need lots of whisky for this one."

<hr />

"You're saying that Purgatory, where Mercy's coven is trapped, was created by Tatyana herself?" I asked. "Why?"

Kris took a large gulp of her drink. "It's another dimension that prevents the creatures of Hell from taking over Earth. Tatyana learned the Devil was sending his demons, specifically Misha, to this world. She went to Earth to prevent the takeover. But she messed up by unknowingly helping Misha create the half-breed."

"A vampire," I stated.

"Exactly. After Tatyana helped create your kind, she designed a place to save vampires' souls and create a barrier between Earth and Hell so the demons wouldn't continue to come here. So, she not only prevented the demons of Hell from possessing humans and taking over their world, but she also created a place to trap what makes vampires ... well ... good."

I huffed and threw back the whisky. "Tatyana thought she could try to save our souls from going to the Underworld?"

"Becoming a vampire doesn't make you evil, Maurice. It's what you do as one that makes you a monster."

"Right ..." I said. "Define evil, Kris. Do you believe I deserve to burn in Hell, or that you do, for that matter?"

Her lips formed a flat line. Not that I expected her to respond. Witches had an arrogance about them and a superiority complex regarding other supernatural creatures in this world. Friend or foe, she still looked down on me as if I were a demon from Hell, and she was simply doing the universe's work.

"What else did you learn?" I asked, pouring myself another glass.

She straightened her back. "Mercy was trapped in Purgatory after she died in 1692. Kylan knew it, Misha knew it, and the Devil knew it. They did everything they could to get to her, but Tatyana's power prevented the walls of Purgatory from ever being breached."

Kris glanced down at her feet, clearly nervous about finishing her thoughts.

"What is it?"

She inhaled deeply, let it out, then continued. "When I read Kylan's mind, I saw that he'd tried to pass through Purgatory and back to Hell, right when Julian performed the spell to pull his spirit from Cami and transfer it to Clara. For a moment, he crossed through Purgatory and entered Hell before Julian pulled him back."

I blinked rapidly. "What are you saying?"

"He couldn't do that unless Purgatory were no longer pro-tected," she explained. She poured herself another whisky and slammed it back. "The walls of Purgatory are down."

Understanding washed over me. "Because Tatyana became mortal. When she no longer had the magic used to create it, the power to keep Hell from crossing over no longer existed."

I wasn't sure how I felt about this. If Hell took over Earth, I'd have no power here. All my ambitions would be burned away by the coming tide of the Underworld and its inhabitants.

"So, now the gates of Hell are open, and every soul from every vampire, along with Mercy's coven, is standing in Hell's path, unprotected?" A nauseous feeling sank into my stomach at the mere thought of what could happen. It wasn't that I wanted my soul back ... ever. But I liked the fact it was tucked nice and safe in a sanctuary where nothing could touch it.

"That's what I read from Kylan's mind," Kris said. "Do whatever the hell you want with that."

I mulled this over briefly until the realization hit me. I looked over at Kris, who slammed another shot and set her tumbler on the bar top. "If Hell consumes the souls that live in Purgatory, Mercy's power to reunite a vampire with their soul wouldn't actually work, then, would it?" An unhindered smile crept across my face. "There'd be no soul to save. And Mercy will never get her coven back."

Kris's gaze shifted to the ceiling as she appeared to contemplate my words. "In theory, yes. But we would set the Devil and all his demons loose into the world and—"

"And I'd have no power here ... unless we stopped them before that happened."

"Stop the Devil?" Kris asked. "Have you gone mad?"

I threw back my head in laughter and then gulped down my last drink. "Oh, Kris, if you only knew." My finger swirled around the edge of my empty glass, then I straightened my back and stretched my arms out wide. "It looks like I must kill the Devil. Demons need a king, don't they? So, let me give them one."

CHAPTER 28

MERCY

I paced the floor for what felt like hours. "Joel, please say something."

Joel leaned against the sofa, a look of astonishment clear on his face. "So, let me get this straight. My niece, who's an immortal witch, now has the magic to raise the dead. Not only that, but on top of being a vampire hunter, you used to be a witch hunter."

Hearing Joel say those words out loud stopped me from pacing. The realization of the situation I was now in hit me head-on.

I steadied my breathing and looked down at my stable, outstretched palms. "My magic seems to have changed color as well. I can pull a bright white power through my hands now."

He stifled a laugh. "Lily's going to lose her shit. Do you realize what this means?"

"It doesn't mean anything. I may not even use this power."

"But you are," he said. "You're going to use it once. Just once."

"Four times, actually. I'll use it four times. Then I'll give it up forever."

Joel planted his hands on his knees. "You saw yourself kill a witch in your past life?"

"Actually," I added, shame burning my insides, "I saw myself kill hundreds of witches."

I hadn't shared that information with Dorian. In fact, I hadn't thought I would share it with Joel, but the words just came out, as if I were confident that he would accept that part of me. The only one who knew what I did back then was Roland.

"Mercy," Joel said, "you ..."

"I was born to rid the world of evil. Tatyana gave me this ability so that I could usher in peace to humanity. The justice system in place cannot hold a witch or a vampire. Our laws will have no impact, and imprisonment won't stop anything. If we allow vampires or witches who practice dark magic to roam free, we will be as good as dead."

Joel gave me a pointed look. "You're talking as if you've already accepted this part of you."

I sighed and plopped down on the sofa next to him. At this point, it didn't matter what I said. It wasn't like I could erase my memories or personality from the seventeenth century.

"Yes, I have. I remember everything and not just the memories. I remember wants, needs, and dislikes. It's as if I closed my eyes at the gallows and woke up in this life. Nothing has changed."

Joel pushed away from the couch before I could say anything else and ran a hand through his hair. His jaw was set, and he clenched his fists. "It can change. We can find another way."

I held up my hands and gave him an exasperated look. "How? Tell me how we can save our world from monsters without killing them, and I'll gladly give this up."

"We create a prison," he said. "It can be like Raven's but more secure. We can start our own government within the witch community. If the human justice system and prisons can't hold supernatural beings accountable for their crimes, *we* will."

I scoffed and looked away from him. "If it were only that easy."

"We can try," he said. "Your grandfather's inheritance was enough to take care of our family for years to come. It isn't like we've used it much these last few years."

I looked at him again, that time with mild frustration. "In time, yes. I'm open to it. Believe me. The memories I have of taking the life of someone just like me aren't pretty. It never felt good."

Joel's shoulders dropped, and he sighed. "Now what?"

My face softened, and I shifted closer to him. "I'm not the same woman anymore. I don't feel the same. The world needs the Chosen Ones, and the traitors of our kind will meet their fate. So, I'll bring back the coven. Then we go from there."

The look on Joel's face shredded my heart into a million pieces. He didn't recognize me anymore. I knew that. I barely recognized myself, but it didn't matter.

With that, Joel crossed his arms over his chest and gave me the tiniest of smiles. "Okay. What do we have to do?"

———

I retrieved Joel's spell book from his bookshelf and flipped it to the blank pages in the back, where we'd written our own spells. I copied the spell I had hidden in my memories, which I had created in the seventeenth century, on resurrecting someone.

I placed my hands on the open book, and the pages lit up, sealing the spell into the Book of Shadows.

"What exactly do you have to do to bring them back?" Joel asked.

I regarded him. "You won't like it." I turned the book to face him, so he could read it himself. After a few minutes, his jaw dropped, and his eyes went as wide as two moons.

"Fuck," Joel cursed and then looked up at me. "And knowing this doesn't give you second thoughts?"

I shook my head. "No. I know I have to do this, but—"

"Are you afraid it will change you?"

"It already has, Joel. This isn't my first time," I reminded him.

"Yeah, you said that." His accusatory tone pulled at the pit of my stomach. I leaned back and placed my hands over my face. "I need to talk to Roland."

Joel's chin rested in his hand, and he slowly rubbed his fingers over his face. "We can't keep this from Lily."

"I know. Honestly, I'm terrified to tell her," I admitted.

He grabbed his phone and sent off a text. "I let Lily know we're on our way."

———ele———

Lily was behind the counter, handing a customer their coffee, when she spotted us. She held up a finger and pointed to a table near the back. As we approached the cash register to order, Desiree appeared from the back room of the café. "Mercy! Joel! Hey, guys."

She may have been centuries old, but I loved that she still had a childlike spirit. Despite what she had gone through, she was always happy, even during these last few weeks after learning of Abigail and Caleb's deaths. It was as if joy was the only way to get through it.

"Hey, Desiree. How are you?" I asked, and though she frowned, there was still light in her eyes.

"I'm doing okay. I still think of Abigail every day and what happened to Caleb, but I'm here. Alive. I'm alive because of you."

I gave her a weak smile but straightened up when the bell over the door jingled, and a couple walked in. "Um, we will have two lattes, and later on, we can talk about anything you want."

She nodded, typed in our order, and waved us off to the side, refusing our money.

Lily soon joined us at the back of the café and set our coffees on the tabletop. "Welcome back, Mercy. What did you find out?" she asked.

The next twenty minutes were probably the most difficult minutes of my entire life as I explained to Lily what kind of person I truly had been in my previous life. The idea of me bringing someone back from the dead wasn't what seemed to shock her. It was the fact that I was okay with taking another life to make it happen. Well, that and the fact that I would take the lives of our own kind.

"They aren't innocent, Lily," I explained, almost trying to convince myself more than her.

"I understand that. But that isn't you anymore, right?"

I shrugged and snuck a glance at Joel, who had his arms folded, leaning back in the chair. He was probably hoping I would say, "Nope, not me anymore," but we all knew that wasn't true. It *was* me.

It is me.

I quickly changed the subject. "Joel has this crazy idea that we create a prison system once we bring the coven back. We would use this system to hold traitorous witches accountable for their crimes, since normal prisons won't work at all."

She perked up. "Honestly? I like that idea." Light came to her eyes for the first time since our conversation had started. Her expression then turned somber. "I get why you had to do it, though. If you hadn't, so many more people would have died. But Mercy, these are different times. It can't be an eye for an eye. We can't be the judge, jury, and executioner. We have to bring them to actual justice. Our family has the money and resources to do this."

I shrugged. "Maybe, although I'm not sure this is what Mom had in mind when she set up the trust for me. But it's going to take time, and right now, the only thing we need to be focusing on is getting the coven back and killing Maurice."

Lily smirked, and Joel joined her that time. "*That* I can get on board with," she said.

Joel nodded toward Lily. "Go on. Tell her what you have to do."

I shifted uncomfortably in my chair.

"The spell?" Lily asked.

I nodded. "I'm going to need your help to trap the four witches I must kill to bring the coven back." I frowned. "I hate to involve you in this, but we're going to need all the power we can get. These witches only use dark magic."

She reached out and rested her hand on top of mine. "Anything you need."

I squeezed her hand gently then released it and sat back in my chair. "I have a plan to get them to follow me to the field by the mausoleum, but there's a chance it will fail, and we all need to be ready to jump through that portal and enter Maurice's lair to fight until we take them out."

"I would give my life if I had to. You know that," Lily said, her voice low and serious.

I stared at Joel, and he nodded slightly, as if permitting me to share the rest of it with Lily. "I know, but mostly, I need you to hold yourself together when you see what I have to do to the witches," I explained. "I'm ..."

She turned in her chair and looked me in the eye. "It's okay, tell me."

"I'm transferring their life forces to the coven. Their bodies will shut down and keep aging until they die. You'll hear them scream until their hearts stop beating. It's not like I'm snapping my fingers. We will be watching them suffer until they go to the Underworld. That is, *if* they go there."

"Like ... Hell?" Lily raised an eyebrow.

"It's as if you didn't hear me say that I have to suck the life out of four witches," I said, more sharply than I meant to.

"Oh, I heard you," she said. "I'm still processing that part."

I let out a heavy sigh, and Lily looked around the shop, ensuring we were alone. "And Maurice?" she asked.

"I'm going to take my sword and cut off his head. I will put an end to that son of a bitch once and for all."

As the words left my mouth, complete and utter satisfaction hit me at my core. No more waiting for Maurice to corner me. No more fearing he'd retake me. There will be no more death at his hands. Maurice was going to fucking die.

Lily looked surprised by my statement, but after a minute of processing how serious I was about what I had to do, her shoulders relaxed, and she smiled, sending a wave of relief washing over me.

Though Lily hated violence and anything remotely related to dark magic, we all knew what we had to do to save our world. I may have had the powers of all the elements, but they didn't belong to me; they belonged to my coven. And though I was able to harness their powers, it wasn't the same. The balance was off, and my coven wasn't meant to be trapped for eternity in Purgatory.

"We're with you. Let us know what you want us to do," Joel said, and Lily nodded with him.

"You're not going to like this next idea that I have," I said, spinning my coffee cup, unable to meet their eyes.

Joel pressed his lips together. "Probably not, but we trust you. What is it?"

"I ..." I paused, not believing what I was going to say next. "I need to confront Kris and trick her into reading my mind."

"What? No!" Lily looked around her and then lowered her voice to a whisper. "She'll know everything."

Yes, that was the hard part, but I'd learned enough from my father about how to control my thoughts in those three weeks I had stayed with him. The techniques were different from what I did to Kris when they attacked us at Dorian's home. If a mind-reading witch was to take over my mind, I knew I could pull it off. The tricky part would be getting her alone to hear me out.

CHAPTER 29

MAURICE

I stepped back as the large moving truck reversed to the front entrance of the hangar that I had purchased last month.

Everything I'd planned in the last year was finally coming together beautifully.

The hangar was about twenty thousand square feet and would be used for our training grounds and vehicle storage. We had been working night and day to get it ready. Attached was a large building we would use as office space, or in other words, a prison for our captures.

If we were to do this correctly, I'd need a structured operation.

Julian lifted the tailgate on the truck and pulled down the ramp once our driver put the truck in park. My men grabbed the dollies and unloaded large wooden boxes, rolling them into the hangar. Once a few of the shipments had been placed on the floor, I signaled for them to stop. I needed to check the product inside and make sure every piece was accounted for. After prying open the lid with a crowbar, I pulled out a silver bracelet. It looked just like the ones I kept in the lair before Tatyana destroyed them all.

I signaled for Julian to come over. "Here. Put this on."

He briefly hesitated but reached out and grabbed it, wrapping it around his wrist and securing the lock. "Okay, now try to use your magic."

Julian lifted his hands, presumably to levitate the box in front of me, but nothing happened; he lowered his hands and grinned widely.

"It works. It's as though my magic doesn't exist," Julian said, taking a key from me and unlocking the bracelet. "Brilliant."

"Then we're back in business," I said as I thought about all the lives that would soon be mine for the taking.

The boxes with blue markings held the bracelets, and the boxes with red markings had chains. Most were meant to secure around someone's neck, but a few were shackles for wrists and ankles. We'd use those chains to secure the werewolves, and once the silver did its job to contain them, we'd slaughter them one by one.

Werewolves served no purpose for a vampire. Their bite could drive us into madness, causing us to drive a stake into our hearts to end it all. Their blood tasted atrocious to vampires and weakened our strength significantly.

I had hoped the wolfsbane would be enough to dismantle them, but if it didn't bring them to their knees, we'd have to put the wolves in shackles just long enough to use a silver sword to cut through their necks.

"How many did you order?" I heard Courtney ask as she approached us from behind. I looked at the twenty-foot truck in front of us.

"Each truck contains what we need to secure five hundred humans."

"That's it? Are you sure that's enough?"

I hissed at her. She was new to how I ran things, and she hadn't quite figured out that questioning my methods was on the list of things never to do unless one wanted their head ripped off.

"No, of course not," I said, trying to contain my annoyance. I needed this witch's power, so I couldn't kill her ... yet. "This is only the first arrival ... you imbecile." I smiled viciously as I watched Courtney's mouth drop and her eyes fill with terror.

She'll learn.

"Twenty other trucks will arrive this week," I continued. "I suspect most humans and witches won't exactly cooperate with us. They can either join us, be imprisoned, or die."

"What do you need me to do?" Courtney asked.

"Excuse me?" I snarled, reminding her to whom she was talking. She gulped. "What would you like me to do, Master?"

To be honest, I fucking hated that title, but for years I had felt it was the only way for those who served me to show their respect.

"Better." I turned and placed my hand on her cheek, caressing her soft skin with the backs of my fingers. "You'll bring me a little witch named Desiree. You'll find her living with Lily, Mercy's aunt. If she's not at their house, check a little shop on Main Street in East Greenwich called Lily's Café. She's a powerful one. Don't underestimate her based on her size. She has magic that can turn you to stone."

CHAPTER 30

MERCY

I didn't blame Lily and Joel for looking at me incredulously. Once we settled back at Lily's place and Desiree had gone into the living room to read, I explained in vivid detail how we'd get Kris away from the rest of her coven and make her listen. To her, it would look like I'd be negotiating, but in actuality, I would be feeding her lies through my mind, making her believe that I had slipped up in shielding my thoughts. Then, I'd trick her into following me through the portal and into the mausoleum where my coven was.

According to Noah's report, Kris, Julian, Marcus, and some black-haired woman met for coffee each morning before reporting to Maurice at his new lair. That window of time would be our best opportunity to pick them off one by one, starting with her.

Lily wouldn't stop shaking her head with every word that came out of my mouth, but she always doubted any plan that might end up with me hurt or captured again.

I continued. "If I can intercept—"

"It's too risky," Lily interrupted. "We don't know what other powers she has!"

"I'll risk any surprises. I need them to be in proximity to my coven to perform the spell. Trying to knock out and capture four witches so we could drag them there would be a hell of a lot tougher. I need her to believe she's one step ahead of us and go there of her own free will, along with the rest. Then we trap them."

Lily's hands trembled, and her foot tapped the wooden floor before quickly standing. A loud crash came from the living room, causing us all to jump. We stood motionless for a few seconds and then sprinted to the foyer. The front door was wide open, and one of Lily's vases had shattered on the floor.

"Desiree?" she called, but when Desiree didn't answer, she hurried to the back of the house. "Where is she? Desiree?" Panic filled her voice. She flapped her hands violently, as if trying to shake away her terror.

Maurice.

We ran outside and looked around frantically. A few blocks down, I spotted a car speeding down the road, skidding around the corner, and heading eastbound.

"We won't catch them before they get lost in the city. Grab the locator spell ingredients," I said.

Joel ran back into the house, and we joined him after he gathered three bundles of herbs. We moved quickly, holding hands and using our powers together to locate where they had gone.

"I don't feel anything," I sighed, losing hope that we would be able to see where they had taken Desiree.

"Shit! Me neither," said Lily.

"They must have cast a cloaking spell on her," Joel added.

I put my hands down on the table and closed my eyes tightly in frustration.

"What the fuck does Maurice want with Desiree?" I asked, but it was a rhetorical question. We couldn't know Maurice's twisted plan. He was unpredictable. That's why he was so hard to stop.

"It must be her power. It's unique," Joel said.

Since I had given Desiree back her humanity, which allowed her to use her powers again, I had been in awe of how incredible her magic was. No other witch I knew could do what she did.

"This changes things," I said.

Joel turned to me. "Do you have a Plan B?"

I looked them both in the eyes. "I always have a Plan B. You're just going to hate this one a lot more than you did the first one."

CHAPTER 31

MAURICE

"Let me go, you pasty leech!" Desiree cried as she tried to twist out of my firm grip on her arm.

Pasty leech? Well, that's a new one.

I glanced down at her, ignoring her futile struggle as I dragged her down a long hallway that connected to the office building.

She was a little thing, but she wasn't a child. This witch could turn us all into statues if Courtney didn't ambush her and snap that bracelet on her wrist. Desiree had lived through several lifetimes, but when it came to experience and power, I was far superior. Maybe I'd be able to tame the little beast before too long.

"I think we all underestimated you, Desiree. None of us realized what kind of power you held until I sent my men to follow Mercy around these last few weeks. I've always known you were once a vampire, but this ... this power you have is unlike anything I have ever seen."

My eyes lit up at the mere thought of her freezing our enemies where they stood, becoming true testaments to my might and power. She'd be quite useful if she'd agree to join us. We reached the end of the hallway that led to the prison cells, where I had planned to keep freshly caught witches and humans who resisted me and my new empire. Desiree would be my first guest of honor.

I leaned down and lifted her chin. "Is it true that you were among the first of the witches to have this power? And that your bloodline goes back to the infamous Medusa?"

Desiree scowled at me. "Fuck you," she cursed. Despite her rage toward me, her voice trembled with fear.

My eyes narrowed at her as I fisted her hair, pulling her head back. "Will your hair turn to snakes?" I drew out the end of that question, making a slithering sound with my tongue.

She glared at me, her eyes turning black with hatred.

Oh, she despised me, all right.

"Courtney! Put her in the holding cell on the second floor," I ordered. "I'll deal with *her* later."

Courtney grabbed Desiree again and escorted her away from me.

Once they were out of my sight, I turned to Julian. "How many do we have now?"

"We have about twenty witches and two hundred vampires. Everyone is devoted to fighting by your side as long as you keep them safe when the portal to Hell opens."

"Excellent," I said, clapping my hands together. "But I expect that number to grow, Julian. Do you understand me?"

He nodded. Like everyone else in his coven, Julian knew that once those gates of Hell were open and I became the new king, they'd be fools to challenge my new order of things. I was draped in wealth, clothed in power, and I possessed the inability to feel mercy toward my enemies. I had used these tactics my entire life, and it was the only way I'd survived this long. It was the only way I'd have control. If I had to use manipulation to do it, I would.

Kris joined us in the hangar, and I pointed to the building where Desiree was now confined. "Go. See what you can fish out of her head."

"You got it, boss," Kris said, leaving me standing alone with Julian again.

"I've finished creating the symbols on the ground in the left wing of the hangar," Julian said, gesturing in that direction.

"And the Devil won't be able to cross over it?" I asked.

"Correct. Kris extracted a trapping spell from Kylan's memories that can be used on the Devil. It was one of Kylan's contingency plans if the Devil came to Earth to confront him. Once the magic activates and he steps inside, he won't be going anywhere."

I smirked at how simple this all seemed, but nothing was *that* simple when it involved magic. Perhaps I felt that uneasiness, because I wasn't, and had never been, a witch. I didn't quite understand how it all worked and what could go wrong.

The threat of the Underworld breaking through the veil and into Earth complicated things for my worldwide takeover. But now that we had the trap spell and the little stone witch, I wasn't too worried about getting things back in line. Especially since I would soon become the new Devil King and gain an even grander army.

I sauntered to the bar we had installed in the hangar and poured myself a glass of pinot noir. Julian joined me and poured himself a glass of whisky.

"Cheers to defeating the Devil," I said before slinging the liquid back in one large gulp and then slamming the glass down, the remaining wine sloshing like exquisite blood.

CHAPTER 32

MERCY

Roland slid a shot glass toward me, but I didn't touch it. "Drinking won't bring Caleb back, Roland," I said. He glanced over at me. His eyes were more bloodshot than when I first had to drive his ass home from a heavy night of drinking. After Caleb and the coven died, Roland had been living inside a bottle.

He shifted his gaze back to the shot glass, which was meant for me, raised it, and tossed it back. "And you will?" he asked. "You're the reason he's dead, after all."

"Kind of dead," I corrected, trying not to take his words personally. "And that's a cheap shot, asshole." I folded my arms across my chest and narrowed my eyes at him. "I have a plan this time. You just have to trust me."

"Ha!" Roland slid the empty shot glass to a male bartender as he walked by. "Another."

"You're done, Roland," the bartender said. "Let Mercy take you home."

"Here." I handed the bartender the cash I had in my purse. "Does that cover it?"

The bartender nodded and snatched up the money.

"I said, another," Roland barked, but I grabbed his arm before he made a scene and yanked him off the barstool. Dragging a guy across the bar with my petite frame brought on a few nosy stares, but I didn't care. I had to get him home so he could sleep off his self-destruction.

"Stand up," I demanded as we neared the bar's exit. "I may be stronger now, but this still fucking hurts. You're dead weight right now."

He stopped dragging his feet and stood up, inching closer to me until I felt the heat from his breath on my face. It smelled like an ashtray. Roland didn't use to smoke, but I guessed he'd picked up a new habit these last few weeks to help numb his pain.

"You want to know what Caleb's last words to me were?" Roland asked as I was about to question him about the cigarettes.

I held my breath as I shook my head. "It doesn't matter. We all say things we regret—"

"He called me a traitor," he said, stumbling over his own feet.

I blinked, not knowing what to say. I hadn't been there, but Melissa had. All she'd said was that the coven had a fight with Roland, and he took off. From what I gathered, it wasn't just a disagreement; the coven had threatened him with their magic. She didn't understand what was happening, and it scared her, so she ran.

According to Melissa, Roland fed me to the wolves. I couldn't believe that Roland, someone who had once loved me as if I were his own daughter, would betray me like that. Now that I had my memories of what he and I had done to witches all those years ago, I understood. But, at the same time, I didn't know if this was the best time to bring it up.

Now or never, Mercy.

"Are you a traitor?" I asked.

He wouldn't look me in the eye. "Yes."

"Was all of that secrecy truly for the goal of finding witches who have betrayed us?"

He staggered but caught himself from falling over and raised an eyebrow. "Melissa told you what happened?"

I instinctively reached out to help steady him. "Not only that. I remember. Every memory from the past. I found the tree that held my true power. I went to that island—"

"You ... you ..."

"Easy," I said, grabbing his shoulder to lift him again as he started to fall.

"Mercy, what the fuck were you thinking?"

I gritted my teeth. Drunk or not, Roland didn't have the right to chastise me.

"I wasn't. The point is, I remember," I said casually. "And now I have that power back."

Roland scrunched up his face, looking as if he were about to toss up everything he'd drank.

He took a deep breath, relaxed his face, and looked up at the clouds forming above us. "How do you feel about me now, remembering everything I made you do to those witches?"

I took his hand and squeezed, forcing him to meet my gaze. "They deserved it, right?"

I waited for him to agree with me.

"No, Mercy. We should hate ourselves for what we did."

I rested a hand on his shoulder. "I don't think we knew any other way back then."

Roland furrowed his brow and huffed, looking toward the ground and around the parking lot—everywhere but at me. Once he spotted my car, he staggered in its direction, stumbling over his feet, and sat down on the gravel near the tire. He leaned against the car and looked up again, still not making eye contact with me. He only stared off into the distance.

"I knew what Maurice had been planning these last few months. I didn't know everything, but I knew enough. I shared information about the coven and your powers with Marcus, and all the while, he was working with Maurice right under my nose. He played me."

My stomach hardened. "You knew Maurice was going to take me?"

Roland didn't feel shame for what we had done all those years ago. He didn't feel hurt about what Caleb had said to him the last time they had spoken. Roland felt self-pity, because he'd allowed himself to be fooled by Marcus and for allowing Maurice to kidnap me.

His fucking pride is wounded.

He finally looked up at me and into my eyes. "I didn't know what he was going to do to you, Mercy. I swear it. But over the centuries, hundreds of witches have turned their backs on their own kind, and I made it my mission to find and stop them. Without the witches Maurice recruited, he won't be able to take us down. We're stronger than a clan of vampires, but not when he's got witches in his corner. They're his only source of power. We take them down; we take Maurice down."

"Why not tell me their plan and leave it to me and the coven to stop them? Why go behind my back like that?"

"I couldn't risk you getting killed. The dagger was still missing, and I had to make sure things stayed in motion," he said, as if he were trying to justify that reason as an excuse for his behavior.

"It doesn't matter!" I threw my hands up in frustration. "God, Roland! People died because of you. You remembered everything. I didn't have that luxury. If I knew ... if you had just told me what you were doing ..."

Roland ran his hand down his face and leaned his head back against the car. "I didn't think you'd be willing to kill a witch, not without your memories. You're not the same as you were back then, even now that you remember. You're still not the same."

"I think I am because I'm willing to kill to bring the coven back," I said. "But I need you to sober the fuck up and help us. I have an actual plan this time."

He started trembling, and his eyes became wet with tears. "Get my son back. I'll do anything you ask me to. Just get him back."

"I swear it," I said after a beat. "Don't ever lie or deceive me again. Do you understand? You're the only father I have left."

I wiped a tear that had fallen down my cheek and kneeled next to him. I sat with my back to my car and rested my head on his shoulder, and we were silent for a moment.

"Can you forgive me?" Roland asked, choking on tears.

"I already have, you idiot," I said teasingly. "Let's get you home to sleep this off and go kill some witches."

CHAPTER 33

MAURICE

"You... you what?" Desiree asked, her voice trembling.

"I want you ... to turn the Devil ... to stone," I said slowly, leaning against the steel bars between us.

"You've gone mad," she said. Then she glanced at Julian. "You're *all* deranged."

I tilted my head so she could look me in the eye. "You see, if we don't, there's no telling what will happen if he were to breach the walls of the sacred circle. You'll be saving humanity. If you truly think about it, we're doing the world a favor."

She stared at me deadpan, and her hands balled into tight fists.

"Oh, you want to turn me to stone right now, don't you? That anger burning inside of you—how does that feel?"

"Go to hell," she said through gritted teeth. "And I hope you burn there. All of you."

I smiled and chuckled to myself. "Desiree, you're going to help me, regardless of what you want. You're also helping me in more ways than one."

"What are you talking about?" She stood and inched closer to me. She was a brave little one. I had to give her that.

"Mercy's going to come for you," I said. "She won't succeed, of course. Then I'll retake her and use you as leverage to ..." I paused for dramatic effect. "... do whatever it is I want her to do."

Desiree stared at me defiantly. "She'll never agree to that. I'm just one person. Mercy will sacrifice me for the greater good when humanity is at stake."

"You underestimate how much she loves the people in her life. She'll yield."

"You're a monster," she said. "I can't wait to see Mercy stake you through your cold, vile heart."

All I had to do was reach my hand through the bars and grab her little throat. I thought about what that would feel like, taking her tiny neck in my hands and squeezing so hard her bones would creak, and she'd pass out. But I wasn't going to let a little witch piss me off today.

"Think about it," I said. "I'll protect you from what's coming; if not, you'll be joining your mother." Desiree's face grew hard, and her nostrils flared. I snapped my fingers at Julian. "Let's go. We have a meeting to attend."

Julian followed me as we made our way to the hangar. As we entered through the door, I looked out at a crowd of supernatural beings who had chosen to fight for me.

Julian leaned close to my ear. "Each witch out there has a unique power. They left their coven to find one that would free them from oppressive rule and allow them to use their dark magic openly."

I turned to him and smirked. "They're in the wrong place, then," I said.

He huffed and shook his head. "You need to understand something, Maurice. Kris and Courtney may yield to you, but you're not a witch. If you want to have the witches on your side, you can't bark orders at them. I have to lead the coven. Not a vampire."

"And if they defy me?"

"Then *I'll* deal with them."

I looked out at the gathering crowd. "And the rest are vampires?"

"Yes. But they're not my concern. My job is to ensure this new coven of witches following you know the consequences if they cross us." He paused and looked out into the crowd. "But you have to promise that when those gates open, you will command the demons to stand down."

I narrowed my eyes at him, and my lips formed a tight line. "Of course."

I raised my hand to silence the crowd and walked up the platform at the back of the hangar.

"Thank you for being here and trusting that this new clan of ours will protect you from what's coming," I said, turning to Julian. "Julian is my right hand. To the witches in the crowd, he's also your coven leader. And to my fellow vampires, I am your king." I waited for a beat, remembering what Julian had said. "To the vampires, bow to me and show your allegiance."

A murmur went through the crowd, and I could see looks of confusion and hesitancy on many of the vampires' faces. This may have been the first time many of them had ever joined a clan. It had taken me years to train the vampires in my own home to refer to me as Master. But I didn't have that luxury of time to train these fledglings to obey me. It would have to be immediate fidelity or severe punishment.

I noticed that several of the old clan members were in the crowd. They were my loyal servants because I was all they knew, but after

I failed to protect them from Mercy and Tatyana, I wasn't sure they'd show up today.

Calvin, from my old clan, pushed past the others and walked to the front line. He stood in front of the platform, bent his knee, and bowed, showing me the respect that I deserved.

Once the vampires in front of me saw Calvin's loyalty, one after another, they walked to the front. I waited with my arms crossed over my chest and my chin held high as more vampires followed and bowed. There were a few who still hesitated.

"Julian," I said. "Deal with them."

Julian walked up to a blond-haired man whose eyes were round with fear. "Is there a reason you're not bowing to your master?"

The man's shoulders heaved. "I ... I didn't think this was what we were doing."

Julian scoffed. "And what did you think was happening today? What's your name?"

"H-Harry."

"Harry. Do you know who that man is on the stage?"

He stared at Julian blankly. "No." Despite his steady gaze, his eyes betrayed his terror.

"Maurice is about to open the doors of Hell and essentially become the new Devil. Do you really want to stand against him and not show your loyalty?" Julian asked.

Harry was stunned. "He's what?"

I didn't intervene. Julian had the situation under control, but when Harry's eyes met mine, I stared him down without blinking.

"You will call him King, Master, Sir, or whatever he wants. But you will kneel, or you can leave. But if you leave, he won't protect you from being torn to pieces when the demons climb out of my portal and into Earth."

Harry gave a terse nod, but his feet wouldn't move. He was terrified. He must have been a new vampire because his outlook on the supernatural world seemed all too fresh and terrifying to him.

I continued staring at this weakling of a vampire as he stood silent. If he were to join me, I would have a lot of work to do to make him understand how it would be to live in my world.

Harry took a deep breath and slowly stepped toward the front. Once he reached the stage, he lowered his head and took a knee.

Behind him were the last of the vampires, who had also been reluctant to follow, but once Harry did as I asked, I now had a hangar full of my kind on their knees, willing to serve me and worship at my feet.

Honestly, I didn't care about the praise. I didn't need anyone to bow to me, but it made my job much easier to know that when the time came, if the vampires were willing to take a knee, then they were willing to sacrifice their own life if needed.

If we weren't powerful in numbers, then humans would continue to rule and wipe us out of existence.

Julian finished addressing the witches and informing them about Mercy, her coven, and her powers. They needed to be prepared if they were to come in contact with her or her allies. We also instructed them that if they went into battle with Mercy, they were not to hurt her. The new coven's orders were to subdue the witch and bring her to me. Once the gates opened, their mission would be to kill the werewolves and whoever else got in our way. Once the last hindrance to my plan was removed, the conquest of Earth would finally become my reality.

"I know many of you have homes of your own, but soon, you will find no safe haven there, so my goal is to acquire several properties in Salem to house you and keep you safe." I smiled, full of pride. "And I'll provide you with a gift if you prove your loyalty to the clan."

Several of the vampires looked at each other. A few shrugged, and soft murmurs filled the hangar.

"Aren't you curious about what that gift is?" I asked.

I focused on Harry as I said, "I will grant you the gift of walking in the daylight, Harry. I will give it to every vampire who follows me, and if you betray me, I will turn you to dust."

CHAPTER 34

MERCY

Lily opened the door to the mausoleum, and we moved inside, staring at the four coffins in front of us. As we looked at their lifeless bodies, silence filled the chamber, and I felt a knot forming in my throat.

I then turned to Roland, who stood in the doorway, refusing to enter. It was the first time he had visited the coven's resting place, and I could see his hesitancy.

Perhaps he wasn't ready to do this.

"Roland," I said, reaching out, but he only stared blankly at my hand. "Come on."

After a slight pause, he wrapped his fingers around mine, and together, we walked up to Caleb's coffin. The coven looked so peaceful lying there, but I knew that Purgatory was anything but peaceful. It was now exposed, in danger of being taken over by the Underworld.

"Alright, I'll give you a min—"

"Please don't leave," Roland said quickly, and his eyes met mine. Once I gave him a nod that I was staying, he placed his hand on Caleb's cheek and began to weep. I wanted to give Roland a chance to grieve in private, but seeing him in this state, he needed someone.

Wiping his tears, he turned and looked at me again. "Okay. What do you need from me?"

I glanced over at Joel and Lily. "I need you to help *them*. The moment I come back through the portal, you need to join hands in a circle. My goal is to get the witches I'm using for the sacrifice to follow me through the portal. Once they do, we need to use our powers to keep them grounded, so they can't run off when they realize it's a trap. Joel and Lily will teach you the spell." I placed my hands on Roland's chest. "We need your powers. The stronger the magic, the easier it will be to hold four powerful witches, especially ones who use dark magic."

Roland didn't even hesitate before answering. "All right, but what if they don't follow you through the portal?"

I gave him a knowing smile. "Oh, I don't know, Roland. How do you get four powerful witches who want to kill you, to follow you through a wormhole?"

He smirked. "You offer them bait."

"Exactly," I said with a curt nod. "And if everything goes as smoothly as I'm hoping it does, and we get the coven back, we will all go through that portal and fight against whatever Maurice has planned on the other side. According to Noah, he's been building up an army, and my guess is that the gigantic hangar he just bought is their new hideout." I turned to Joel. "Where are the wolves?"

Joel nodded over my shoulder, and when I turned around, Riley, Amber, and what looked like hundreds of werewolves entered the field near the cemetery. Some were in human form, but most had already transitioned.

Holy shit.

When my eyes met Riley's, I ran out of the mausoleum toward him with my arms outstretched, pulling him into a tight embrace. "Thank you," I said, leaning back to put a little space between us. "I can't believe how many you recruited for this!"

"We fight with you until the end," Riley said.

Amber walked up to me, smiling. "Two hundred and ten wolves are standing behind me. We *all* stand with you."

I looked around again, amazed at how many trusted us. Each stood proudly in their wolf forms, their eyes bright and fierce, awaiting my command.

"You lead them, Amber. When I give the call, *you* lead them. Not me."

"Just say the word."

Dorian caught my eye as he walked through the crowd. Circling above him was a giant and glorious eagle. It was Noah.

Dorian hurried to me and placed his hand on my cheek. "I don't like that you're going in there alone," he said. "He's going to hurt you."

"I know," I said. "But I won't be going alone. I promise I'll come back to you. I will always come back to you."

He leaned down and kissed me on my forehead. When he pulled back, my eyes darted over to Davina. She stood with her long arms folded around her waist. Her beauty caused me to feel an inkling of jealousy despite Dorian's promise never to leave me and to always fight by my side.

I knew there would always be a connection between them, and it wasn't his fault he felt that way. They shared a blood bond. I had to accept that part of him now and trust that his love for me would never fade and that she'd never try to take him away.

I looked at the crowd of wolves again, and I took a deep, satisfying breath, feeling my lungs expand, and then slowly released it.

"Joel, it's time," I called. He came to my side and took my wrists in his hands. "Let's give this spell a go." I closed my eyes, and we began to chant. A white light wove between us, creating a link. The spell connected our powers, connected our spirits, allowing us to become one.

When we opened our eyes, Joel smiled. "So, this is what it feels like, huh?"

"It's overwhelming, I know."

"We'll be connected for as long as we allow it," Joel said. "I'll feel what you feel, and you'll feel what I feel. Your magic, mine, and my magic, yours. The moment you ask for help, I'll pull you back through the portal."

"Okay. But only if I give the word. I'll take whatever punishment Maurice gives me. Please do your best to contain your anger when it happens. Don't get emotional or react. Got it?"

Joel's jaw clenched. "I'll try."

"No, Joel. Promise me that no matter what Maurice does to me, you will not react or pull me back. Kris will hear you through me, and that will compromise everything."

He was quiet for a moment before sighing. "Fine. I promise. You may not even get caught. That's the plan, though, right?" he asked. "You'll try to get Desiree back and trick Kris into reading your mind. That's it."

"Well, that's the plan, yeah. But now that we're connected, the spell to mask my scent is down. If there are any vampires there, especially Maurice, they will probably smell me. I'll be as quick as I can, but I have no idea where they're holding her. If I'm caught, we move into Plan C."

"Which is what?"

"You pull Desiree back through the portal once I give her coordinates, and I play the damsel until I can get away."

Joel frowned. "You make a terrible damsel."

I shrugged. "We'll see how convincing I can be. Here we go." I turned to Dorian one last time and mouthed a quiet goodbye and "I love you."

Joel moved his arms from side to side, opening his portal, and I stepped inside.

CHAPTER 35

MERCY

"*I see four others around Maurice. They're talking about something, but I can't hear what they're saying.*" I spoke to Joel through the bond, each word vibrating through my mind, fortifying our connection.

"*Get closer if you can,*" he replied.

I inched around the hangar and peered into the window closer to them.

"*They're going to smell me.*"

"*Are they witches or vampires?*" he asked.

I shrugged.

"*Can you feel me shrug?*"

"*Yup.*"

This is wild, I thought to myself.

"*I only recognize Julian, Marcus, and Kris, who are witches. Not sure about the other one. It's a woman. Her features seem a little too humanlike, so I'm guessing she's the other witch Noah told us about.*"

"*Well, it looks like you have your four witches.*"

I gulped, realizing that within the next couple of hours, I'd be taking the lives of four living, breathing humans. I had to remind myself that it was for the greater good. This was something I had to do.

"Hey, relax, okay?" Joel said to my mind. *"I'm having a tough time controlling the emotions you're projecting right now, kiddo. My heartbeat won't slow down."*

"I'm trying." I inhaled and exhaled slowly, willing my heart to ease. As I did, Joel relaxed with me.

Deep breaths.

"I'm going in," I said aloud.

"I can hear you when you speak out loud, too," Joel said.

"Oh, good to know." I opened the back door to the hangar as carefully as I could.

I noticed a set of stairs off to the right, but I'd have to walk around on tiptoes to stay quiet enough. They were too close, and I suspected Maurice would be able to catch my scent and probably hear me, given his enhanced predatory senses. But I didn't have a choice. Desiree had to be in the building next door, as I didn't see her anywhere inside the hangar. The building had two floors, but I had to cross through the hangar to get to the stairs that led to the second level.

I bent down, removed my shoes slowly, and placed them on the ground. I padded barefoot past the bathrooms and over to the stairs. No one had turned around so far, so I kept moving toward the steps. I wanted to sprint up them as fast as I could, as every second counted, but they'd hear the patter of my feet, so I forced myself to walk cautiously. At least ten minutes passed before I reached the second floor. The staircase was at the very end of the hallway, so I could only go one way. I picked up speed as I ran down the hall on the tips of my toes. I slowed down at each room I passed and looked inside. She wasn't in any of them. As I approached the last room, I immediately noticed steel bars and a lock. It wasn't just a room, but a cell.

Once I reached the steel bars, I saw Desiree crying on the floor with her arms around her knees.

I whispered, "Psst, Desiree."

She looked over her shoulder, and her eyes went wide with shock.

"Joel, she's on the east side, on the second floor in a small cell—"

I stopped mid-sentence when I noticed her eyes widen even further, and she stared over my shoulder. My breath caught in my throat, my stomach twisting in a sickening knot.

Slowly, I turned around, seeing Maurice stare at me, stony-faced, and for a moment, every thought and word escaped me. I was unable to move. That was until I felt my powers ignite on their own, shaking me out of our deadly stare-down. I raised my hands and blasted Maurice across the hall.

I rushed at him, but Julian stepped into my path, blocking me. I didn't realize Kris was right behind me until she grabbed my head, trying to pull my thoughts out, but I fought her off, using my telepathy to shoot barbs into her mind, repelling her away. She let out a curse and released me before I quickly kicked her away and squared off with Julian.

Maurice was already on his feet and pulling a bracelet from his pocket. My mouth went dry.

No way in hell I'm putting one of those on again.

He crept toward me, but he only smiled as I raised my hands, magic pulsating from my clenched fists. His sadistic laugh made me pause. "Oh, come on, Mercy. You're caught. You know I'll kill

Desiree if you don't obey. Be a good girl and put this on of your own free will. Now!" he said, holding out the bracelet.

"Well, if you demand it like that and use coercion, is it really my own free will?" I said, taunting him. "Or are you just afraid that if you attempt to do it yourself, I'll break your face again?"

Maurice and I both knew I'd comply with Desiree's life in his hand, so he held out the bracelet with his smug grin, as if I hadn't just thrown out an insult and waited.

I knew by now that Joel was aware Maurice had caught me, so we would have to move into Plan C. Being captured wasn't a "what if," now. It was a certainty.

I had to be careful communicating with Joel from here on out. Kris stood against the wall ... listening.

The only thing I could do now was attempt to distort each thought that naturally made its way into my mind. To confuse Kris and even myself so that she couldn't make out our plan. It was tough, but I had practiced repeatedly with Joel before I came here. Not to mention, my father had made sure I perfected this skill before I returned to my coven. Magic or no magic, Kris was not going to be able to read anything from me.

"Kris, anything?" Maurice shot her a questioning glance.

She shook her head, her mouth forming a straight line and her nostrils flaring wide. I was clearly frustrating her.

"Very well. This is the element of Spirit we're dealing with," he said, walking closer to me. I instinctively backed up, running into Julian, whose hands gripped my arms tightly. "You use your powers on me again, and Julian will use his power to make Desiree turn you to stone. Then I'll gut her right in front of you with my teeth."

My mouth fell open, but I quickly closed it, not giving Maurice the satisfaction of knowing I was terrified of what he'd do to her.

I stretched out my arm. "Alright. I'll put on your fucking bracelet. Only if you don't harm Desiree in any way."

With a wicked grin, he said, "Fine. Thank you, darling."

I grabbed the bracelet, my fingers lightly touching his icy hands, making me recoil in disgust. I gulped as I clamped it around my wrist. The hard lump in my throat stung as he walked over to Desiree's cell, unlocked the door, and pulled her out by her hair.

"You said you wouldn't hurt her, dickhead!" I seethed through my teeth.

"Oh, I'm not going to hurt her. I need her for something much bigger than you."

My eyes narrowed on Maurice as he yanked her out into the hallway. She yelped but didn't fight back. It took every ounce of control not to lose my temper, run up to Maurice, and kill him with my bare hands, but I knew there would be no way to get his coven of traitors to where I needed them if he was dead.

Maurice brought Desiree to my side and released her. I immediately threw my arms around her tiny frame and hugged her tightly. "You're safe, okay? I'm going to get you out of this."

My promise was all I had right now, even if I wasn't confident that my plan would work the way I wanted it to. All I was able to do was give Desiree the promise of hope.

"Break it up, now," Maurice said. He turned to Kris and Julian. "Take Desiree down into the hangar. I need a moment alone with Mercy."

Kris nodded and grabbed Desiree's arm tightly, pulling her away from me. Julian followed closely behind her. After they descended the stairs, Maurice turned to me, flashing his playful yet sinister smile that I remembered so vividly. I fell for that charm when I was under his control, but I knew the deeper, darker meaning behind it. His smile was a threat of pain, deception, and violation.

He inched toward me slowly and placed his hand behind my neck, caressing it, while his other hand gripped my chin, his fingers snug against my jaw. "I've missed you."

"Fuck you."

His brows bounced. "Man, so much tension exists between us. We should hash it out in my bed later."

Maurice moved swiftly behind me, using vampire speed. I felt his lips against the back of my hair, and he inhaled deeply. Was he actually sniffing me?

What the fuck?

"Mm, I missed your scent. You have no idea how hard it is not to sink my teeth into your flesh. The fragrance of your skin—your blood—is all I can think about ever since Joel took it away from me, depriving me of what is mine."

"I'm not yours, you delusional psychopath. Never have been and never will be."

His obsession was worse than I thought. I tried to step away from him, but he gripped my shoulders, his sharp nails digging into my skin, causing me to wince.

"This has to be torturing you, huh?" I asked, ignoring the pain. I attempted to look over my shoulder to make eye contact, but his nails only dug deeper.

"Me not having you?" he asked. "I *do* have you, Mercy. I finally have you again and this time, you can't escape me. It's as simple as that—"

"No ... not that."

His nails eased up their pressure.

"I'm the element, Spirit, Maurice. Tatyana linked my powers to every soul on this earth, including yours, when she created me. My light is reaching your humanity, tethering to your soul while it waits in Purgatory, begging me to set it free. You're drawn to me purely due to your soul wanting to become human again."

I waited for Maurice to laugh at my theory from his bizarre obsession, but it didn't come. He had to have thought about it a million times, wondering why he suddenly cared for someone, and not just anyone, but for his greatest enemy.

"It's not me you want. It's the part of you that *used* to love. That used to care for others. The tiny, last bit of humanity you lost when Valentina turned you."

As he pulled my backside closer to his chest, I grew still.

"Interesting theory," he purred into my ear. "Perhaps you're right. But soon, that little soul of mine will be gone forever. I guess we'll find out soon enough."

I swallowed, unsure what he meant by that.

He loosened his grip and pulled my hair to the side, lowering his lips to my neck and kissing it gently. My skin crawled as if it was covered in thousands of bugs, and bile reached my throat. I shuddered at the thought of what he could do to me, and I wouldn't be able to fight him off.

"I'm right here, Mercy. I'm right here," I heard Joel reassure me in my mind. I stifled a sigh of relief. The bonding spell was still working, despite my powers being cut off.

Joel hadn't left me, but I wondered how furious he was right now and how much it was torturing him to feel what I was feeling—to experience my fear, hatred, and disgust and not be able to do anything about it.

As I felt Maurice's grip on my arm tighten, I said, "Wait." He paused. "Can I please turn around and look at you?"

He released my arm and slowly turned me to face him, flashing a bemused smile.

The surrounding energy shifted as Maurice glared at me with undeniable hunger burning in his eyes. His upper lip curled, and he flashed me a taunting grin. I flinched and turned my head away from him, but his hand reached out, grabbing my jaw tightly, so I'd meet his eyes.

"Don't shy away now," he said.

I backed up just an inch to give us some space, and once his hand dropped, I slapped him hard against his chilled cheek.

Man, I've wanted to do that for so long.

He placed his hand on his cheek, his lips parting into a smile. "You're stronger than you used to be."

Maurice was utterly unfazed.

Next time, I'll punch that grin off his face.

"Let us go, Maurice," I said. "If you think you're going to win this, you're insane."

"I've already won, darling," he said. "I'm excited to show you what I have planned. This world is about to change, and you'll have no choice but to join my side." He placed his hand around my throat but didn't squeeze. The tips of his fingers brushed my skin from the bridge of my neck and down to the center of my chest. "Be my queen of darkness and rule this world with me. I'll spare your family's lives and let Desiree go. I swear it."

The seriousness in his tone made me almost believe him, as if there were a small inkling of humanity inside him, and he would indeed spare my loved ones' lives.

"You belong to me, and you'll soon realize it's better to be on my side rather than my enemy. If you choose not to follow me, I will trap you for eternity in a prison so isolated you'll pull your own eyes out, begging me to set you free."

And just like that, he was back to that soulless, merciless monster.

A bitter taste soured my mouth, but I stared at him without blinking to show him I was unafraid.

"Very well," he said with a shrug. "I hope you said your last goodbyes to your friends and family, because I'm about to open the gates of Hell and release the Devil and demons into this world."

My breath halted, and my body went completely numb.

No.

The black mist that attacked me and the trembling sound of the ground beneath my feet in Purgatory ... was that the creature he was going to set free? Was Maurice *that* fucking crazy?

Panic rose in my chest. If the Devil were about to cross Purgatory and walk the earth, my coven was directly in his path.

CHAPTER 36

MERCY

Maurice dragged me by my arm down the stairs and into the hangar. He threw me to the ground, and before I could scramble to my feet, I looked down at a ritualistic witch circle directly in front of me, drawn in white chalk. The ring contained a pentagram at the center and at least ten different symbols around it.

"What is this?" I asked, pointing at the macabre drawing.

Marcus walked up to me and smirked. "That, Mercy, is where we plan to trap the Devil."

"Trap him?" I laughed aloud, rising to my feet. "You think you can *trap* the Devil in that?"

"Watch it, bitch," the black-haired woman said, but when Maurice hissed at her, she lowered her head and retreated.

Julian stepped closer to the pentagram and pointed at one symbol. "Those symbols *will* trap him. Once that happens—"

"Desiree will turn him to stone," Maurice finished. "Then we'll create a cage around him using the circle, and here he will stay nice and cozy until we figure out how to kill him."

"Why? His demons won't take kindly to you trapping their master," I said, but the moment the words left my lips, I realized his plan.

He's going to be their new leader.

Maurice smiled as he approached me again, placing his hand on my cheek and rubbing it softly with his thumb. "You understand now?"

I fought the urge to spit in his face. "You're going to get everyone killed, Maurice, including yourself. You're going to burn in Hell, right next to your brother and Kyoko."

A frown replaced his confident smirk, and I realized I'd hit a nerve.

"Oh, sorry," I said in a mocking tone. "Too soon?"

The sting from the slap that came next burned my cheek. I opened my jaw and felt a pop, but the dislocated joint quickly repaired itself. I let out a snort of laughter.

"A pathetic slap from a pathetic man."

His face twisted right as the black-haired witch asked, "Sir, may I?" Her tone was calm and unsettling.

"Who are you?" I asked as the witch approached.

She cocked her hip to the side and smiled at me wryly. "I haven't introduced myself yet. I'm Courtney. The two of us are related, you know? My mother's great, great grandmother was also yours. I'm descended from your former sister, Faith."

Great. A psychotic, distant cousin. That also meant that she most likely could conjure Spirit.

I glared at my soon-to-be-sacrificed victim, hoping whatever punishment she was about to dole out was enough to help me not feel remorseful for taking her life.

As Courtney inched closer to me, the others in the room backed up.

"What are you going to do ... cousin?" I asked, trying with all my might to disguise the pain I suddenly felt inching up my spine.

"Do you feel it yet?" she asked, her voice calm and steady.

"Feel what?" I said, pretending that the sharp sting under my flesh was nothing but a minor annoyance.

Her face contorted when she stopped walking. She shot a glance at Maurice, then back at me. She closed her eyes as if she were focusing harder on what she was trying to do.

Whatever she did the second time, I could no longer hide it. I suppressed as many of my emotions as I possibly could. Whatever Courtney was doing to me, I couldn't let it reach Joel.

I felt my blood warm to an unbearable temperature, and needles of pain pricked my skin again. That time, it fucking hurt.

It felt as if shattered glass was stabbing me behind my arms. The heat coming off my body was unbearable, but my body repaired itself with every explosion she conjured beneath my flesh.

The searing heat made me feel faint, causing me to lose my bearings, and I fell to the floor, my knees striking the concrete full force.

I looked up, masking the intense pain coursing through my body. "This is child's play." I forced myself to grin at her.

She flipped her hands up, and her eyes started glowing a crimson red.

"Courtney, that's enough," Maurice warned.

She stepped closer, ignoring his command. "I'm boiling your blood and making your vessels explode inside your body. If you weren't immortal, you'd be dead right now. Instead, I get to watch you suffer!" she said through gritted teeth. "I like that you heal so quickly. It makes the torture much more enjoyable, because I can keep at it for hours."

I dug my nails into the concrete, feeling like someone had dipped my body in molten lava. I could feel blood seeping into my mouth, but I swallowed it down quickly. I was not about to let this bitch see me bleed.

"I said, enough!" Maurice screamed.

I reached forward and dug my fingers into her exposed ankle so deeply that I felt the flesh of her skin split open under my fingernails. She yelped and tried to move away, but she didn't stop torturing me.

I looked up as Maurice grabbed Courtney by the back of the neck and yanked her backward, flinging her body across the hangar like a rag doll. The pain immediately stopped, and the internal damage was repaired.

The sweat seeping through my pores soaked my entire body from head to toe. I tried to rise to my feet, but my vision swam, and I felt like I was going to pass out, so I sat back down. From my peripheral, I saw Desiree being held back by Kris, her eyes wide with terror and her body shaking. I offered a smile to Desiree, trying to convince her I wasn't in any pain.

Courtney slowly stood, wiping dirt from her face, and walked back to us; her head hung low, but fury still burned in her eyes.

Why does she hate me so much?

"Let me help you up," Maurice whispered, reaching out his hand to help me to my feet. His tone was gentle, and it almost sounded like he was concerned about the level of pain Courtney had put me through. I scowled at him, smacked his hand away, and stood on my own.

Ignoring Maurice, I turned to Courtney. "What the fuck is wrong with you? What did I ever do to *you*?"

She just sneered at me, raising her hand in a vile gesture.

Nothing. Courtney is pure evil, and she thrives on torturing others, just like Maurice. I won't feel bad taking her life later.

Maurice stepped close enough to me. I could feel his cool breath on my cheeks. "I want you to understand something," he said, looking over at Desiree. "What you just experienced is what Desiree will go through if you ever deny me." He smiled in her direction. "And she won't survive it."

I looked him dead in the eye and the feeling of complete horror flushed over me. It made me feel dark and alone, even though in the back of my mind, I knew that I wasn't. Joel must have sensed what I was feeling. The sensation of a warm embrace covered my skin like a soft blanket. It was Lily. I felt her arms around Joel, giving me the comfort and sense of peace that I needed.

I wanted to thank them for that moment, but I was too afraid Kris was still listening to my mind, so the voice inside my head stayed silent.

Maurice inched even closer, and my body tensed as I saw a sick hunger in his eyes.

I would rather die.

I turned my head, trying to hide the grimace on my face, because Desiree's life depended on my being calm. He grabbed my chin and turned my face toward him, and I immediately closed my eyes. I was so disgusted that I couldn't look at him any longer, so they stayed firmly shut as his lips touched mine in a delicate kiss. He fisted my hair to keep me from pulling away from him. My entire body went numb as he deepened the kiss, his tongue gliding over mine. All I could do to help myself relax was to picture Dorian's face as his hands slid up my hips, lacing his fingers along the waist of my pants. I felt Maurice's nail scratch against my skin right before he pulled me closer, our chests colliding, and a soft moan escaped his lips.

He released the kiss and rested his forehead on mine. "Not all relationships have to be fairy tales."

He truly is deranged.

He wasn't smiling as he released me, but he wasn't frowning, either. His expression was unreadable.

"It's time," Maurice said, turning away from me and snapping his fingers at Julian.

I ran to Desiree and clung to her, whispering as quietly as I could. "We're going home. Be ready."

She gave an almost imperceptible nod before Marcus grabbed my arm and yanked me away from her. Maurice held out his hand for Desiree. She hesitated at first but reluctantly placed her hand in his, and he escorted her to the symbolic circle on the ground. Julian walked with them and unclamped her bracelet.

"You try to use your powers on us, and we'll torture Mercy again," he threatened. Desiree's eyes went wide, and she rubbed her wrists, nodding her head in agreement.

Maurice and Julian backed away from Desiree, leaving her alone right outside the circle. She and I both watched in horror as a portal, much larger than what Joel or I had ever created, opened before us.

The center of the portal resembled a black hole, stretching into nothingness. Suddenly, a blood-red ring of pulsing light appeared. It spun so rapidly that it looked frozen in time. As the red light grew stronger, I tried to shield my eyes, but I wasn't able to break my gaze. It was mesmerizing.

Julian lifted his hands, and the circle drawn on the floor lit up like bright, glowing stars.

He began to chant, and Marcus, Courtney, and Kris soon joined in.

"Joel, you need to pull us back now."

I was in such a panic I didn't shield my thoughts. The second I realized this, I froze, and my gaze shifted to Kris. Her eyes were wide, and I knew immediately that she had heard me.

"Maurice!" she yelled, but the sound of high-pitched, demonic screams emitted from inside the portal, drawing everyone's attention toward it.

Oh my God.

Maurice couldn't look away from the portal. He stood, frozen, staring at the strange sight. The same black mist from Purgatory crept from the hole in one long, rope-like shape. It swirled around the circle on the ground, and Julian moved his hands from side to side, controlling where it went. My jaw dropped, my breathing hitched, and my stomach twisted until I could no longer move.

"Maurice!" Kris screamed again. She looked at him and then at me, but Maurice still didn't look away. She ran toward me, which snapped me out of my panic and allowed me to get my thoughts back under control. I braced myself, waiting for her to strike, but she only grabbed my head, pressing her hands on my temples.

I felt a vibration against my skull, but I didn't shield myself from her that time. It was now or never. I offered my bait. I let my thoughts deceive her and let her see where the coven was laid to rest, making it seem as if I had messed up and revealed something I didn't want her to know. I cloaked the vision of the army that awaited them. Kris released me when she thought she had retrieved enough information. She shoved me backward and ran back to the circle to alert Maurice.

When I looked over at the portal, the black mist took the shape of a body at the center of the circle. I saw a pair of black eyes begin to form and settle into sockets surrounded by red, reptilian skin. The Devil's bat-like wings were sharp at the tip. Black horns protruded from the top of his head, curling around his ears and against his cheeks. A loud roar filled the hangar, vibrating the metal walls.

I'm not seeing this. I can't possibly be seeing this.

The Devil looked around, keeping his gaze on Maurice, then dove toward him with his arms outstretched. We all jumped back, but an unseen force yanked him backward, plummeting him to the ground. He growled and stood back on his feet; his eyes shone a ruby red, and smoke poured from his mouth, rising high above him and up into the air. It didn't get far as the magical force above the circle pushed it back down and into his mouth.

The Devil's upper lip curled as he opened his arms and unfurled his hands, revealing long, sharp fingernails. Gray, cloudy smoke left his fingers and enveloped him, swirling around like a tornado.

The floor shook below us, and I had to plant my feet to keep from falling over. Several stacked crates crashed to the ground, spilling out silver bracelets and chains. Above us, the skylight shattered, shards of glass raining over us. Courtney and Kris stepped back, looking as if to bolt from the scene, but Julian turned to them, snapping his fingers to bring them back.

When I looked up, the Devil's face transformed into something else. Something ... human. His scale-like flesh smoothed out to porcelain, human skin, and his eyes turned a brilliant shade of green. He was naked, exposed, and eerily beautiful. The horns from his head had blended into silky, dark black hair, and his wings folded back into his body, disappearing.

He looked like an angelic being, so different from the horrific sight we all had just witnessed crawling through the portal.

I remembered from my previous life stories that the Puritan church had told us about the Devil.

Long ago, the Devil had once been an angel but had fallen from grace, cursed to rule the Underworld with fire and endless pain. He was who Tatyana and the angels fought against. He had been my enemy, and now, he stood before us all, showing us that his fight against good wasn't over.

"He's taken on his true form," Julian said. "Just as we had hoped. It's the only way Desiree can trap him."

"Now, Desiree, or he'll kill us all!" Maurice shouted, barking his command at her.

As much as I didn't want her to obey Maurice, at this moment, I wanted her to abide by his command. The Devil couldn't be unleashed.

Without hesitation, she lifted her hands and released her power into the magic circle. The Devil screeched and screamed, and I muffled my ears to block out the harrowing sound. When I glanced up, Julian, Kris, and Courtney were doing the same. The piercing noise coming from his throat was unlike anything I had ever heard. It was a truly unholy sound, not of this world. The Devil tried to move forward again, but his foot was locked into place as gray stone crept up his toes and surrounded his ankle. The power moved up his legs, turning every inch of his body to rock until it covered his head, and he became a frozen, angelic statue.

Julian removed his hands from his ears and chanted the last of the spell, encasing the Devil in the magic circle and trapping him inside.

Desiree fell to her knees and sobbed. "I'm so sorry, Mercy. I'm so sorry."

As Kris stepped up to Maurice, I ran over to her and kneeled by her side.

"She fucking did it!" Maurice said, his eyes not leaving the Devil's stony figure. "Desiree did it. We won." He didn't seem to notice the increasing cries and screams coming from the still-open portal.

Something else is coming.

He didn't win anything. It was only the beginning of Hell on Earth.

CHAPTER 37

MERCY

"Maurice, listen to me, dammit! I know where they are," Kris yelled. That time, Maurice turned his attention away from the Underworld portal and glared at Kris.

"What are you talking about? You know where who is?"

"The coven. I know where their corpses are." She pointed at me. "She's also telepathically connected to her uncle," she said.

Kris now had Maurice's full attention, and his gaze snapped over to Desiree and me, still kneeling on the floor, embracing one another.

"*Now, Joel. Center hangar, below the skylight.*"

Within seconds, I felt a breeze on my face as a portal opened next to us.

"Grab them!" Maurice barked, but it was too late for anyone to reach us. I gripped tightly to Desiree and yanked her with me into the vortex.

We landed hard against the ground on our backs, hurrying across the grass and backing away from the portal. I half-expected Maurice to come tearing through the opening at any moment, but he hadn't yet.

"Go to the wolves, Desiree! Now," I said. "Be ready." Roland, Lily, and Joel clasped hands, forming a circle while Desiree bolted to the wolf packs, ready to fight with us.

"I need to get this off me," I said, pointing to the metal bracelet on my wrist.

I couldn't use magic to unlock it since the bracelet prevented that from happening, but Lily could. She released Joel's and Roland's hands and quickly approached me. She placed her hands on the lock and used her magic to unlock it, letting the bracelet drop to the ground. My magic rushed back to life, and I sighed in relief.

"Thank you. Okay, go!" I shouted. "Joel, keep the portal open!"

I ran back to the entrance of the vortex and waited. After a few minutes, my hope faded when I realized that neither Kris nor any other person, for that matter, had followed me through the portal.

Where is she?

I was certain that she would have been close behind. Kris believed I exposed my coven's location, and now she and the others could track them down and eliminate them for good. The yawning silence within the portal had me growing even more nervous. The way was open. This was their opportunity to stop me.

Suddenly, the light around the portal pulsated, and Kris came tumbling through the hole. She regained her balance and met my gaze. Before Kris made a move, she looked around and saw that there was an army of werewolves staring down at her. She whipped her head around and saw Lily and the others standing in a circle.

I smiled grimly at Kris. "How does it feel to be caught unaware for once?"

Kris's eyes grew wide, and she turned to run back through the portal. I raised my right hand and summoned the nearby tree roots to tear through the ground and wrap themselves around Kris's ankles, yanking her down into the dirt. Once I knew she was secure, I raised my other hand and pushed my powers through the portal until I felt the cold, open air of the hangar. Using my telekinetic senses, I created ropes of light and moved them around until I connected with Julian, Marcus, and Courtney. Once the connection was made, I wrapped the magic ropes around them and pulled the three of them through the portal. For extra measure, I slammed their bodies into the ground, leaving them stunned next to Kris.

My hands remained outstretched, waiting for Joel and the others to activate the spell and trap them in place. "Joel?" I called out, my arms growing weary.

"We're working on it, Mercy," he shouted back.

Lily, Joel, and Roland began to chant the trapping spell. I saw that Julian and Marcus were already on their feet and rushing toward me. Using another surge of my power, I threw out a blast that knocked the two men back down.

"Joel! Now!" I screamed.

Blue light rushed from the circle and flew toward Kris and the others, trapping all four inside an unbreakable sphere of power. They screamed from inside the shield, banging their fists against the pulsing blue energy. But it was useless.

I released the binding ropes of magic from the four and moved toward the entrance to the mausoleum. I took my position and raised my hands to the sky. Physically exhausted as I was, my powers were stronger than ever.

I closed my eyes and chanted the spell that would drain their life forces. White light filled the darkness behind my eyelids. A stream of power left my body, and I could feel the magic enter the sphere and surround the witches. Even from inside the shield, I heard their pain-filled screams as I stole their essence. I could open my eyes at any moment, but I didn't want to. I knew that if I did, I'd have that image burned into my mind forever. I already had too many of those scarring memories.

It felt like the screams lasted hours, but it was only minutes.

When the screams had stopped, and everything fell silent, I opened my eyes and watched in horror as Kris, Courtney, Marcus, and Julian collapsed into heaps of aged skin and broken bones on the ground.

I pressed a hand to my chest and fell to my knees. Suddenly, I felt the coven's elemental powers leave my body. An empty feeling consumed me, as if I had lost a part of my soul. I stared blankly at the doors to the mausoleum and waited.

Please be alive. Please be alive.

CHAPTER 38

MERCY

The spell had exhausted me, where I could no longer regain my strength. I kneeled on the grass, taking heavy breaths to help settle my nerves and my powers, which were still zipping around in my body like a ball inside a pinball machine.

I looked up as Joel rushed past me to the mausoleum doors and pulled them open. My heart leaped out of my chest when I saw Caleb, Leah, Ezra, and Simon standing in front of us—alive.

My legs moved faster than my mind could process what was happening. I jumped into Caleb's arms, and he squeezed my waist so tightly I could hardly breathe. His powerful arms engulfed me, and he had to ease up a bit for me to catch my breath.

"Sorry," Caleb said.

"You're alive!" Tears flowed freely down my cheeks, but I didn't bother to wipe them away.

I felt Desiree push between us, wrapping her arms around Caleb's waist. The three of us embraced for what felt like hours. I knew we didn't have that kind of time for sentiment, but I couldn't let go just yet.

Caleb buried his face in my shoulder and squeezed Desiree tightly. "You did it, Mercy."

I turned to the rest of the coven and pulled them in close. "We all did." After pulling back from our group hug, I said, "This isn't over. Maurice managed to capture the Devil, intending to become the demons' new king! But he didn't cross through the portal."

"We know," Leah said. "And they're coming."

"Who?" Lily asked.

"The demons of Hell. They crossed through Purgatory before you pulled us out," Leah explained. "We need to close the portal that Julian—"

"Fuck," Ezra and Simon cursed in unison, looking past me.

Leah's eyes opened wide as loud screeches filled the air. I whipped around and saw a portal ripping through the air right in front of the cemetery. It was pulsing red, like a fresh, gaping wound, and I could see a multitude of long, skinny demonic arms clawing through the vortex.

"Run!" Simon shouted.

We bolted toward the field where the werewolves were waiting. As we crested the hill, I saw Dorian standing next to Noah and Davina. I waved my arms frantically to get their attention. "The Underworld has broken through Purgatory. They're coming!" I screamed.

Once I reached the field, I looked on to a gathering of witches that Noah had successfully recruited, mixed amongst the werewolves, ready to fight with powers ignited and weapons ready.

"There's so many," Lily said, looking around.

I gave a quick nod. "We fight together now."

A loud, tearing noise drew my attention, and horror filled me as the demons tore through the cemetery, heading to the field.

Ezra let out a low growl, and his magic lit up around his fists. Caleb looked at me with determination shining in his eyes.

"They're here," I said, giving him a quick nod. "It's time."

Dorian and Davina shifted into their wolf forms, and Noah leaped into the air and flew into the sky in his giant eagle form. The coven, Desiree, and I ran to join the front lines. I could see that some members of our supernatural army were watching in terror as more demons spilled from the portal, charging us.

Even with the number of witches and werewolves standing behind me, I didn't know if there were enough to fight the demons of Hell, as well as Maurice's clan. What we had originally planned for was going through Joel's portal and confronting Maurice and the people he had recruited, not the demons of the Underworld.

Reaching within my element, I used Spirit to amplify my telepathy and reached out to every witch who had joined us. I instructed them to use myself and the coven as conduits for their magic. I told them to tap into our elements if they needed to or if their abilities were to become weakened. We would fight to keep them safe from the evil that threatened our home, our world. Our elements were with them until the very end.

A roar came from the crowd as everyone stood ready to fight. They were fighting for the safety of humanity, even if it meant giving up their lives for the cause. The screeching and screams of the army echoed over the field as they drew closer. I looked at Leah and squeezed her hand. Even though night had swallowed the world, the full moon glowed in the starry sky, washing over the field and the faces of my allies.

"Mercy!" Joel shouted over the din of screams. I turned to the sound of his voice as he flung my sword to me. I caught it midair and swiped it down. Caleb and Leah stood to my right. Ezra and Simon were to my left. Our powers danced at our fingertips, and I kept my sword gripped at the hip.

Lily, Joel, Roland, and Desiree formed a circle, linking their hands together as they chanted the words to a barrier spell. A thick, barely visible wall of energy formed across the field, which we hoped would slow down the demon army. When they approached the wall, my heart thudded heavily against my ribs, and I prayed the wall would hold.

The demons slowed down as they charge for us. They were only a few feet from the pulsating barrier now.

Thank God. We can buy some time.

One demon broke from the horde and moved closer to the wall. It raised its spiky, twisted head and made eye contact with me. Sweat beaded on my forehead as I stared this creature down, refusing to blink. Tilting its head, it raised a disfigured, scaly arm ....

Silence.

Steady silence ...

Suddenly, the creature's claws went through the barrier, ripping it wide open. *Shit.* A bellowing cry echoed in my ears, and the demon army continued toward us, rushing even faster than before. They were now at the bottom of the hill, almost upon us.

"Amber!" I shouted. "Get ready to charge at my signal."

Amber, in her wolf form, let out a chuff of agreement. I raised my hand over my head, and a ball of white light flew into the air like bursts of falling stars.

"Attack!" I screamed.

Amber let out a long, piercing howl before Riley joined her, and the werewolves charged forward. They were much faster than us, and several leaped at high speed, slamming down on the demons and ripping at them with their sharp fangs. The witches soon followed, their magical powers lighting up in the darkness like a prism.

Two demons tried to pounce on me, so I extended my left arm and summoned a bright beam of white light, which evaporated them into a gray mist. Spinning around, I brought my sword down on two more, slicing them in half. The field was now a sea of chaos. I couldn't focus on anything but the horde of demons coming toward me. I sensed my coven's power flying past me, and I prayed again that we would be strong enough to defeat this evil.

Another demon lunged at me, its eyes blazing red, and tried to sink its teeth into my exposed arm. It was too close for me to use the sword, so I seized its horns and blasted my power into its body. The surge caused the demon to explode from the inside, and it quickly disintegrated. Sharp claws dug into my back, and with a scream, I swung around, driving my sword in a backward stab. I caught the demon's midsection, and it vaporized around my blade.

I saw Desiree several feet ahead of me, surrounded by a couple of demons. She threw out her hands, and gray energy swallowed up the encroaching attackers. They all froze midair and crashed to the ground, breaking into piles of rubble. Pride swelled within me. Despite only being a witch again for a little over a year, Desiree was a master of her magic.

There were so many werewolves on the battlefield that I lost track of who was where, but I hoped that wherever my loved ones were, they were safe.

I hope Dorian is safe.

Roland came up from behind and blasted a massive red fireball past me, and I had to duck as it flew at lightning speed and slammed into four demons that were about to grab a black werewolf. The demons were immediately reduced to a pile of ash. The werewolf nodded in thanks, lowered its muzzle, and charged toward another demon, taking it down in a flash of fur, fangs, and scaly skin.

A human scream came from the far left, along the edge of the nearby forest. I could see a woman on her back, trying desperately to shove a snarling demon away from her neck. I broke into a sprint, summoning the trees to grab it off her. Realizing that the branches wouldn't be able to save her in time, I threw myself into the monster, knocking it to the ground. With a sweeping arc, I severed his head from his body, and he exploded into gray powder.

As strong as my powers were now, my sword was much quicker.

I looked back at the fallen witch, but she was already back on her feet, running into the fray of battle, purple lightning crackling from her hands. Once there was an opening in the fighting, I searched for any sign of Maurice.

Where the fuck is that coward?

I cast my eyes along the length of the field when I spotted movement at the southern end of the forest. That's when I saw his army of vampires slowly emerging from the trees. In their hands were purple glass spheres. One vampire lifted a sphere and threw it into the battlefield. It exploded into a cloud of purple smoke, and my insides went cold.

Wolfsbane.

One by one, werewolves caught in the cloud collapsed to the ground and transformed back into their human forms. They were left exposed, defenseless, and vulnerable.

No!

I tried to run in their direction, but with every step I took, another demon would lunge for me. I cut down each one that faced me, my sword moving with deadly swiftness against their mere claws and teeth.

"Simon! Simon, can you hear me?" I shouted in my mind, knowing I had to act quickly.

"I'm here! What's wrong?"

"Maurice has armed vampires with vials of wolfsbane. See that purple smoke? That smoke is disabling the werewolves and leaving them defenseless. I need you to summon a gale over there right now."

"You got it!"

The surrounding wind picked up, causing the trees to shake and creak from the force. The stream of air moved through the battlefield and to where the wolfsbane smoke was. As I watched the smoke clear away, my eyes widened as someone else emerged from the dark forest, the moonlight shining over his features.

There he was ... Maurice.

He stood on the outskirts of the field, watching the battle with blackened eyes, wearing a sinister grin as if he had already won. I could see that his features had changed, he was more twisted, and darkness seemed to pour out of him. We locked eyes, and I raised my sword in front of me. It was time to end this, once and for all.

Maurice glanced over his shoulder, where more vampires were appearing from the forest. There were at least fifty of them. They all were carrying vials of wolfsbane. Each one tossed their glass simultaneously, smoke billowing up from the ground. The wind was not enough to keep all the smoke away from the wolves.

Son of a bitch!

All I could do now was run to the vampires and confront Maurice head-on. I gripped my sword tightly and sprinted as fast as my legs would carry me. More wolves were dropping from the effects of the wolfsbane, and I knew I wouldn't make it to Maurice before his vampires slaughtered them. I called upon Earth to help me cross the field. I felt the roots of the trees respond, moving quickly beneath my feet.

The roots broke through the soil, taking me airborne. I looked down and saw the intensity of the battle continuing beneath me. There were large splashes of blood in the grass, and the iron smell made my stomach lurch.

I have to end this. Now!

The roots carried me through the plumes of smoke, and I spotted Maurice standing alone. He looked up at me and let out a guttural hiss, baring his fangs. I jumped down, raising my sword in front of me and taking an offensive position. "Maurice!" I screamed. "This war ends now!"

Maurice let out a laugh as he dodged my sweeping cut. "Heartless? Look around, darling. My war is succeeding, and as soon as the last of your werewolves is slain, I will take you and my victory over this world. I rule the demons now. I am their king. Not even you can stop me."

I leaped at him again, slicing down toward his neck. Maurice whirled and caught the tip of the blade with his bare hand. The blade had sliced his flesh but didn't cut through the bones, nor did it draw any blood. When I looked closer, I saw his fingers were now blackened, with pulsing veins of red moving through them. He flashed his teeth as I yanked the sword from his grip and stepped back.

It became all too clear that Maurice now possessed the full might of the Underworld. But I couldn't stop now. I had to fight. Despite the fear that threatened to consume me, I took up my stance and lunged again. Maurice moved with impossible speed, kicking out his leg and slamming it into my left side. The force of the blow cracked my ribs. I fell to one knee, gasping and coughing, trying to draw air back into my lungs. I climbed to my feet, the bones already knitting back together, but the pain was still radiating through my chest. Through the smoke, I could hear the laughter of the other vampires.

Maurice clicked his tongue. "Darling, you won't be able to lay a finger on me. Not now, not when I command the forces of the Underworld. Just admit defeat and become my queen. Become mine forever."

"I would rather be hanged again. Your existence is a disgrace to all things good in this world, and I cannot allow you to taint it any further." I slashed again at Maurice, but he quickly sidestepped the sword and lashed out. His sharp nails sliced across my right arm, drawing blood.

I staggered back, giving myself enough space to heal the wound. The nearby vampires growled as the scent of my blood filled the air. As the blood ran down my wrist and soaked into the hilt of the sword, I felt a flicker of hopelessness in my heart.

Maurice moved closer to me. "Well, then. Let's finally end this."

Panic flooded through me as he lunged with demonic speed. Right before he could reach me, time came to a halt, and I heard something like a voice echoing through my mind.

By the blood of the Blessed, good will shine through. Use these words to sever the darkness and banish the Devil's horde.

The sword ... the magic from the sword was speaking to me. As I looked down, I saw the runes glowing. Understanding flooded my mind. This sword's power was more ancient than the Chosen Ones. This energy was as old as the Gods themselves. Joel had theorized that a knight may have owned it, and I was thinking maybe he was right.

This must be a Templar Sword, blessed by the Upper World to slay monsters.

I swung the sword high above my head, the light of the moon flashing over the silver. Using my left hand, I poured my magic into the runes. The blade glowed with white light, and a green aura flowed along the edges.

With a deep breath, I closed my eyes and recited the words the voice had told me.

I call to the power of Spirit, the bringer of life, nature's ultimate magic. Sharpen my blade and shine. Cut through the evil, and spill the blood of the creature before me.

With those words, a radiant light burst from the sword, wrapping me up in its power. Maurice let out a loud cry and fell back, his body smoking from the intensity of the magic. I saw my opportunity and leaped high into the air, kicking off the tree beside me. Maurice looked up into my eyes and snarled, raising both hands to deflect my blow. As I descended, I brought the brilliant sword down with one swift slice. When I looked up, Maurice's arms had been severed, and his head separated from the rest of his body. His face wore a hideous grimace of disbelief, and his head rolled across the grass, stopping short of the vampires who had watched the fight.

My eyes went wide, my breath caught in my throat, and utter relief washed through me.

He was dead. Maurice ... was finally dead.

I reached down and seized Maurice's crumbling, severed head by the hair. I raised both the head and sword up high and let out a warrior's scream that carried across the entire field. The vampires that were about to sink their fangs into the unconscious were-wolves froze. "You have no master and no protection. Stand down and surrender!"

Their eyes widened as they saw their leader's head in my hand crumbling to ash.

The fear was written across the vampires' faces. They were cow-ards, and the one vampire who promised them protection was now dead. From the battle, the other vampires had also paused their attack and had taken notice of what I had done to their king.

One vampire dared to flash me his fangs and growl as if he could take me down. I raised the sword again, and the light of my power glimmered at the tip of the blade. Behind me, the trees rustled aggressively, and the branches extended toward the vampires like sharpened stakes.

"You must not have heard what the trees did to the last set of vampires who challenged me?" I said, recalling the night of the ceremonial feeding ritual in Maurice's lair when I commanded the trees outside to impale the hearts of the clan with their pointed branches.

I smirked as the wind carried Maurice's ashes away.

"Last warning. Stand down, or I will burn you until there is nothing left but your teeth."

The vampires halted and looked at each other, and one by one, they turned and fled into the forest.

I'll hunt them down later.

I stuck my sword into the ground and looked out over the battlefield. The demons had not ceased their violent attack on my army. They didn't seem to care that their new leader was dead. The vision was a fucking nightmare. As bloody bodies flew through the air, I spotted my coven amidst the carnage. They were standing in a circle with their backs to one another, moving and attacking as one. Caleb and I made eye contact, and he signaled for the others to run and join me.

When everyone had gathered, I quickly checked each one of them, making sure they were all in one piece. Despite the streak of blood down Ezra's face, he was grinning from ear to ear. Relieved, I let out a heavy breath and said, "There are too many demons for us to take down. We need to somehow close the portal that Julian opened in the hangar and the portal by the cemetery."

"I agree," Caleb said. "We need to send them back and seal up Purgatory, so they're trapped again."

"How?" Ezra asked.

We turned around to look at the fighting behind us. Everyone, myself included, was completely exhausted. I looked around at the group, trying to catch my breath, when a thought struck me.

"Roland once told us as kids that the Chosen Ones were sent here to create balance on Earth and restore what was once pure. Demons don't belong here, so we have the power to send them back. They were never, and will never be, a part of this world. We can use our elemental magic to create that balance again."

Caleb nodded and grabbed my right hand, and our group formed a circle.

We held on tightly to each other's hands, and we began to chant. The coven and I spoke the words of a spell none of us knew, and our powers flowed together like the waters of a river. When our chanting stopped, our heads flew back, and our eyes turned white. Our hands remained locked together as light beamed from our eyes and into the dark sky above.

Then I felt the sky crack, and the Upper World opened all at once. A brilliant, golden light shone down upon us. Goosebumps covered every part of my body, and I sensed that thousands of angels were covering us with their wings for protection.

The screeching of demons pierced the air around us, and I felt the force of energy pull them from where they stood. As that happened, Hell's portal opened at our feet, the ground trembling beneath us. The screams grew louder and louder as our power pulled the demons toward the portal and sucked them all back into the Underworld. When all the demons had vanished, the vortex at our feet closed, and I released the circle.

All light and power diminished into complete silence and serenity. Dawn was approaching the eastern skyline, a soft periwinkle blue against the dark sky.

I looked back at the field. Mangled bodies were scattered in the grass, but not many. Witches helped other witches back on their feet, and werewolves transitioned back into their human forms. Everyone who could stand tended to the wounded, gathering torn pieces of cloth for makeshift bandages.

I spotted Dorian about halfway across the field, who was trying to help Noah to his feet. Noah's torso was soaked in blood, and as soon as he stood, he collapsed back to the ground. Noah was badly injured.

I hurried over to them and kneeled at his side. "Stay still, Noah."

There was a four-inch wound across his stomach, deep enough that I could see sinew and muscle tissue under the torn flesh. A demon must have taken a massive bite out of him during the fight.

"Jesus," I muttered.

I placed my hands on Noah's stomach and used my healing magic to close the wound. After a minute, the torn skin had knitted together, and aside from some pink skin, it looked as though he had never been injured. To my surprise, the healing magic was glowing green, like how my powers once were before I touched the tree.

Noah let out a deep breath at the sudden release of pain. "Mahalo, my queen."

His choice of words made me laugh. I was far from a queen. "I need to check on our allies and see if anyone else needs help," I told Noah. "Spread out and look for any survivors."

I worked my way across the field, healing the injured and instructing the other witches to help gather the bodies of those for whom it was too late.

A small crowd caught my attention, and I went over to see what was going on. When I got closer, I saw Dorian kneeling on the ground, holding Davina's lifeless body. He wasn't crying, but the look on his face was empty and lost. It didn't matter how long he'd known Davina. They had a connection I would never understand.

I stepped back and let Dorian and his pack mourn the loss of their Alpha.

As morning approached and the sun peeked over the tree line, everything around me seemed to slow down. I leaned back against a tree and fell to my knees. We had defeated Maurice, but this war was far from over.

Sixteen heroes died as we fought Hell on Earth, and though my family was safe and my coven was alive, the Devil was still a threat the longer he remained here.

After a few minutes, I rose to my feet and walked over to where my coven and the others were waiting. Desiree held Caleb's hand tightly as if she were afraid that, at any moment, she would lose him again. Roland draped his arm over Caleb's shoulder, pulling him close. Tears were running down his cheek, and his expression of joy seemed to have lifted years of pain from his face. My heart melted watching this reunion, but I knew that as happy as we all felt, even though this part of the fight was over, we still had a Devil to send back to Hell.

Riley and Amber gathered the packs and headed back into the forest. They were going to hold a funeral service for Davina. The other covens who joined us expressed gratitude and promised to be here the next time we needed to fight, though I hoped that day would never come. But it was good to know we had an army of witches on our side fighting for the same cause.

Joel and I opened several portals to send everyone back to their homes. The dead were gently carried through to be buried with honor by their families. Lily and Joel then teleported back to Joel's home, and Dorian and Noah went with them so that Noah could rest.

I closed my eyes and visualized the left wing of the hangar, where the Devil remained frozen in stone. When the portal opened, I gripped Desiree's hand, and with my coven, we jumped through.

Once we landed, we looked up to see the Devil was still encased in stone. Julian's portal was still open, but no more demons were climbing through.

Thank God.

After I closed our portal, Desiree lifted her hands and recited her reversal spell. The stone around the Devil's body broke apart, crashing to the ground. The magic circle had been broken when the Underworld had climbed through, so we had to act quickly. Before the Devil could become fully animated, we all joined hands and blasted him through the portal back to Hell.

The coven and I then called upon our elements to create a new barrier around Purgatory, where the souls of vampires would remain until their bodies were destroyed on Earth, or I reunited the vampire with their human soul.

CHAPTER 39

MERCY

I t was almost sunset, but my coven and I wouldn't leave each other's sides. After checking in with Joel and Lily, we left Desiree in their care and went back to the house that the coven and I shared. We were beyond exhausted, no matter how much power and strength we possessed. We spent the entire day close together as if, at any moment, we might lose each other again.

Dorian wrapped his arms around my waist and buried his face in my neck. I smiled when his lips touched my skin, and chills snaked down my back.

I looked up, embarrassed, but everyone was so caught up with being able to finally touch each other again, they couldn't care less what I was doing.

When I looked around the room, I noticed Caleb wasn't with us.

"Dorian, give me a minute. Okay?"

"Of course."

I looked through the front window, spotting Caleb perched on the porch swing, staring blankly at the street.

Something is wrong.

"I'll be right back," I said, heading to the door.

Stepping onto the porch, I made my way over to him. "Hey, you," I said gently. "Are you okay?"

Caleb turned to face me but was unable to meet my eyes. "I'm sorry for everything, Mercy."

I frowned, placing my hand on his. "There's nothing to apologize for."

I didn't want our first time together after reuniting to be filled with guilt and self-pity. I wanted him to know that I forgave him for the secrets he kept from me.

"I've lied and hurt you in more ways than one," he continued, his shoulders hunched. "No one should ever hurt the ones they love as I have. My actions resulted in you being killed and us being trapped in Purgatory while you suffered alone."

"What are you talking about?"

"I didn't tell you about the tree. Not because I knew it contained your powers, because I swear I had no idea."

"I know."

"I just—" Tears filled his eyes, and he placed his hand over his mouth as if to stifle a sob.

"Caleb, don't do this."

His hand dropped to his knee, and he finally looked up at me. "Let me explain, okay?"

I pressed my lips together and nodded.

"All I knew was the consequences of using the powers from that tree. Watching Molly die over twenty-two years ago has haunted me, regardless of her willingness to sacrifice herself. I knew that if you ever used that kind of power—"

"But I *did* use that power. If anyone should apologize, it should be me. When I was thirteen years old, I used that kind of power over and over again against other witches until I met Dorian. I used it with your father and didn't tell you or anyone else in the coven what I had been doing for seven years." I reached down and grabbed his hand, squeezing it lightly. "That isn't me anymore. Okay? I swear to you. I will never resurrect another human being again."

He sighed and sat back on the porch swing, but he didn't speak.

I leaned forward and brushed a stray hair away from his eyes. "We forgive each other. We forgive ourselves. And from here on out, we move on."

Caleb placed his hand on my cheek, but I didn't move away. I loved him. I did. I wouldn't be alive today if it weren't for Caleb and my coven. But my love for him was more profound than any romantic relationship. He was a part of me, and I was a part of him. It didn't matter if we loved someone else, because that part of us was eternal and unwavering.

"Forgive yourself, Caleb," I repeated as a tear slid down my cheek.

He wiped it away when suddenly we heard Melissa calling Caleb's name.

Melissa stood on the walkway by the house, her eyes locked on his.

"I called her after we got back," I confessed.

Melissa stepped closer to us, her eyes glistening with tears. "Caleb, you're—"

"Melissa," he whispered as he ran toward her, lifting her high above his head and wrapping his arms around her hips. He slowly lowered her until their faces met, and he pulled her in for a kiss.

I looked away and smiled to myself, walking back into the house to give them their privacy.

Dorian was laughing with the coven at one of Ezra's lame jokes when I entered the family room again. His eyes watched me as I sat next to him and scooted closer. He wrapped his arms around me, pulling me between his legs and up against his chest.

He leaned in, kissing my lips gently and lacing his fingers under my hair, creating butterflies in my stomach once again. I pulled away slightly and looked into his beautiful eyes. I could hear Leah giggle in the background, but I ignored her.

"I'll love you until I take my last breath," I said, and Dorian smiled, knowing that hidden meaning. "And whatever happens, whoever tries to destroy us, that love will never falter." I placed my hand on his cheek. "Promise me a lifetime of this."

His brow arched. "How about eternity?"

I gave him a knowing smile. "Someday, I'll have to say goodbye to you, but until then, we have this." I looked down and placed my hand on his chest. "We have now."

I felt Dorian's hand on mine, and I looked up at him.

He leaned in and whispered in my ear. "It doesn't matter what happens tomorrow or what happened yesterday. We move forward together, because all we have is now."

For a long beat, those words resonated with me. I lifted my hand to Dorian's cheek and repeated those words. "All we have is now."

EPILOGUE

MERCY

Two years later

I n a time of battle, soldiers must prepare themselves to fight their enemy in the darkest of hours.

But what if those enemies aren't enemies at all? They're just like us, but perhaps they're lost in the struggle to be a good person and wanting to give in to their evil desires.

The world almost ended two years ago. I tried not to think about what would have happened if we hadn't succeeded in sending those demons back to the Underworld or finally putting an end to Maurice and his evil schemes.

Thankfully, we'd won, but there was a long road ahead of us, ridding the world of vampires, who still wrought havoc in this world.

No new leaders of clans had surfaced, that we knew of anyway. My archenemy was dead, and each week, there were handfuls of vampires coming to me, asking me to free them from the nightmare of the undead.

My coven and I, along with Dorian, Noah, and Melissa, moved to Paris about a year ago. Hundreds of witches throughout Europe had called upon us for help since news of our battle against the Underworld had spread. As the universal elementals, we felt a strong obligation to be a part of this new revolution of witches who were ready to fight with us against vampires.

As far as the witches who had turned against their kind and succumbed to dark magic, we had a place for them that didn't require me to end their lives.

Roland had worked night and day to build our own magic prison in the heart of Boston.

Of course, we had to keep everything we did behind closed doors to keep our secret from the human world. My family and I used all our resources to create a prison that held or rehabilitated witches who would do the world harm. It took us a year and a half until we could make such a space, but since then, our streets and homes have been safer places, primarily free from dark magic.

Roland once again resumed the mission of tracking down traitorous witches, and Desiree was more than happy to assist him in bringing them to justice. There were still dark witches out there, and they needed to be found.

Lily met a guy named Thomas, who was also a witch. They started dating and, about six months ago, moved to New Orleans, where she opened her own witch shop. Shannon, of course, was happy about having others she looked at like family so close to her again.

Joel finally reunited with Derek, and together, they moved back to New York and reopened their art gallery.

Riley and Amber grew their pack to great numbers and joined forces with the pack in Providence, which no longer had their alpha, Davina, because she had sacrificed her own life to save Dorian.

Cami spent three months at Raven's and now works at a marketing firm in Newport, so she wouldn't have to leave her mom again. She told me that, though she felt normal enough to return home, Cami's days sitting with a therapist were far from over, and she was okay with that. After all, she did still see the darkness of Hell while she slept.

Then there was Dorian and me, sitting across from each other at a café in Paris, waiting for our server to bring us our food.

"Voulez-vous plus de vin?" our server asked, holding a bottle of pinot noir.

"S'il vous plaît," Dorian responded, and she filled both our glasses.

Dorian kept his eyes locked on mine. "Mercy?"

"Yes?" I said, bringing the wine to my lips and tasting sweet, black cherry and vanilla on my tongue.

"Remember what we said to each other a couple of years ago, after we defeated those demons, about 'living in the now?'"

I thought about it for a moment. "I think we said, 'All we have is now.'"

I can't believe I remember that. It's as if it happened yesterday.

He gave me a goofy grin.

"Why are you being so weird?" I asked.

Dorian reached under the table and pulled out a black velvet case. When my stomach lurched, I looked up to meet his eyes. "Dorian?"

He opened the case, and I looked down at a beautiful, sparkling black diamond ring.

"In 1691, I met a woman who saved my life. Not only that, but centuries later, she literally saved my soul. I had endured centuries of pain and feared that I would never find that kind of love again. When I heard Caleb brought you back into this life, my entire world stopped moving, and the only thing I thought about was having you in my arms again and never letting you go."

As Dorian pulled the ring out and set the case aside, my heart pounded with excitement. Of course, my answer was going to be yes, but I had difficulty finding my voice.

Dorian carefully took my left hand and gave it a gentle squeeze. "Mercy," he said, "will you marry me and never let me go?"

ABOUT THE AUTHOR

D.L. BLADE

D.L. Blade grew up in southern California and studied at the California Healing Arts College, working as a massage therapist for thirteen years, then on to real estate. D.L. and her family moved to Colorado in 2015, where she now writes full-time.

Blade always loved writing, concentrating on poetry and music rather than novels when she was younger. That changed, however, when she had a dream one night and decided to write a book about it. Aside from reading and writing, she enjoys hosting parties, wine tasting, rock concerts, and spending an enjoyable weekend in her cul-de-sac with her neighborhood besties, drinking cold sangrias.

In the future, D.L. hopes she can continue writing exciting novels that will captivate her readers with twists and turns and all our favorite tropes.

www.ingramcontent.com/pod-product-compliance
Lightning Source LLC
Chambersburg PA
CBHW051125190726
48290CB00006B/1690